PENGUIN BOOKS

Don't Let It Break Your Heart

Don't Let It Break Your Heart

♡

MAGGIE HORNE

PENGUIN BOOKS

PENGUIN BOOKS

UK | USA | Canada | Ireland | Australia
India | New Zealand | South Africa

Penguin Books is part of the Penguin Random House group of companies
whose addresses can be found at global.penguinrandomhouse.com

www.penguin.co.uk
www.puffin.co.uk
www.ladybird.co.uk

First published in the USA by A Feiwel and Friends Book, an imprint of
Macmillan Publishing Group, LLC, and in Great Britain by Penguin Books 2024

001

Book design by L. Whitt
Title page artwork by cherriielle
Printed and bound in Great Britain by Clays Ltd, Elcograf S.p.A.

The authorized representative in the EEA is Penguin Random House Ireland,
Morrison Chambers, 32 Nassau Street, Dublin D02 YH68

A CIP catalogue record for this book is available from the British Library

ISBN: 978–0–241–63810–1

All correspondence to:
Penguin Books
Penguin Random House Children's
One Embassy Gardens, 8 Viaduct Gardens,
London SW11 7BW

FOR GABI, MY BEST-EVER BATHROOM KISS

LET'S ADMIT,
WITHOUT APOLOGY,
WHAT WE DO TO EACH OTHER.

WE KNOW WHO
OUR ENEMIES ARE.
WE KNOW.

"DETAIL OF THE FIRE", RICHARD SIKEN

♡

ONE

When I was eleven, Sydney Demarco told me that the nail polish she was wearing was called Princess Purple. She fanned her skinny little fingers in front of my face and said that her mom had taken her to an *actual* spa and the women there said that she had beautiful hands and she looked at the ragged pink skin around my thumbnail and asked if *I'd* ever been to a spa.

I don't want to be a dick, but maybe that's where Sydney peaked, because she's never stopped painting her nails Princess Purple.

I painted her nails for her, once, before a party. At Olivia Reiner's kitchen island. She splayed her *beautiful hands* across the white quartz, and when I took off the old polish her nails were yellow and brittle underneath because they never see the sun, and then I covered them up again while we drank coolers and Olivia winged my eyeliner and asked me all about what it was like to sleep with Ethan Gray.

Sydney's never stopped painting her nails Princess Purple. Same way Olivia's never stopped throwing parties.

Now, though, there's no pregame. The coolers are still

here, but my hands skip over them in favor of a vodka bottle's shiny red cap. There's no nail painting, but there *is* a bottle of Princess Purple on the same island. That's where Sydney did her nails while everyone was getting ready. Olivia wouldn't have been the one to paint them for her, but maybe someone else, Savannah or Jordan or Kennedy, someone, peeled back the chipped purple and replaced it with the exact same shade. The same, always.

I haven't seen Sydney or Olivia, yet, but I know they're around together somewhere. Olivia never goes missing for too long at her parties; she sparkles and glows when enough people look at her. At her house, she can make all the rules. And you can't have an Olivia without a Sydney, who only ever wants to laugh at your jokes and remembers, sharply, everything you've ever told her.

It feels like everyone in the world is in Olivia's kitchen. It's sticky-hot, too hot for Maine in September. Olivia's sliding glass door is open so the boys can smoke outside, and the humidity is creeping in, thick and suffocating like the rest of the party. My hair is starting to stick to my forehead. It must be going frizzy because I wasn't here to get ready and borrow one of Olivia's ten thousand products for it. A drop of sweat is slowly making its way down the center of my back.

If this was last year, I'd yell at the boys to stop, tell them they're giving us all cancer even though it's probably just pot, end up marching myself out there and finishing off whatever they have in their vape pens, tucking myself under Gray's arm while he or me or both of us get more crossfaded than intended.

Logan Bailey comes in from the outside, and I try not to look at him, but I still see he's holding a beer and a cider he pulled from the cooler. They're dripping all over the floor. He starts walking toward me and it feels like something in my stomach melts.

"Hey, Alana."

"You sure your delicate sensibilities can handle both of those in one night?" I ask him instead of saying hi back. You have to one-up Logan, always, or he'll beat you to it.

Logan hasn't quite known how to talk to me since last year, but he used to do this, would bring me drinks while we waited for Gray to arrive, and it wasn't ever my favorite way to spend an hour but it was something. Maybe this is something.

"This one isn't for me," Logan says, and there it is again, the melting, the corners of my mouth lifting.

He looks around, over my head, past me at the brass pendant lights hanging perfectly in Olivia's equally perfect kitchen. He still isn't looking at me when he speaks again. "Where's Gray?"

You can never let Logan know he's made you feel small. He's the type to pounce—on girls who give him the time of day, on teachers who think he's a Nice Young Man, on the joke, always a joke, at your expense—and if he smells blood, it's over. Even if the half smile on my face freezes, even if my gut twists, even if my cheeks glow red, he can't notice it.

That's Gray's drink, that cider, and Logan is Gray's friend, and he wasn't my friend when I was Gray's Girl, so why would we be friends now?

"He's not here yet." I cross my arms over my chest and

swallow hard, because Logan *fucking* Bailey can't know that he hurt my feelings.

If Logan really was Gray's friend, he'd probably know that Gray's not here yet. But I bet he thinks texting Gray to ask when he's going to show up is "gay." Guess it's only fitting that he asks me, then.

Gray would have laughed at that, if he was here now like he said he'd be.

"Nice shirt." Logan's smirking now, in the way I used to find funny. He takes a look at me, dips his gaze up and down my body like he has a right to it, the way he has a right to everything. "Nice shirt, nice hat, nice jacket."

It's even hotter in the kitchen now because I'm trying to tell myself that I don't want to hit Logan Bailey, except that I do, I *so* do. I haven't cut my hair all summer, so it's down past my boobs now, spilling out from under Gray's hat and wavy-messy because I haven't brushed it all day. I'm glad for it right now, covering me up, hiding me away from where Logan's eyes stick to me for just seconds too long, sizing me up like he's trying to peel away layers until he figures out what Gray ever saw in me.

"What, did you come out just so you could keep wearing Gray's shit without having to sleep with him? You can tell me, I won't say anything."

Logan's laughing because this is a joke, because we're friends, aren't we? Friends make fun of their friends. It's a joke, it's *fun*, we're *friends*, come on, Alana, *god*, this is supposed to be a *party*.

I don't respond, and he wanders off in that way drunk boys

do when you aren't serving a purpose and they forget that they have to at least pretend to have manners. I tip my cup sarcastically at his back, and Jordan, stumbling inside with a vape cloud surrounding her like some kind of grimy angel, sees it and shoots me a confused look on her way by.

Someone cheers from a few rooms away, a big, loud boy-shout that feels familiar and a million miles away at once. Gray's shirt is soft, worn with use. It's one of my favorites, faded black and perma-wrinkled because I always tuck it into my bra when I wear it out. If I look down at myself and listen to the party, it almost feels the way it felt last year. Same Princess Purple on the counter. Same Alana, same party. Just waiting on her boyfriend.

The difference is, last year people would be talking to me. Logan might have stayed, might have offered me one of his drinks because everyone's nice to Gray's Girl. My makeup would be cuter because Olivia would have done it, and she can be an almighty bitch but she knows her way around a beauty blender.

I put both my hands on the island to feel the cool stone, to prove I'm still here. No one else has noticed Sydney's nail polish there, wedged between two bowls of chips. No one would notice it if they didn't know what it was, if they hadn't felt the glass, hadn't picked up Sydney's hand like it might explode because everything always felt so much like a test back then.

It's not that no one's looking at me. It's that everyone's trying so hard not to.

I watch my hands reach over and stuff Sydney Demarco's bottle of Princess Purple into my back pocket.

The kitchen tile is sticky because all the other drunk kids are spilling their drinks, and the music and the talking and Sydney shrieking somewhere else in the house is all too loud, so I can't hear the way my flip-flops peel slowly away from the floor, but I can feel it. It's too hot to be wearing Gray's jean jacket, but it looks good with my outfit. We've both worn it enough that it smells like the two of us. I'm about to take it off (not because of Logan, but not *not* because of him, either) when I hear another voice.

"Nice jacket."

It comes from behind me. The comment should make my shoulders rise, make me feel small and angry like Logan does, but instead everything melts away and I smile for the first time all night.

"Nice dick," I counter when Gray slings his arm over my shoulders and squeezes me close. Broad shoulders, brown skin tanned dark and beautiful, smile like the sun, like a homecoming. I lean in, arms around his waist, take a breath and smell minty gum and that boy-scented bodywash they all use.

"You would know," he says down at me.

I cackle, bright and familiar but foreign at once. Gray must have snuck a couple of beers in before coming here; he hasn't joked like that before. I picture him silent on the car ride over, his mom dropping him off before her shift tonight and him desperately trying to play it cool. My laugh is part genuine, part relief.

Gray grins, and I grin back, and the kitchen doesn't feel too hot anymore. Everything is normal again. I can breathe again.

Sydney's never stopped painting her nails Princess Purple.

Same way Olivia's never stopped throwing parties. Same way Gray and I never stopped loving each other.

"I can't believe you made me sit here alone for an *hour*." I follow him to the drinks table and watch him mix dark rum and Sprite. It's too strong for him and he's going to make me finish it off later, I already know, but even that's comforting. The knowing. It's not a party without Gray. Everyone thinks so.

"You only texted me fifteen minutes ago, drama queen," he says. "Besides, I figured you'd be doing all your pregame shit with Olivia and them."

I take a very, very long sip of my drink.

"Well, you haven't missed anything," I tell him instead of disclosing my lack of pregame invite this evening. It's true that Gray hasn't missed anything tonight, as far as I know, but I'm sure by Monday we'll hear all about how someone pissed their pants and fell down a flight of stairs or something.

"I've missed *you*," he says, jabbing his fingers into my sides. I double over and laugh again, loud enough that people look our way. It all clicks into place, and it's so good that I remember why I faked this for as long as I did.

"You're the best boyfriend ever," I tell him. I mean for it to come out as a joke, but I end up sounding too sincere. Gray makes a face like there's something caught in his throat for a second and then laughs me off.

"You're just saying that because I'm the only one you'll ever have."

"You don't know that!" I chirp. "I could have an exploratory phase in college and find me a good old-fashioned himbo jock to settle down with."

Gray gives me a look. I ignore it.

"He'll treat me well," I continue. "His name is *absolutely* Josh."

Gray tries to glare at me, but he laughs instead, so I laugh harder and take the drink he's just going to pass off to me anyway.

We do a lap and find ourselves in Olivia's crowded living room, standing off to the side and watching everything, me tucked under Gray's arm as if it's not a billion degrees in Olivia's house. She and Sydney are both in here, Syd's legs in Olivia's lap while Logan sits on the arm of the couch and looks down Olivia's top so obviously it even makes *me* feel violated.

"Do we know her?" Gray asks after a second. He nods his head in the direction of a girl wearing ripped jeans, without a drink in her hand. She's standing uneasily beside another girl—a sophomore, I think—who looks much more comfortable than she does. I consider making some kind of joke. *Anxious and out of place. You have a type, huh?* But I already feel like I'm pushing my luck with Gray tonight, so I bite my tongue, say what he wants me to say.

"I think she's Rachel Milner's cousin." I don't know for sure, but anyone new at Olivia's house is almost definitely someone's cousin or neighbor or childhood best friend who's just moved back from somewhere.

Gray and I haven't done this yet. We don't quite know how this works. I've spent years of my life dealing with the fact that nearly every girl Gray comes into contact with wants to be with him. Before, I was always more worried about making sure people knew I didn't like it than I was about the wanting itself. Gray would never. Not even when, secretly, in the middle of the night, I wished he would.

But it's different now. Now Gray has all of this wanting right in front of him, and he knows that if he wants any of it back, all he has to do is ask. He just doesn't know how to yet.

"Maybe we should invite her to play beer pong with us," he says, not looking away from her. He has to dip his head and crane his neck to keep staring because there's always this frenetic energy in Olivia's living room, everyone nearly vibrating, constantly darting in and out of conversations and people and locations, wondering who's going to do whatever it is we'll be talking about tomorrow.

"Ah, yes, that beer pong game we were mere moments from playing."

"Yeah, that one."

I guess it's better to get this one, this weird first whatever-this-is-going-to-turn-into interaction with a girl who isn't me, out of the way before the school year actually starts. Gray and I haven't spoken about protocol yet, but we've put ourselves in an extremely fucked-up spiral where neither of us feel like we can do something like this without the other around. Nothing says *hook up with me at a party* like your ex-girlfriend chaperoning the entire thing, right?

I roll my eyes, but walk up to the girl and her friend. The floor here is less sticky than the kitchen, deep brown hardwood that's usually covered with these impossibly fluffy white rugs. Olivia would have made Sydney roll them up, stashed them away in her room so no one could spill on them.

"Are you Rachel's cousin?" I ask the girl. I guess the drinks I pounded while I was waiting for Gray worked better than I thought they did, because subtlety left the building a while back. "You look familiar."

The girl's friend hides a laugh behind her hand and I realize what this looks like. Oh my god.

"My friend thinks you're cute." I nod back at Gray, probably too quickly, probably too jerky, but the girl's friend drops her hand and gives her The Look, so I know it worked.

We play beer pong, badly. I never liked beer, but I learned to like it back when I thought that: A) liking beer would make boys think I was hot, and B) I wanted boys to think I was hot. It's fine until Gray picks up Rachel's Cousin (I should probably learn her name, but a mean part of me doesn't want her to stick around long enough for it to matter) when she sinks her first shot, spins her around and I get dizzy.

It's when the lights start to blur and my head starts to pound along with the music and Gray has his arm around Rachel's Cousin's waist that I know it's time for me to go. If I squint at the two of them I can put myself back there, can feel Gray's hand touching the skin between my shirt and my ripped jeans.

Sydney's nails are still Princess Purple. But I'm not Gray's Girl anymore.

"Gray," I call out from across the table, too quietly. He's murmuring down at Rachel's Cousin and she's pretending that she doesn't care. "Baby."

He hears that, looks up at me like I woke him up from

something. I walk around Olivia's glossy dining room table so I don't have to keep shouting.

"Leaving."

"I'll walk you home."

I wave him off. "It's down the street."

This isn't a new conversation and it won't have a new ending. Gray picks up my hand, presses his lips to it, squeezes twice.

"See you tomorrow," he says against the thin skin on the back of my hand, and I'm suddenly that drunk kind of exhausted where my legs are heavy and it feels like it takes a million years to get out of Olivia's house, let alone make the five-minute walk to mine. We all live in the same new-ish part of town, got packed up by our parents when we were too little to remember and plopped into houses with construction-white insides and new turf in the backyard. Grew up alongside the limp saplings they planted in front of each carefully planned house. It used to mean that you never had to worry about leaving a textbook at school, there was always someone nearby you could borrow from. Now it means that when I need to get out of Olivia's house, when it feels like I could drift away from the whole world, I have a quick getaway, a short walk under the streetlights, hidden away under Gray's hat.

My parents leave the door unlocked for me. They're friends with Olivia's parents, because all the parents are friends here, have been since they were our age. They like to think they're cool, better than their parents before them, so they let their kids drink on hot September nights and leave the door unlocked.

I text Gray *got murdered* when I get in, and he replies with a thumbs-up. When I close my eyes, I can still see him. Surrounded by our friends, everyone hanging on his every word.

Just another thing that never changed.

TWO

My dad drops me off for the first day of school. We stopped doing the whole pictures-on-the-front-porch thing back in middle school. There's no little chalk sign that says *senior year!* but I still get a ride on the first day. That's the rule.

We pull up to the building, clean white brick and glass stairwells because it's still new, not even ten years old, not the same school our parents went to. All our parents love to tell us that, love to talk about how the old high school had asbestos in the walls, wooden lockers with graffiti practically from the Middle Ages. One time, they swear to god, a rat fell from the ceiling. Now we have this tall shiny thing nestled in with all the houses, unearthly green lawn stretching out in front of it and 1,500 of us swarming in and out like an ocean tide. A great school when you don't have any other options for miles—and our parents don't—busing kids in from three towns over if they have to.

We pull up, and it's not like it's this huge difference between last year and now. It's not like I'm expecting some ridiculous teen movie moment where I walk down the hall in slow motion and everyone stops what they're doing to stare at me. Everything that happened last year happened before summer. I've been this version of myself in this school before, so it shouldn't matter that it's a new year. But it does matter, I guess, somehow, because I can feel the way it does, clattering around in my chest. I shove a big breath out of my lungs, let it trill my lips like when we used to pretend to be horses and Olivia would insist that *she* was actually a *unicorn*.

"Are you gonna be okay?" my dad asks, in that voice I'm still not used to. The one that seems to have no idea what I need.

"Guess so!" I say, and hop out before he can keep talking, before he can ask me something else or look at me for too long. I don't particularly know what I need, either.

When I was younger, I hated the first day of school because I could never see the point. If we weren't going to just get on with it and start doing work, why have this day, this week, dedicated to filling out worksheets about our summer activities and favorite colors?

I'm feeling that again now, a bit. It would be so much easier if we could sit down and get yelled at about verbs and not have time to talk to each other.

Or talk *about* each other, as the case may be.

It's exactly the same as the party last weekend, exactly the same as every other party since last year. Suddenly, I don't know how to walk through a hall and wait around for a class to start. I don't know how to answer those stupid first-day-of-school questions teachers make us answer, don't know how to *tell us one interesting fact about yourself* because I think everyone already knows the most interesting thing about me, and honestly, I'm getting a little sick of repeating it.

Gray isn't in any of my morning classes. He's got Business

and Law and Politics and Accounting because Gray's known that he's going to be a lawyer since he was a little kid. Meanwhile, I have the *no fucking clue* special, a generic math, science, and English combination that works for me most of the time and hopefully is going to work for my UMaine app, but it means that I don't see Gray until lunch.

"There's my first lady!" Gray hollers when I walk into the student council meeting room. He bops over and wraps me up in a hug and my shoulders unlock a bit from where they've been hovering at my ears all morning.

"You're such a dickhead." I laugh, pushing him away. "Not only am I not your first lady anymore, I'm *literally* the VP."

It made so much sense, last year. Gray would be the president because he was always going to be the kind of guy who was senior class president. I would be vice president, because I went where Gray went.

That's still true.

I don't really know why we have student council meetings, since there are only four of us and we're all friends because high school student council elections are, in fact, a popularity contest. Sydney's here, giving Gray and me a funny look because no one seems to be able to comprehend the fact that we still love each other the way we do. Logan shows up late, because he doesn't think being the treasurer is that exciting ever since he found out that he doesn't actually get paid for the job.

"Teacher incoming, please stifle all hormones and swears," a voice says. Mrs. Davis-Garcia, my eleventh-grade math teacher, student council advisor, and token faculty lesbian breezes into the room in a pair of mustard corduroys I actually really like. Not that I would ever say that.

Mrs. DG nudges Gray out of the way and steals his spot at the teacher's desk at the front of the room. She immediately pulls out her phone and gets sucked into something on the screen, scrolling endlessly. Gray clears his throat and she looks up.

"Sorry," she says. "My wife's at home waiting for someone to come fix our toilet and they haven't shown up yet. I'm trying to figure out if I need to call someone."

I ignore the way her saying *my wife* so casually makes my heart leap, just the tiniest bit, same as it did last year before I fully knew why.

"Ugh," Mrs. DG says now, still looking at her phone. "Okay, this is a phone call. I'll be right back. Maybe. Realistically, I don't do much here and you guys know it. Gray, you're in charge."

I groan internally. You never tell Gray he's in charge. It immediately goes to his head.

"Order in the student council room!" Gray booms as soon as she's gone, making me and Sydney jump. I smack him on the arm and he smiles winningly at me.

"Syd, can you please note that demonstration of violence from our vice president, and also jot down the fact that I would like a gavel for our next meeting."

"I'm not your secretary." Sydney rolls her eyes. Normally I would agree, except for the fact that Sydney *is* the senior class secretary.

"Correct," Gray says. "You are *everyone's* secretary. The people's secretary, if you will. And we all love you for it."

Sydney laughs at that and starts writing things down, and Gray's saved the world again.

"Quick meeting! Only one thing to talk about," Gray says. "Then you can get back to terrorizing the local community, Bailey."

Logan gives Gray the finger and I snort into the sleeve of my hoodie.

Gray's hoodie. Whatever.

"The state's doing this new thing for . . ." Gray reads aloud from a pamphlet on the table in front of him, putting on a faux-fancy voice. "'*Maine's best and brightest high school students looking to enrich their academic careers.*' It's a camp that runs the weekend of Thanksgiving break; teachers are nominating five kids to go and hang out in the woods listening to CEOs give inspirational speeches with kids from other schools in the state. It also says that they're doing speed networking. Apparently, they tried it in a couple other states and all the kids who went got into their top-choice college and are now, like, curing cancer and making flying cars and shit. We're supposed to spread the word and try and get kids excited about it so they'll kiss teacher ass this semester."

"Five kids," Logan muses. "So, what, us four and some random, right?"

Sydney laughs and I grimace, but Logan's only saying what we're all thinking.

"Bremner may have implied he'd be into nominating me,"

Gray admits, but that's not a surprise. Bremner's only been principal since last year, but he's been obsessed with Gray since he got here.

"And you'll just have to talk to Linney, huh, Syd?" Logan nudges Sydney and she laughs again, but nods. Ms. Linney basically thinks Syd is a Rhodes Scholar in the making, and she's not shy about letting people know.

"And . . ." Logan turns his face to me. That mean little smile from the weekend comes back and my stomach drops.

Before I can find out exactly how Logan was planning on making fun of me (though I could guess: I'm sure his jokes about why Mrs. DG might want to nominate me would be hilarious and not at all offensive), the door is yanked open and a girl is in the room.

And . . .

And . . .

And . . .

That's all, really. A girl is in the room. But that's not all. A girl is in the room and something makes my gut twist. A girl is in the room and I can't look away from her. A girl is in the room, and, somewhere, something blinks into clarity for the first time.

She's tallish, just a little taller than me, in ripped jeans and a cropped hoodie. Her hair is dark and curly—*curly* curly, not like those girls who sleep with braids in and then talk about how hard their curls are to *maintain*—wild and hanging over one perfectly winged eye. She's looking at all of us, carefully, one by one, and I jolt. I think she said something.

"Is this the senior student council meeting? Mr. Bremner said I'd find it here."

"Yes, it is!" Gray says, standing up at his desk just a little too quickly so his chair falls over. "I'm Ethan Gray, senior class president."

Oh, he's *Ethan* now. Of course. I stifle a slightly hysterical laugh behind a cough.

"Tal," the girl says. I watch her tongue flick down from the roof of her mouth to form the sharp *T* sound and then I want to slap myself.

"I'm new this year," she continues. Half our school is new this year, everyone being bussed in from these shiny developments a few towns over. But none of the other new-this-years look like *her*. None of the other new-this-years have inspired this awful combination of dread-and-longing nonsense going on in my chest right now.

"This school's a fucking labyrinth," she's saying. "My schedule is all over the place and Mr. Bremner said you guys could help."

If it was somehow possible for me to not have known Tal was new, I'd know it now. Because now she steps toward me. Now she flashes a tiny but blinding smile my way. Now she tilts her head down so slightly that no one else probably even noticed it.

"How is it possible that I have Art in room 210 and English in 211, but those rooms aren't, in fact, across the hall from each other?"

Disarming. That's the word. *That's Tal*, I think, and then feel stupid for thinking that. Who am I to say who Tal is? Tal's said one sentence to me, and I'm making it weird, the way I must be looking at her. What, like I've never seen a hot girl in real life before?

(Except I don't know if I have, really. I don't know when me googling "girls kissing" when I was ten turned into me scrolling through some actress's Instagram turned into me coming out turned into this, here, now. Seeing a girl and knowing that I think she's hot.)

Gray laughs like that was the funniest thing he's ever heard and I just barely suppress the urge to roll my eyes at him.

"I know, this place is wild," he says to Tal, coming up beside me and swinging an arm around my shoulders. He shoots Tal the kind of smile that makes you feel like the only person in the universe, leaning forward and bringing me with him. "But if you show me your schedule, I can definitely help you out. Believe it or not, the 210/211 thing isn't even the weirdest part of the layout."

Gray holds out his hand and Tal passes him her schedule. If there was even the faintest brushing of hands there, I'm going to be hearing about it for the next four business days. He's using his Grown-Up Voice. There's only one reason for Gray to turn on his Grown-Up Voice, and that's when he's trying to impress a girl. Also, the 210/211 thing is *totally* the weirdest part of the layout. He's just looking for an excuse to talk to her.

Tal smiles up at him the way I've seen a million other girls do. Looking up through her eyelashes, head tilted, shy but knowing exactly what's going on. I know it. I *know* it. Because that's how girls look at Gray. That's how *I* looked at Gray.

"If you want, I can walk you to your next class?" Gray's saying now, and it sends me right back to earth. I know my cue when I hear it, know when it's time to leave something alone and let Gray work his magic. It just hasn't happened like this yet.

Tal looks at me one more time, just for a second, just long enough to meet my eye and make me feel like there's static electricity in my fingertips. I force myself to remember the smile she just gave Gray, to think about Gray's posturing and his Grown-Up Voice.

"I'll see you guys later, nice to meet you, Tal!" I say, too quickly, too desperately. I get the fuck out of there. I flee, honestly, because Gray's using his Grown-Up Voice and Tal loves it and they were two words away from forgetting I was even there. Lunch isn't over for another ten minutes, but I have a feeling Gray's not going to notice when he's looking at Tal.

I'm halfway down the hall before I can think too hard about the fact that Tal is the first girl outside of the internet who's made my stomach feel like that.

THREE

"She is so fucking cool, Luke."

"Don't call me Luke," I say automatically.

"She is so fucking cool, Ms. Alana Lucas, Esquire."

"Better."

Gray showed Tal around for the rest of lunch, brought her to the cafeteria that's always too cold and the track out back where half the student population sneak out to smoke and the other half earnestly run laps or have picnics when the weather's nice. Then it turned out that they're in the same English class, so Gray took it upon himself to become Tal's unofficial first-day-of-school buddy, already showing her off like she's Gray's Girl 2.0. I heard someone in fifth period say *of course Gray already claimed the hot new girl*, and the first day only ended twenty minutes ago. Dozens of new transfer kids, but Gray's already found the best of them.

"We were supposed to talk about our favorite poets, and, like, who has a favorite poet, right? Tal does."

I swallow something bitter stuck in my throat when I hear Gray say her name.

"She's from Portland, which, y'know, automatically makes her cooler than any of us, right?"

"I guess."

Gray squints at me.

"You guess? What's your issue with her?"

"I don't have an issue with her!"

"But . . ."

But I wonder if her hair's as soft as it looks and what she smells like and how her voice sounds first thing in the morning.

Jesus, that's not good.

"But nothing!" I rush to say. "I'm glad you've found someone new and exciting to chase around."

"What makes you think I'm going to be chasing?"

I catch myself before I say something stupid like *the, like, everything about her?* Because I can't imagine Tal chasing anybody, but I can very easily imagine people chasing after her. Like Gray. Like me, in a different universe where she looked at me the way I saw her look at Gray earlier and where I'd actually have the guts to talk to someone like her in real life and have it mean something.

"I'm sorry," I say. "I forgot who I was talking to for a second."

Gray grins at me. "I'm six one, y'know."

"I know."

"Girls like that."

"So I hear."

Gray laughs and swats me on the arm. It's after school and we're in the big gym with the A/C the school's said they're fixing twice a week since freshman year. My hair is sticking to the back of my neck. All around us, dozens of freshmen are playing badminton with a zeal the sport has never seen before, our conversation punctuated by yelps and screeches and big look-at-me laughs.

"So," Gray says grandly, sweeping an arm across the stunning landscape. "That brings us here."

I look around us. Two of the badminton players are having what appears to be a lightsaber battle with their rackets. They're making the *schoom* noises and everything.

"Here to . . . intramural badminton?"

(When Gray and I were still together, it made perfect sense for us to volunteer to be the student council reps for the badminton team. All we'd have to do is sit around and watch people swinging rackets at each other, right? Now that we aren't together, it's still nice to hang out, but I can call him a dickhead more freely for choosing the world's most annoying sport based solely on the fact that he likes to giggle at the word *shuttlecock*.)

"Here to the *plan*, Ms. Alana Lucas, Private Investigator!"

Oh god, he has his notebook with him.

I groan. "Why do we always need *plans*? Can we not do something without written documentation?"

"These are our glory years, Ms. Alana Lucas, Certified Life Coach," Gray says. "One day, you'll thank me for the written documentation."

I give Gray the finger and he gasps, putting his hand up to shield it from the eyes of the impressionable badminton freshmen.

I know that I'm not actually going to say no to whatever it is Gray's asking. We don't say no to each other, ever. It's just that Gray seems to ask for shit more often than I do.

"What's your incredible plan?" I ask.

Gray's eyes light up, because he truly loves a plan. He opens the notebook.

"Okay, so our whole thing is a little . . . bizarre, right?"

"I don't know what you're talking about, ex-boyfriend whose house I spend forty hours a week at."

"Right! So I bet people might be intimidated! I think the key is going to be easing Tal into us, a bit. We can gradually work up to the two of us hanging out alone, and by the time we *are* hanging out alone, she'll be in love with me and she won't even know how it happened!"

The annoying part about this plan is that he's right. No straight girl within a mile of Gray can resist him, and they don't even know why. Even, unfortunately, straight girls that make my heart pound.

"Allow me to add that you're very nice and pretty," he says after it's been just a second too long since I responded.

I honk out a laugh and a freshman girl shares a look with her friend. I want to stick my tongue out at them, but maturely refrain.

"If you're so sure she's perfect, why can't you just ask her out?"

Gray gasps, putting a hand to his chest.

"I can't just *ask her out*, Ms. Alana Lucas, Registered Dietician. I need to make sure we're on the same page! I need to make sure our energies align! I need to make sure she's not one of those absolute *aliens* who think Coke and Pepsi taste the same!"

"Wouldn't you find out all of that by talking to her?"

"Well, yes, in an ideal world. But we don't live in an ideal world."

"Clearly."

Gray takes a breath. He sniffs out a weak little laugh at himself. He looks away from me.

"I don't really know how to do this," he admits, scratching at the back of his neck. "It's not like I've done any of it since . . ."

Since he took me into his backyard in the middle of the night the summer before we started high school and kissed me. Since he told me he'd been in love with me for a year. Since he asked me to be his girlfriend and I said yes because why wouldn't I want the thing that every girl we knew seemed to want?

"And I made it easy," I say, because if I don't make a joke I won't be able to look at him. "Basically just dropped into your lap."

"I should have sent your mom Mother's Day cards," he agrees.

Gray's fiddling with the hem of his shirt. The skin around his thumbnail is raw and bleeding. There's a deep line between his eyebrows that's going to be permanent one day, a hunch in his shoulders and it's only the first day back. When you want things the way that Gray wants things, you need to have someone to help you get there. I think he'd combust otherwise.

"We could invite her to the pool this weekend," I say after

a pause. It's not like Tal was ever going to like me. It's not like I would have ever done anything about it. So I might as well do this. I might as well keep being Gray's Girl. Gray just grins and I roll my eyes and shoulder-check him.

"Funny you should say that . . ." he says, letting the sentence trail off into the air.

Oh, this asshole.

Gray waves at someone over my shoulder and all the air rushes out of my body. I have to force myself to sit up straight so that he doesn't notice. Tal's waving back, hiking her banged-up backpack up on her shoulder and dodging a particularly unfortunate serve. She catches the wayward shuttlecock without even trying and then laughs with the poor guy who chucked it at her in the first place. We watch him fall immediately in love with her.

I glance sideways at Gray. I'm pretty sure we have the exact same look on our faces.

"This is amazing," Tal laughs, making herself comfortable beside me on the bleacher. "Thanks for the hot tip, Gray, this is clearly the place to be."

Gray grins, ducking his head and, *Jesus*, I haven't seen that face since middle school.

"Hi again," Tal says, turning to me. She's looking directly at me and I still have to resist the urge to turn around and see if she's talking to someone else. That's how pathetic this baby-crush has gotten in the three hours since I met Tal. Is this what happens to everybody? I'm suddenly struck by a deep understanding of why everyone got so weird once we hit middle school.

"Hi again," I parrot. I smile, closed-mouthed, polite.

"Oh, sorry!" Gray says. "You guys didn't get a chance to really meet each other earlier, did you?"

"I was whisked away," Tal confirms, and Gray laughs like they're in on a cute little joke together.

Tal's looking at me, and I squirm before I even mean to. A few extremely long seconds pass when we're just looking at each other, the sounds of the rowdy freshmen fading away.

And then I realize that Tal is waiting for me to officially introduce myself, and I look like a creep just staring at her.

"I'm Alana," I blurt out. "Sorry."

"Alana Sorry," Tal says. "A beautiful name."

That's such a ridiculous dad joke that it should make this better, make Tal feel less untouchable. Instead, I just get this sick little thrill at Tal saying my name so close to the word *beautiful*.

"So did you guys draw the short straws or something?" Tal asks. She leans back on the bleacher behind her, taking it all in.

"I, unfortunately, have to take credit for this one," Gray says. He's doing that aw-shucks-I-can't-stand-how-charming-I-am schtick that I hate.

"Extracurriculars don't need a faculty advisor if they have senior student council supervisors," Gray explains. "It's a way to give people a bit more freedom."

I scoff. "It's also a way for teachers to not have to sit through intramural badminton."

"So Mr. President roped you into it, huh?" Tal asks, that laser-focus back on me again for a split second before she turns to Gray. "Surely you could let the poor girl off the hook for this one."

It does a couple of things to me, that. I don't really know which one to focus on.

For one thing, it's so deeply strange to speak to someone who doesn't know about me and Gray; who doesn't see us as institution and myth and haze. But then, if Tal doesn't know about me and Gray, that means that Gray hasn't been telling her about me, and of course Gray doesn't have to tell people about me anymore, but it still vaguely stings to know that he wasn't thinking about me all afternoon.

"Nah," Gray says with a carefully practiced ease. "We're a package deal."

He says it lightly, just exactly the way he wanted to say it, but I see the waver below the surface. Because Gray's not kidding. Because this is the first girl he's liked—*really*, actually liked—since me. You can see it in everything about him, if you know how to look for it. And we *are* a package deal. If Tal can't deal with that, then whatever's between her and Gray won't last the week.

Tal looks at the two of us for a second, eyes darting back and forth. I can see the faintest hint of panic rising up behind Gray's eyes, worried that he's scared her away.

"Cute," she says eventually. It does pretty much the same thing the whole *beautiful* debacle did to me.

The three of us sit for a minute longer, breathing out laughs at the expense of various freshmen trying extremely hard to make badminton their Thing in high school. It takes Gray a second to ramp up to what is clearly phase two of his plan.

"Hey," he says, to me but really to Tal, "do you mind if I head out early? My grandma's coming over and I told my mom I'd clean before she got home from work."

I narrow my eyes at him. He's not lying; I've known Granny Gray was coming over tonight for weeks. *I'm* literally coming over for dinner as soon as badminton is over. But Gray's definitely only talking about it now so that Tal sees what a great guy he is.

It would probably be more annoying if it wasn't true.

"Go forth, perfect son," I say. I hold my hand out and Gray kisses it before either of us can think about it. I see my panic mirrored in his eyes at the thought of Tal thinking we're something different from what we are. But she's smiling at us.

"Sorry to bail," he says to Tal, but she just shrugs. I watch Gray watch her and then wave—*wave*, big and embarrassing and smitten—goodbye on his way out the door.

"He's cute," Tal says after he's gone. She's smiling, because of course she's smiling. How can you not smile at Gray like that, perfect and shiny, just enough of a peek under the surface to see that it's all real? Like I said, no straight girl within a mile.

"He tries," I say, and Tal laughs.

"How was your first day?" I ask after I pointedly look away from the curve of her mouth when she laughs.

She shrugs with her whole body, leaning back on the bleacher behind us again. "It's been fine," she says. "My old school was way bigger, so I'm used to kind of just being a face in the crowd. It's not that much of a difference, really."

I nod, hum. We both sit there and it feels like I can tell exactly how far away she is. Down to the inch. Down to the molecule. I need to say something or I'll combust.

"Oh!" I say, like I've only just thought of it. It sounds so fake and I cringe but power through. "I don't know if you've seen the town pool? It's, like, kind of tucked away, off Liberty Street in the south end? It's closed for the season now, but Gray's aunt owns it and she lets us hang out there one extra weekend every year. She doesn't let us call it a party, but, like, it's a party. Gray told me to invite you."

That's the key, I think. *Gray told me to invite you.* The magic ticket. I don't have to worry about Tal figuring out how much I want to see her there as long as I'm clear that Gray invited her.

"Oh yeah?" Tal shakes a hand through her hair and smiles sideways at me. I know that smile, that trying-so-hard-not-to-look-too-excited smile girls do when Gray talks to them.

"You should come," I say, but halfway through I have to look straight ahead because I feel like my face will melt off if I look at hers. I hate myself. "I can't promise it'll be fun, but someone usually throws up in Gray's aunt's office."

Tal gasps, putting her hand to her chest.

"And that could be *me!*" she exclaims, but it's not mean. She's not bored with us yet. "When's it start?"

I shrug. "It's during the day. Like one?" We don't do times, because no one's ever new enough to need to know when it's time to go to the pool or Gray's garage or Kennedy's living room. You just go and usually there's one or two people already there and you kind of fold yourself into them. "Hope you don't mind day-drinking."

"Aw, you have so much to learn about me," she says, and then.

And then.

She stands up, turns around. Tilts her head at me and smirks.

"Does everyone have to do that goodbye with you?" she asks.

It takes me a second, but when I realize she means my Gray goodbye, means her lips on my knuckles, all the blood rushes from my face.

Tal grins, huge, would-be-scary if it wasn't her, all her teeth on show. She throws her head back and laughs on her way out and she's laughing at me, of course she is, laughing at her own audacity to flirt with the gay girl, and I know I should hate it but I'm left staring at the space she just occupied with my mouth hanging open.

I walk to Gray's house once badminton's over because his grandmother is the cutest woman on the planet. She gives me a hug and $5 that I try to sneak back into her purse when she's not looking, but Granny Gray is always looking, and she gives me such a glare that I hastily stuff the money into my pocket and thank her.

"How was school?" Granny Gray asks while Gray's mom and I dole out plates of spaghetti. I eye Lianne carefully when she takes her first bite, because I made the sauce the other day and I've been experimenting with sugar quantity. Thankfully, she doesn't seem to hate it and I haven't ruined family dinner.

"I met the girl of my dreams," Gray announces. "Present company excluded."

What a coincidence, my brain says helpfully. *So did I.*

"And it's only the first day," Lianne says dryly. "Imagine what you might achieve if you came home talking about actual schoolwork."

Gray shrugs off his mom and barrels ahead, telling all the stories he's already told me about Tal. Tal, who has a favorite poet. Tal, who actually had fun at intramural badminton. Tal, who leaned back on the bleachers and her hoodie rode up and showed a sliver of skin that I wanted to touch so badly it almost hurt. Tal, who was definitely making fun of me when she asked to kiss my hand and Tal who I should hate for that but don't, can't.

Okay, so maybe I added the last couple.

"What about you, Alana?" Granny Gray asks. "Any girls of *your* dreams kicking around that school?"

We almost didn't tell Granny Gray about me, when we broke up. We had a whole plan to pretend we were still together when she came over. I couldn't bear the thought that she might take it badly, that she would stop calling me her *favorite granddaughter* and reminding me to stretch my neck because *you kids and those phones are going to destroy your own spines, and for what?* But then one day Gray and I were talking about it and she overheard us, and the next day she dropped by Gray's house wearing a little button with pink and orange stripes on it and she said, *I think this is the lesbian one, is that right?* And I said, *I have no idea* and we both laughed, and then I cried in the bathroom between dinner and dessert.

"Luke's saving herself for UMaine," Gray says. I kick him under the table because I really don't need for him to say anything about *saving myself* in front of *Granny Gray*.

"You do know that you'll have to actually study when you get to college, right?" Lianne asks.

"Not all parties and girls," Granny Gray adds, but her and Lianne are smiling because they know Gray would never in a million years blow his chance in college. The two of them take turns teasing Gray, and I sit back and watch, let the food and the familiar smell of Gray's house and the sound of his family laughing blanket over me. The TV's on in the other room because Granny Gray says we need to always have the news on in case we miss something exciting, and one of the three lightbulbs overhead is burned out so everything has a yellowy glow to it, and if I focus on this, only this, I can forget what Tal even looks like.

♡

FOUR

It's late when I finally get home, takeout containers in the sink because my parents never really learned how to cook for themselves. It's part of their charm. They aren't anywhere to be seen, maybe across the street with the Rosses drinking wine on their back deck or in town getting dessert somewhere or in another one of the million places around town they've marked for themselves in that grown-up, weirdly official way.

I throw my backpack on the kitchen counter and we stare at each other for a good, long minute. I know, technically, that there's math homework in there. I also know, technically, that I could probably finish it in the library tomorrow at lunch before class. I also *also* know, technically, that there's probably enough time to make myself something sweet before I have to go to bed and deal with the Tal-shaped dent in my brain.

Gray drove me home, like he always does, but there was this new bright light in him that made the car feel smaller than usual. He couldn't stop talking about how *cool* Tal was, how *amazing* it was that he felt like he already knew her, how *amazing* it is that she just happened to transfer to our school in time for the two of them to meet. He's already talking about her like they're together, which is annoying for a *number* of reasons I don't have the brain capacity to think too hard about right now.

I shake my head, trying to dislodge the look on Tal's face when she told me she thought Gray was cute. No thinking about that. We have heavy cream and three pints of strawberries Gray and I bought the other day, and that can solve everything, maybe.

"Hey, baby," I say to my stand mixer, because it's never hurt me and even if it did, it's under warranty. The eggs come out and I spend way too much time separating them by hand just to feel something working, dropping the whites into the stainless steel bowl and smiling serenely once the whisk attachment starts whirring away.

Meringues were the first thing I learned how to make that didn't come out of a box. It's magic, the way the eggs go from clear to bubbly to white to glossy, the way a little sugar and vanilla turns them into something perfect. I know that you're supposed to do other stuff while you're waiting for egg whites to form peaks, but it's too mesmerizing for me to look away. As long as I get everything right, the same thing will happen every time. If even a speck of yolk had fallen in, I'd be standing here forever, uselessly. But it's perfect. Because of me.

Once my meringue's in the oven, I throw the heavy cream in my mixer and watch that magic, too. Thick and frothy. There's something glamorous about it. Vanilla makes it real whipped cream, and I help myself to a generous finger dollop of it before I start slicing up the strawberries. The cutting board and my hands and under my fingernails are red, red,

red when I'm done, and I take my time licking the juice off because I know in about thirty seconds it's gonna be winter, again, and strawberries are going to cost $11 a pint and come from Walmart already overripe.

I add *eggs, heavy cream, vanilla* to the running supply list I keep stuck to the fridge. The meringue is basically done, and I think I've just about gotten away with it when the front door opens and my parents come in laughing slightly too loudly. Which means I know exactly where they were.

"How are the Rosses?" I ask.

"They say hi," my mom says, then eyes up my bowl like I'm behind the counter at McDonald's at 3:00 a.m. "Whatcha got there?"

"A dessert I made from scratch by myself *for* myself."

My mom pouts. "That's very rude."

I snort. "Oh, sorry I didn't think to make drunk munchies for my parents at nine p.m. the day after Labor Day. Isn't there decorum about that kind of thing?"

"We're not drunk," my dad interjects. "We're carefree."

"Footloose and fancy free," my mom adds. "And we aren't wearing white. Isn't that the only post–Labor Day rule?"

"If you wanted to convince me you aren't at least a little tipsy, you should probably have removed the phrase *footloose and fancy free* from your vocabulary."

My parents laugh, and it's so loud and ridiculous that I laugh, too, and then I feel bad that I didn't make enough dessert for them. Not bad enough to do anything about it, but still.

"How was your first day?" my mom asks, sitting at the

breakfast bar and watching my dad rip into a bag of frozen fries and lay them out on a baking tray.

I know the joke here. I know that parents love to laugh about how, whenever they ask their kid how school was, they say *fine*. I know about the books and blog posts and videos people make to try and teach parents how to get their kids to *share* with them, to avoid that *fine*.

But my first day was my first first day of high school where I wasn't Gray's Girl. It was the day I realized what it was like to want in real life and the day Tal looked at Gray the way she did, so it was also the day I remembered who I was and what I do now. My parents have never been anything but supportive, but there's this *thing* I put between us now, just in case something ever changes. Every word has a double meaning, every *how was school* turns into *so have you kissed a girl yet?* in my head.

I could tell my parents about Tal and about Gray and about how Gray's roped me into making Tal and Gray Tal-and-Gray. I could tell them about Tal's sharp teeth and big laugh and curly hair. But it's like coming out all over again, that step between telling them I like girls and *showing* them.

So I say, "Fine," and pretend I don't notice the look they exchange when I retreat back up to my room.

I'm thinking about calling Gray (honestly, more to show off my dessert than anything else), but when I'm tucked into my room, door shut, under covers, lights dimmed, he calls me first.

"So I've planned it all out," he says. We don't say *hi* or *bye*.

Why would we need to, when we're attached to each other 24/7?

"My murder?"

"You wish."

"I *do* wish. If I was dead, you wouldn't be able to rope me into your Tal plan."

Gray ignores me, but I knew he would. "Did you invite her to the pool thing?"

"I am but your humble servant."

"Ugh, you're the best," he says, and it makes it worth it but also makes me wilt because I'm not sure he'd think that if he knew what I was thinking about Tal a few hours ago. "So first she gets to know everyone in a group, that way it's not like this big serious thing."

I nod, mouth too full of meringue to speak. They're a little brittle, but also it's eggs, sugar, and vanilla. It was never going to be *bad*.

"Then hopefully she becomes just, like, part of the group, y'know? Maybe she's hanging out in Ken's garage with us, maybe she goes to one of Syd's parties . . ."

"Maybe your best friend stops speaking to you because you're treating this relationship like a PowerPoint presentation . . ."

"I'm not trying to hear that," he says, in a frankly scary accurate impression of Dionne from *Clueless*. "Then, once she's comfortable with all of us, we see if she'd want to go to homecoming. As friends, y'know?"

Our school's homecoming is low-key. For whatever reason,

we missed the memo about parades and banquet halls. It's in the gym and people barely bother to even bring a date. Gray and I have always gone with our friends in one big group, even when we were dating.

"*Then*, we can start hanging out with her."

I cough and little specks of whipped cream launch out of my mouth and onto my phone.

"*We* as in you and me?" I ask, wiping my phone's camera with Gray's hoodie sleeve.

"Yeah, of course," Gray says. "Obviously. If she's gonna last, she'll have to be okay with our whole thing. What better way to make sure that happens than to make her part of it?"

It feels like there's still whipped cream in my throat. *If she's gonna last.* Gray wants Tal to last. Gray wants Tal to last, and I think I might be jealous but I can't figure out if it's of Tal, taking Gray's attention from me, or Gray, getting to soak in all of Tal's light.

"And then, eventually, I can ask her out and everything will be perfect forever, the end."

I snort. "I'm glad you're being realistic about it."

If I was feeling meaner I'd call Gray out on this, tell him it was stupid to create such a drawn-out plan to avoid actually talking to Tal, tell him I've already seen the way she smiles at him and how I seriously doubt she'd turn him down if he asked her out now. But Gray has to do what he has to do to feel okay about stuff, always has, and this is one of those things.

And if it means I get to wait a little longer before I have to watch him and Tal all over each other, so be it.

♡

FIVE

I get to the pool late on Saturday, just as Rosie's leaving in her yellow VW Bug. She'll have already stood in front of everyone and glared at them all individually, told them that if there's so much as an extra bit of chipped paint on the pool floor, then these parties are over, she means it, seriously this time, *Ethan*. She honks the horn at me, rolls her window down, and makes me squeeze through it so she can hug me.

"Here I thought Gray finally chased you off for good!" she says.

"He'd have to try way harder than that."

I see Rosie twice a year. Today, and the day after Christmas, when I go to Gray's house and we sit with his mom and eat nothing but candy all day while his family bustles in and out. She's so happy to see me, and it feels so the same, that for a second I'm worried that no one's told her about Gray and me, that I'm going to have to come out to her when I thought someone had already done it for me, and the thought makes my stomach hurt even more than it already does.

But then Rosie says, "You look good, babe. I hope you

were late because you were prettying yourself up, not because anyone in there's giving you a hard time."

It perks me up, knowing that she knows and seeing that it's the same. But I deflate again when I remember that it's not, actually, that if things were the same, then I wouldn't have freaked out over what I was going to wear to this because Tal's going to be here, and then I wouldn't have freaked out over freaking out, because if I was freaking out, then that means I care, and if I care, then that means I'm an asshole.

"I'm good," I tell Rosie. I smile, and she definitely doesn't believe it, but she pats my cheek and I let her drive off and I steel myself and I walk out to the pool.

It's another stupidly nice day, hot like the middle of July. We're due a thunderstorm, one last massive summer storm, but it doesn't look like anyone else is thinking about that right now. Syd's on Logan's shoulders in the shallow end, sunning herself like a lizard while Olivia and Kennedy dip their legs in, lean back, and let bikini straps slip off their shoulders.

"Hiiiiiiii," Ken drawls up at me as I walk by. I think she's the last person on the planet to get the skin cancer/tanning memo. She spends every summer half-naked in her backyard trying to brown up. As it is, she's currently a crispy beige that'll fade just in time for her to bring down the house at whatever this year's musical is. If we were actually talking, she'd have told me already, would have made me listen to the cast album while we drove around in her mom's CR-V and then yelled at me when I inevitably knocked my fries all over the floor. I nudge her in the back with my foot but don't say anything because she's already turned back to the others, and they don't acknowledge me except for brief, tight smiles.

I haven't actually hung out with these people sober in months, but I'm only just realizing that. I've got my bathing suit on underneath the button-up shirt Gray lent me when we repainted his room two years ago, but I don't want anyone to see me. I'm too afraid of exposure, which is stupid since it's *beyond* clear I've already been exposed to all of these people.

My instinct is, as always, to scan the crowd for Gray. I find him off to the side, by the changing rooms, drink in hand. He's leaning against the wall, talking to Tal.

Tal.

Tal's here.

I mean, I knew Tal was going to be here. I was the one who invited her. But there's a difference, I'm finding, between thinking about Tal in theory and being faced with the screaming, shining, life-ruining reality of her.

She's facing away from me, which is good, because it means she won't see the way I've just burst into flames, the way I don't know which way's up. I don't know if this is what Tal does to everyone, if Gray's feeling like this, too, and that's why he's made me go over his master plan three times this week, or if this feeling is uniquely mine.

Tal's wearing an oversize jean jacket with the sleeves pushed up to her elbows and, I assume, a bathing suit underneath because all I can see is leg, leg, leg. She has a drink in her hand—one of Gray's beers, which makes my stomach slosh uncomfortably because he only ever shares his drinks with me—and her fingers are wrapped around the bottle's neck, long, brushing against her own hand. I can't stop looking at them and feeling dirty, heady, and just when I think, *Oh, this is what it feels like when you're attracted to someone, this is what wanting is,* Gray spots me and waves me over, and Tal turns around.

"Shit," I mutter, and then freeze because I didn't mean to say it out loud, but *shit.* What the hell am I doing?

Tal looks, of course, even more amazing from the front, but as soon as I see her, I look away, focus on Gray, smile at Gray, remember Gray.

"She lives!" Gray says, throwing his arm around me and squeezing me close. I should have skipped out on this, should have said I was sick, should have flung myself out of my bedroom window instead.

"Luke is almost never late," Gray explains to Tal, because that's what he does now, explains our world to her so he can invite her into it. "So either she hates you or she was abducted by aliens this morning."

"Don't call me Luke," I say, harsher than I maybe normally would, and I feel bad for it right away because Gray squeezes me again, a *you okay?* and I lean my head on his shoulder because I don't know what else to do.

I try to shake it off. "I was attacked, actually. Are you familiar with the film *Bugsy Malone*? It was a group of small children dressed as 1920s-style gangsters."

Tal *cackles,* throws her head all the way back, makes everyone turn to look at her, and for just a second, just a teeny moment, I think, *Ha.* I think, *I bet Gray hasn't made her laugh like that.*

But then Gray passes her another one of his beers, and she smiles up at him through her eyelashes, and I come right back down to earth.

"How long have you guys been here?" I ask, because I hate myself.

"Not long. You missed Rosie's lecture, but she said that you were, quote, *the only one of you little jackals I actually trust*, so she let it go. I haven't even pushed Logan into the pool yet."

"Logan's already in the pool," Tal points out, then furrows her eyebrows. "Right? Guy sitting in the shallow end with the girls? Not as tall or hot as he thinks he is?"

"Can you please tell him that?" I ask. "And, follow-up question, can I please be there when you tell him that?"

"He's *in* the pool," Gray agrees, ignoring me. "But he'll never go under. His hair gets really fluffy when it's wet. Makes him look like a Pomeranian. Big crowd-pleaser."

Tal laughs and turns toward Gray, which makes Gray turn toward Tal, and I don't think either of them realize they're doing it but suddenly they're two people having a conversation, and I'm getting in the way of it.

"I'm gonna go tell Logan about your nefarious plans," I say.

"You wouldn't dare!" Gray screeches.

I shrug and walk off, but instantly regret it. Where the hell else am I supposed to go, if not near Gray? We've always lived in each other's orbits.

"Alana!" I whip around because it's been a while since someone else called my name like that, but I freeze when I realize it's Logan. Sydney's off his shoulders, but Sav's taken her place, fingers rooted firmly in his as-yet un-fluffy hair, because Logan Bailey's no prize but when there's no one else to compete over, he'll do just fine. Sydney's laughing, kicking too-cold pool water at Logan's bare chest and hissing, "*Stop it!*" Ken doesn't open her eyes, but she always does this, falls asleep while she tans. We used to try and put stickers on her so she'd wake up with untanned patches that spelled out *slut* in little circles on her stomach and she would get so mad at us.

I know this isn't going to end well. Obviously I know that. But I still walk over, still sit on the edge of the pool between Sydney and Olivia and dip my toes, cock my head at Logan like *what now?*

"We need your expert opinion," he says. "Tal."

Don't talk about her, I want to say, like I decide, like she's mine, like she's anyone's.

"What about Tal?" I bring my feet out of the water, hug my knees to my chest, then get paranoid someone will see pubes if I sit like that, so back down they go.

"Think Gray can seal the deal?"

I raise an eyebrow, pretending like I don't know what he's asking, and Logan turns to make sure Tal and Gray aren't looking. Holds two fingers up to his mouth and waggles his tongue between them, and Sav smacks him on the top of his head but also laughs and laughs.

"You're such an asshole," Olivia says, but she's also laughing.

Here's the thing.

Of course I could tell Logan he's an asshole. But it's not the same as when Olivia does it, is it? It's me being difficult. It's ruining the party. Somewhere along the line I became the expert, the arbitrator of what people are allowed to say, and honestly I don't think I give a shit what someone like Logan Bailey has to say about anything.

I think Tal would call him out. Tal would tell him to shut the fuck up and mind his own business, probably.

"Are you asking me if she wants to fuck you instead?" I ask, pretending to stand up. "I'll just go ask her, gimme one second—"

Logan grabs me by the ankle and pulls me back down, exactly the way he would have done months ago. I passed, then.

Olivia leans her head on my shoulder and blinks up at me.

"Hi, baby," she coos, and I put my head on top of hers.

Olivia's always been contact-heavy, with all of us, but it's been weird with me since last year. Not even in the way I thought it would be—Liv's gotten touchier with me, always crowding my space now. I can't tell if she's trying to be daring the same way Tal was, seeing if she can get a rise out of the gay girl. That, or it's a guilty conscience.

"I love your sunglasses," Sav says to me then, and it's the first time she's spoken to me in god knows how long, so I thank her and lean back on my hands, nudging Olivia's head off my shoulder, and let the conversation happen around me, and it's almost enough, almost like I can imagine I fit here.

♡

SIX

Somewhere, between Saturday and now, here, after school during badminton on Tuesday afternoon, Gray got it in his head that I don't like Tal.

"I think you'd really like her if you gave her a chance," he says, reproachfully and carefully because he's so worried about me. So worried that maybe I'm not handling his moving on well, that maybe I want to hold on to him a little tighter before he runs off with Tal, his new perfect girl. So worried that I find Tal threatening.

And I do. It's just I find her threatening in more of a having-to-reevaluate-my-plan-to-remain-celibate-until-college-but-also-hating-myself-because-I-don't-have-a-chance-in-hell-with-her kind of way.

"I do like her," I say around a bubble of a laugh that I have to quickly pop. I *do* like her. "How's the plan going?"

I can ask Gray about the plan now, and it works the same magical way asking him about UMaine, about the leadership camp, about his future, works. I guess as far as he can see it, Tal's the future, too.

"Pretty good," he says. "We talked a lot. I don't think Logan scared her off. Were the girls nice to her?"

I shrug. They were nice to her in the way I knew they'd be nice to her, in the way you're nice to the new animal at the zoo. Tal's still a baby panda, still exciting. The bitching and gossip will come in due time.

"So next is homecoming, right?" I ask, but of course I know that next is homecoming. I'd know it even if Gray wasn't so hell-bent on this plan, because every time I think *Tal* and *homecoming* in the same sentence, my brain zings and short-circuits.

"Funny you should say that," Gray says, and I roll my eyes.

"Were you going to do that thing where you pretend like you just thought about texting her even though you already texted her before I got here and she's on her way?"

"I have no idea what you're talking about, and, apropos of nothing, I'd like to remind you that friends don't read friends' texts that may confirm suspicions those friends may or may not have."

Tal appears on cue. Me and Gray and the freshman guy who almost hit her with the shuttlecock last time all try to carry ourselves taller in her presence. The best part is she doesn't care, doesn't notice, doesn't ask anyone to look at her the way we all do.

"Hi," she says once she gets up to our spot on the bleachers. Her eyes dance over my face, bounce over to Gray's. My nails dig into my thigh and then I'm mad at myself for it. What, she can't *look* at him now?

"How are your cocks?" Tal asks.

Gray's eyes widen. He sputters, looks around like he can't believe his ears, his luck.

"Shuttled," I answer, because that's what she's looking for, the other half of her joke, and she grins at me, tongue between her teeth.

"I'd expect nothing less."

I salute her and then sit on my hands because Gray looks at me and tilts his head, just slightly. Only enough for me to notice. *Who are you and what are you doing here?* he's asking.

"You just missed it," Gray says after he recovers. "Those guys down there tried to play doubles, except each side had to play while piggybacking each other."

"The future is now," I add.

"See?" Tal says. "That's the kind of innovation I come to this thing for."

She pulls a history textbook from her backpack and Gray eyes it hungrily, desperate for any new information about Tal the same way I am.

"Who do you have?" he asks, gesturing at the book.

"Mr. Kurtis," Tal replies, and Gray and I both groan.

"My condolences," Gray says.

"God, he's the *worst*," I say. "And *ancient*. Has he tried telling the class that his ancestors came here on the *Mayflower* yet? Like, A, not true, and B, are we supposed to be impressed that he's related to some of the *first* colonizers?"

I don't know where this is coming from. Before, Gray did most of the talking up front and then, because I was there, because I was Gray's Girl, people brought me along for the ride. This isn't that, and I don't know if me *or* Gray really knows what to make of it.

"To be fair, I think that probably went over better when he first started teaching," Tal says. "Y'know, in 1823?"

"*Anyway.*" Gray clears his throat dramatically. "I bet you're wondering why I've gathered you both here today."

"No one was wondering that," I say.

"I thought we were watching badminton," Tal says. "If we're not here to watch a thrilling match of my new favorite sport, I'm out."

Gray likes a challenge. Always has.

"I am a man of my word," he says, gesturing grandly.

He learned how to do this when we were nine. He used to be so scared, all the time. Of speaking, of being heard, of telling someone what he wanted. We'd get to his mom's house after school and he'd collapse, start crying or breathing too quickly and freaking us both out because the amount of effort it took for him to be okay meant that once he was home, once it was just us, once he felt safe, he shut down. His mom sent him to a therapist and she told him that no one knew what was going on inside his head but him. To treat every presentation, hand raised in class, conversation with a teacher like a performance. If he didn't know what it meant to be Ethan Gray, make it up. If other people didn't know, show them. A switch flipped, and everyone started loving him like I loved him, and he stopped being Ethan and started being Gray. The bigger the show, the more nervous he actually is.

"But as I stand here, at intramural badminton, I cannot

help but wonder"—dramatic pause for effect—"how many more intramural badmintons are there?"

"Well, it's only, like, the second week of school," Tal says. "This happens once a week, so probably . . . a lot?"

"How dare you bring math into this," I add.

"Really ruining the moment," Gray says, but his shoulders have started to relax.

"Oh no, Gray, how many intramural badmintons are there?" I ask flatly.

"Thank you. Our time in high school can only march forward. Before we know it, this will be a thing of distant memory."

Tal mouths *It's September* at me and I snort.

"Distant memory!" Gray continues. "And things like, say, for example, homecoming dances will fade into the past."

When I broke up with Gray, I broke up with dances, with yearbook features and plastic tiaras. Even our low-key homecoming felt further away from me than it was before. But it makes sense that he hasn't stopped thinking about them, I guess. And look, isn't it perfect that we all get along so well, doesn't it all just work out that Gray can ask Tal to homecoming without actually having to ask her?

"Oh no, I had not thought of that," I say in my still-flat voice. "Do you think the three of us should take some sort of action?"

"Why yes, I do, Alana Lucas!" he says, which finally makes me laugh.

"It's this Friday," I say, turning to Tal.

And then I realize that Gray just made me ask Tal to homecoming. She laughs, once, a little awkwardly.

"Sorry," Gray says. "I should have clarified. We usually go to homecoming as, like, a big group. So if you wanted to go, you could come with all of us."

"Oh, so dates aren't really a thing?" Tal asks. She's looking at Gray when she asks, and my heart sinks impossibly further.

"I mean, people *do* go with dates," he says. "If you already have one that's not, like, weird, I just thought—"

"No, it's a great idea," Tal says. "Sounds good. I'll be there."

She smiles at both of us. I gulp and hope neither of them notice.

"To celebrate!" Gray starts waving his arms around again. "I propose a journey."

"There's still, like, half an hour of badminton . . . ing," Tal says.

I point at her. "Look at her, using the terminology already."

I immediately regret saying it, because Tal grins, just for me, and it's so bright I actually blink.

Gray finally sits down again. "Okay, well. After, then," he says. "Let's go be delinquents."

When Gray says *let's go be delinquents*, he means let's go eat candy in the Walmart parking lot, because that's the only thing you can do here. When you get your license, you take your best friend to Walmart. When you invite a new girl to your weird homecoming group date, you go to Walmart. When you're agonizing over the fact that you might be developing something along the lines of a crush on a straight girl who's already into your best friend, you go to Walmart. Apparently.

Gray drives, because he has the car. Tal lets Gray open the door for her and she sits in the front seat and she lets me sit behind Gray and look at her and hope she doesn't notice. But the fact that she doesn't seem to notice, because she's looking around, because she's looking at Gray, doesn't make me feel much better.

"My girl!" Gray says when he hears the song on the radio. It would sound so fake if it came from anyone but Gray. Of course he wants the girl he likes to believe he's the kind of guy who likes Taylor Swift.

Except he's actually the kind of guy who likes Taylor Swift.

It takes three songs and one commercial break to get to Walmart from school, but Gray and I knew that already. This drive, this afternoon, is so like every other afternoon that I close my eyes and when I open them I've forgotten I'm in the back seat, that Tal's right there in front of me and Gray's sitting up too straight as he parks. It makes me dizzy.

"I'm a generous homecoming date," Gray says. "But I also make minimum wage at a hardware store. Thus, I will be paying for one candy or candy-adjacent treat each this evening."

"Wow, thanks, Dad!" I say. I lean forward and kiss him on the cheek and he swats me away.

"So, this is what we do?" Tal asks once we're in Walmart's fluorescent embrace. When I was in middle school, we went to Niagara Falls and we went to a Canadian Walmart and everything was exactly the same, minus the gun cabinet. Walmart, at least, is unchanging.

"Sorry to disappoint," I say, "but this is absolutely what we do."

"It has its own charm," Gray adds.

The night I broke up with Gray, I came here an hour before

closing and walked and walked and walked and walked up and down the aisles until it felt like my knees were going to give out. Everything was so white and bright and clean that when I finally got outside, into that real-world fresh air, my vision went blue the way it does on a snowy day. I walked home even though it took almost an hour, because there was only one person I wanted to come pick me up and I'd just broken his heart.

Most of our visits aren't like that, not least of all because Gray doesn't actually know that happened.

For all we've talked it up to Tal, we don't ever really spend much time inside once we're here. Gray takes the lead and heads straight to the candy section, bright greens and oranges and pinks and reds glowing out at us and making my mouth water like I'm seven and it's Halloween.

"What's your poison?" Tal asks, nudging me with her hip. I hadn't even realized she'd come up beside me.

"All of it," I say. Tal laughs but not in a mean way and I grin.

"I'm pretty sure our dentist is going to make Luke his kid's godmother," Gray says. "They're like this." He crosses his fingers and I kick him lightly with the toe of my shoe.

"We should leave her to it," Gray says. I look up, confused, until I realize he's talking to Tal. They should leave me to it. They should walk away together and leave me here. I don't mean for my heart to pick up speed, and I don't mean for my fists to clench, but it does, and they do.

"Best of luck," Tal says to me, semi-sincerely, and she lets Gray lead her away as if she isn't a teenager in America who knows what Walmart is.

My eyes lose focus, staring at the candy options and pretending like I'm trying to figure out what I want. I strain to hear what Gray and Tal are talking about between the aisles just behind me, but all I hear is too-loud music and the occasional overhead announcement. Someone named Judy is supposed to call Bakery, and it's apparently very important because they make the announcement three times in five minutes.

I hear Tal laugh, and to my absolute horror it almost makes me want to cry. I don't even know what I'd be crying about—Gray leaving me behind, Tal being into it, me being a fucking goner over a straight girl I've known for a week. They're all pretty much as pathetic as each other, so I guess it doesn't really matter.

This is ridiculous. I grab two bags without looking, stare at them like I'm trying to decide between them even though I can barely tell what I'm looking at.

"Still not sure?" Tal's voice comes from behind me and makes me jump out of my skin.

"Told ya," Gray says, and Tal chuckles, because they talk about me now, when they're together and without me and having fun.

I look down at the bags again. Neon green or Barbie pink, sour or sweet. When I realize that Tal and Gray are going to stand there and stare at me until I pick one, I panic and take the pink. Gray cheers too loudly, for Tal's benefit, and when she laughs again I roll my eyes.

But then we get back in the car. Then Gray stops for gas. Then he gets out and Tal watches him carefully. Then she turns around, grins at me, and I grin back too big, too excited, because she's being friendly and I'm trying to find a way to dig my claws into it.

"I'm a generous homecoming date, too," she says.

She reaches into her jacket pocket, pulls out the other bag of candy, and throws it over the seat and into my hands.

Gray gets back into the car and drives off, chattering happily with Tal in the front. I watch my knuckles turn white as I grip the green bag for dear life.

♡

SEVEN

I used to be so good at homecoming.

I did the face paint. I did the gaudy orange bow in my curled ponytail, so high on my head it felt like I was going to fall over if I moved too quickly. After the game Sydney would zip me into dresses two sizes too small and cheer when they closed. Olivia did my makeup because Olivia has ten thousand followers on her makeup Instagram and never lets anyone forget about it. She would hold me still by my chin, pointed acrylic nails digging into my cheek, jerking my head back and forth while my breathing got faster and faster, claustrophobic because if I thought about it too hard, I was sure Olivia was drawing blood as she called me *little bitch* for squirming. Sydney would play music too loudly and her and Olivia would pass a joint back and forth, taking turns sitting at Olivia's bedroom window and blowing smoke out of it that just got blown back inside. Homecoming before smelled like weed and hair spray and Olivia's thousand scented candles all lit at once.

I don't even go to the game this year. My hair stays down and I brush it half-heartedly. I didn't go out and buy a new dress with Sydney, so I'm in what I wore to my cousin's wedding last summer and a teacher would call it *appropriate*, so it's obviously completely wrong. All of this should be telling me that I shouldn't go tonight, that I should fake sick and let Gray not believe it. Let him have his night with Tal and let her do and say whatever she wants to him because it's not actually my business even though yeah, okay, I might want her to be my business.

But then there's a knock at my door.

My parents aren't home. Olivia and Sydney and Kennedy and Sav never knocked. Gray definitely doesn't knock.

Tal knocks. Tal's there when I open the door, in a jumpsuit with a deep, deep V-neck and a gold tangle of necklaces draping her throat.

"Hey!" she chirps, I think, distantly, maybe. I wouldn't be able to say for sure because I'm too busy staring at her, too busy trying to stop my brain from imagining what it would be like if she was here for just me.

It's officially been too long for me to respond normally now. Tal has a confused little smile on her face, head cocked while she watches me watching her.

"I thought we were meeting at school," I say, instead of *hi*, which would have been ideal, or *will you marry me?* which would have been worse.

"Oh." Tal takes a step back and I feel instantly awful. I want to grab her by both of her hands and pull her back inside my house and make sure she knows how happy I am to see her.

But that probably wouldn't be the best idea.

"I mean, hi!" I say. "Sorry, that was rude. I was just surprised."

Tal brightens slightly. "Gray was pretty sure you were—and I'm quoting here, so forgive me—*trying to pussy out.*"

We grimace in tandem. Sometimes—rarely, but sometimes—Gray reminds me that even the best, most strong-willed high school guys are still just high school guys. Every so often, it's hard to forget that Gray's cool because he makes people think he's cool, and talking like that is exactly how most of the other guys we go to school with think someone cool talks.

Still, even now, I feel the need to say, "That wouldn't be his usual phrasing. Promise."

Tal shrugs—not like it doesn't bother her, but like she's choosing to ignore it.

"He suggested I come help you get ready because by now you would be—again, quoting—*more bagel chip than woman.* He's gonna meet us here and drive us, if that's cool?"

"I hate him," I say. Down to the bagel chips? Ugh.

Tal laughs. "He also said you'd say that."

I step aside and let Tal walk fully into my house, and, strangely, there's no power surge or mass extinction event once she's inside. That doesn't seem right. She feels too significant for the whole world not to take notice.

"If it helps," Tal says while I lead her up to my room, "I brought you a present."

We stop at the top of the stairs and Tal swings her backpack around to her front and unzips the main pocket. I peer inside and it's filled with dirty old makeup palettes and loose glitter and, importantly, an almost-full bottle of white wine.

"It was the only thing my parents wouldn't miss," she says apologetically.

"Very recent divorcée of us."

Tal brushes past me into my room like she's done it a million times, and I'm hyperconscious of every detail of this space all at once. The walls, a color the paint company called *Lavender Kiss* (I chose it when I was ten, and my parents keep telling me they'll let me repaint it but we never actually get around to doing it). My bed and its white quilt, its gray flannel sheet with the bloodstain smack in the middle because my period always comes in the middle of the night. The dust and closet full of old dolls and the dresser topped with rings and hair ties and bracelets I haven't worn since middle school. There aren't posters on the walls, just two big discolored rectangles where posters used to be. A pretty boy popstar and a girl model in a brown leather jacket side by side. I took them out of the same magazine that Kennedy left here one summer, pinned them up and thought too hard about that soft leather, how it would feel, what it would have been like if that girl had given me her jacket. I took them both down a few months ago—the boy because it felt like pretending and the girl because it felt like a statement, and I was sick of doing both.

"So you were thinking about ditching us?" Tal asks. She looks at my bed like she's maybe going to sit on it and something flickers across her face like she might actually feel awkward, too, so she doesn't.

I shrug. "You guys should have fun. It's fine."

"No!" Tal says. She looks horrified that I'd think she was rude, because she's perfect. "I want you to come! It wouldn't be fun without you."

I didn't realize Tal had any opinion at all about me, let alone a positive one. I always assumed that when Gray found a new girl, she'd hate me and I'd have to get over it because it wouldn't be right to tell Gray not to date someone just because she didn't like me. Of course, I never assumed that I'd be developing my first real-life crush on the real-life girl in question.

Tal seems to get over her initial awkwardness, because she hops up onto my bed. Leans back on her hands and looks up at me from across the room. My room isn't very big anyway, but it's getting smaller now, with her presence and all the electricity I'm making up crackling away around her.

"So are you going to leave me without a homecoming date, or what?" she asks.

I sigh, just a little. "I don't know how to do homecoming as this person."

I don't mean to say it. Or I do, but I don't know how to make it make sense. It's the same ugly building, the same playlist that hasn't been updated since 2014, the same people. It's a stupid thing to say and I'm about to shake it off, tell Tal I'm just being stupid and of course we'll go, let me grab my bag, but Tal's nodding. She's nodding, and she probably has no clue what I'm even saying, but it still makes me feel just slightly better.

"I hope you don't mind, but . . . Gray told me why you guys broke up."

It freezes me for a few different reasons.

I mean, of course Gray told her. I'm sure she asked. Why wouldn't you ask, when your new potential boyfriend's ex-girlfriend won't leave him alone? When he doesn't *want* her to leave him alone?

Then there's that prickly feeling that's been following me around since last year. That feeling like there's eyes on me even when there's not, like nothing I say is safe and anything I do might end up being used against me, like the walls have eyes and everyone's waiting for a reason to laugh at me. Of course Tal knows that I'm gay, the same way everyone else knows it, but it sometimes feels like I don't have any more room for another person, another coming out story, another reaction, another change. That's why I'd decided to hold off on actually thinking about anything until college. No one there is going to know me one way and then have to be told otherwise. Alana Lucas Is a Lesbian is going to be everyone's base level, not a whisper that gets passed around a hallway.

But then, if Gray told Tal why we broke up, that means that Tal knows. That she knew when she came to my house, that she knew when she walked into my room, that she knew when she sat on my bed. She knows, and there's no awkward phase like with Sydney. There's no overcompensating like with Kennedy. She's just here.

I haven't responded in too long, again, so I clear my throat. "Lesbian ex-girlfriend, at your service."

Tal smiles, but it's not that condescending one I sometimes get now. The you're-so-brave smile. The I-totally-get-that-love-is-love-but-I'm-definitely-never-sharing-a-bed-with-you-again smile.

"What was it like before?" she asks. "Homecoming, I mean."

Tal pats the space on my bed beside her like it's her own and I sit so that I can feel the fabric of her jumpsuit's pant leg but not the heat of the leg itself.

"Loud," I say. "Busy. Homecoming's low-key, but we'd still do the game and all that. Gray isn't, like, a sports guy really, but all his friends are. All the girls did hair and makeup together, and then we'd go back to Olivia's after. Spend the night, usually."

Olivia's basement, with its million blue-white lights in the ceiling. We camped out there last year, each of us making blanket forts out of rugs and couch cushions, extra sheets we found in Olivia's mom's immaculate linen closet. Gray and I left *early* early the next morning so we wouldn't have to help clean up and no one gave us shit for it because he was Gray and I was Gray's Girl.

Tal considers that for a minute. Watches my face and waits for me to cry or laugh or say something else, but I don't have anything else to cry or laugh or talk about, so she finally nods, a little, to herself. Grabs her backpack from my bedroom floor and rips it open instead of pulling the zipper. Stands up. Stands in front of me so her knees are just above mine.

"Close your eyes," she says, and I know what she's going to do, I'm not stupid, but my heart still stutters. I know all the things people do with their eyes closed.

It's not like Olivia. There's no sharpness, no edge, when Tal's cold fingers reach my face, tilt it so gently it makes me shudder.

"Am I hurting you?" she asks. Her voice is quiet and rough and so close to my face.

"No." My lips don't move as I say it. My heart's the only thing that's moving, frenzied but quiet.

Tal works on my eyes for a few endless minutes, the same careful touch, the same quiet ache. I keep my eyes closed. I keep my eyes closed. I keep my eyes closed, sure that when I open them again the world will be different.

Tal's hand is on my cheek. Tal's thumb brushes the corner of my mouth.

I open my eyes and her hand twitches like she's thinking of moving it, but she must reconsider because it stays. She moves her thumb to my mouth again, the center this time, unmistakable, and a rush of breath falls out of me with a soft, deep noise and—

And my door gets kicked in. I leap so far backward I hit my back on the wall, my legs stretched out painfully in front of me. Tal jolts back, and I'm sure she's about to ask me what the hell my problem is, but then she sees Gray, my perfect boy, standing in his dress shirt, his Good Shoes. Grinning like it's all part of his plan, like nothing could ever hurt him.

"So are we going to this fucking thing or what?" he asks, and Tal's watching me like a hawk, like she's not sure who I am or what I'll do, what I might make of nothing at all, but what can I do but smile at Gray and say yes?

EIGHT

Kennedy is staggering, messy, sloppy drunk before we even get inside.

We meet everyone in the parking lot so that Logan can vape and Olivia can pretend it annoys her. The girls are overly nice to Tal because she's still new and interesting, Sav touching her necklaces with one careful finger and making something jealous and sour rise up in the back of my throat. They tell her how much they love her outfit, because when someone's new and exciting, wearing pants to homecoming is cool and ironic and hot. If I'd worn pants, Olivia would have told me that she thinks it's so *cool* that I'm *so brave* and finally being myself, and I think if she tried to say that to me after what happened last year, I'd actually have to hit her.

It's getting colder at night now, the first signs of fall creeping in. I wish I'd worn tights, but we don't wear tights, ever, not to something like this where everyone can see. We'd rather our legs turn blue and fall off than have them wrapped up warm, safe and hidden. I'm praying Tal isn't cold, or at least that she doesn't shiver before we get inside. I know Gray's just dying to take that blazer off, drape it over her shoulders, and tell her not to worry about giving it back. I don't know if I could watch that, knowing Gray's middle school graduation blazer is still hanging up in the back of my closet. My eyes keep drifting to Tal's hand, to the thumb that was on my lips like a kiss barely an hour ago. That thumb wraps around Gray's arm with the rest of Tal's hand when he offers her his elbow.

Kennedy stumbles up to me, grabs my face with both hands, and smashes our noses together so hard my eyes water and I lurch back. She means it cute, but it's not. She isn't done, though, hands still planted. They're icy cold, and between the pain in my nose and Ken's Malibu breath and her loud, pealing cackles, I just want to break each of her fingers, crack them like icicles.

"Ken, fuck off," I say, paired with an eye roll. We all say it to her when she's like this. It doesn't have any heat behind it anymore.

Kennedy leans forward, squishes her sticky glossypink lips onto mine with an exaggerated *mwaaaah*, and then finally releases me, shrieking at herself, at how bold and fun she must be, how chill and interesting everyone must think she is.

"Fuck *off*, Ken," Gray says, stepping in before I even really know what happened.

"I'm fine," I say automatically. "Someone slap her or something before we go in. She's gonna get all of us kicked out if she's that sloppy."

I'm being too angry. I should have laughed with Ken, taken a picture with her even. Kissed her back. Let it become the joke. Gray made me feel like I should be angry, but I know no one else thinks that. Not with the way Olivia's raising her eyebrows at me. Not with the way Logan hides a laugh behind a cough, badly.

"Are you okay?" Tal asks in an undertone when I retreat over to her and Gray. I tuck myself under Gray's other arm, hidden away from the world even though I know how pathetic that looks.

I smile once, tight, quickly. "Fine. She's the worst when she gets like this."

"Clearly."

Tal gives Kennedy a look like she'd be more than happy to be the one to slap her to help her sober up. I'm not drunk tonight—we didn't even have time to touch Tal's contraband wine—but I feel it, now, a little. That warm feeling in my stomach. Knowing it's cold out but not feeling it, or caring. I can't tell if it's rage at Kennedy or something else.

Gray squeezes me tight for a second and I shudder. He's always given off so much heat that being near him is like getting into a hot tub in the middle of winter, but then he lets go, wanders over to Logan and makes him laugh.

"Are you carrying Ken in, or what?" I ask Olivia.

Olivia's been drinking, too. Not nearly as much as Kennedy, but enough that she forgets to hide her curled lip, the way she looks me up and down, her smirk like she's just filing away shit to say about me to Sydney in the bathroom later, like I don't already know Olivia's only ever just waiting for you to leave the room.

"You seem sober," Olivia says. "You guys can carry her. What else is a homecoming throuple good for, right?"

"And *you* seem like a bitch," Tal says, quiet so I'm the only one who hears it, and then Olivia doesn't matter so much anymore.

We finally make it inside twenty minutes later, when literally everyone else has already shown up and the kids who got here first thing are already thinking about leaving. Gray ends up walking with Kennedy, arm around her waist and trying to make it look casual, and she talks his ear off about how she's fine, it's just her *legs* that aren't working, her *head* is *fine*. Mrs. DG is standing at the entrance taking tickets, and she arches an eyebrow at him. Gray attempts an easy smile, his please-just-let-me-get-away-with-this-by-the-way-I'm-perfect-in-case-you-forgot smile, and she rolls her eyes at him but doesn't say anything. Gray drops Kennedy off with Olivia and Sav and then, once his back is to them, mouths *Jesus fucking Christ* at Tal and me.

"She's a vision," I say, craning my neck to look behind Gray at Kennedy attempting to drop it low but getting stuck on the ground and needing Olivia and Sav to yank her back up.

"So glad I girled myself up for this," Tal says. I can't tell if she's being sarcastic or not, but she looks at me like I'm in on her joke, so I laugh, too.

"You look amazing, if that counts for anything," Gray says. That earnest voice, that half shrug, him trying so hard to make it seem like he's not trying. I can't take it. I actually *can't take it*, can't stand around and be a third wheel when we told Tal we didn't do homecoming dates. I was never Gray's homecoming date, officially, so Tal doesn't need to be it, either.

"And?" I say. I twirl. "Anything you'd like to say to your *other* date?"

Gray puts his hands on my shoulders and sways the way we danced at our middle school graduation.

"*You*," he says, "look amazing, too. But *you* are not my girlfriend anymore, so *you* don't get first compliment dibs."

And how fucking ridiculous is it that that hurts?

Somehow, through the magic of stale veggie platters and the sheer energy of drunk teenagers pretending to be sober, the night isn't so bad at first.

Gray's too nervous to focus all his energy on Tal. I know if he had it his way, I would have done weeks more recon on her for him before he asked her to homecoming. If he had it his way, I probably wouldn't be at homecoming, either. I can't blame him, really—she flits between all the girls like she belongs and rolls her eyes at Logan like she's put up with him as long as the rest of us have, while everyone else watches her and thinks she's cooler and cooler and cooler—I wouldn't want to share her, either.

But Gray being nervous around Tal means he doesn't ignore me, means the three of us can dance stupidly and make fun of Sav when she rolls an ankle on the spiked heels she obviously borrowed from her sister who goes to NYU and sells us weed when she's home. Every so often Tal looks at me, flashes me a smile because she's nice and we're friends and we're having a good time, and I'm so embarrassed at how much it lights me up.

Gray disappears for a little while and Olivia marches Syd and Sav and Kennedy over to us like nothing's wrong, like she wasn't a bitch earlier, because that's what we've always done. It's just easier to pretend like nothing ever actually happens.

Tal wants to blow them off. You can see it in the way she moves, the way she puts her shoulder in between herself and them, the way she takes a step back when Sav pretends to grind on her. Just as I start to entertain the fantasy of asking Tal if she wants to leave, the guys come back all at once, laughing and punching each other and talking too loudly, and Sav and Syd and Ken and Olivia follow after them and Tal stops dancing, gives me that easy smile, that nothing-behind-it, casual, new-friend smile that I return because I know I should even though it's not, I can admit to myself in this dark room, actually what I want.

And then the music stops. Then some sophomore on the planning committee is on the stage and she's chirping about how excited she is to announce this year's homecoming royalty.

We aren't one of those schools that do the whole cringey campaigning thing; Liv hasn't been going around telling people to vote for her. People just write down names on little scrap pieces of paper on their way through the door.

But nameless sophomore reads her cue card and makes a face. Looks off to the side like someone cares enough to tell her if she's right or wrong. Laughs nervously as she announces that our homecoming queen is Logan Bailey.

The guys—even Gray, even my Gray—explode, so happy with themselves. It's Kennedy all over again, the same squealing thrill at getting away with something *so* funny.

Logan makes his way onto the stage, pretending to cry like Miss America and waving like royalty. He accepts the sash from the confused sophomore (and looks down her dress in the process), keeps waving, keeps fake crying. The king gets called up, this guy Carter who Gray knows—and I do, too, of course, but everything I've ever learned about him has been against my will. Him and Logan dance, cartoonishly rocking back and forth. Carter grabs Logan's ass and Logan leaps out of the way, punches Carter in the stomach, but they're both laughing. Everyone's laughing and it makes me think that I should be laughing, too. That the twist in my gut is my own problem, that everyone's enjoying the joke. But Gray looks at me from his boyhuddle with bright, flashing, panicked eyes, and when I look around I realize that Tal's halfway out the door.

I don't even think about going after her; I don't make the decision to rush out of the gym without looking behind me once. The gym is near enough to the front doors, down one narrow hallway, that it's easy to catch up to Tal, standing outside the school doors with her breath fogging out all around her. I feel the cold, now that it's just the two of us and she's angry and Gray might have ruined the whole thing.

"Are you okay?" I ask her once I'm finally close enough to touch her, but don't.

"God, are you?" she asks. She grabs both my arms, just above the elbow. All my blood rushes to the exact point of contact. "They've been so fucking awful to you since the second we got here. I can see why you wanted to bail. I should have just stayed home with you. I'm sure it would have been better than this."

I didn't realize they were being awful to me until Tal said it. I didn't realize I was allowed to be mad until she was.

"It's not so bad," I say, even though I don't really believe it. "It's just the way they are. They don't mean anything by it."

Tal looks like she's going to argue with me, but then she just looks sad.

"I'm sorry they make you feel like that," she says.

She's still holding on to my arms and there's no one out here with us, everyone else staying warm inside and laughing at Logan's best-ever joke. Something about that weird feeling of being at school at night when it doesn't feel like it should be allowed and Tal's hands on me (which *definitely* isn't allowed) and the memory of what happened in my room earlier makes me open my mouth to say *should we just leave?*

I can picture what that night looks like, I think. If I let myself do it. It wouldn't be what I want, really, wouldn't be the night that ends with Tal's hand back on my cheek and Tal's mouth on mine, but it would be something. We could watch a movie. We could drink that bottle of white wine even though it'll be disgusting. We could laugh about that. Gray would probably end up happy about it, anyway. What a great opportunity to get more info on Tal, to show her all the perfect things he is. Tal's right; it would be better than this, at least.

But before I can say it, the school doors fly open and Gray's there, eyes frantic like he was sure we'd both be gone by the time he got out here. I tense up and Tal lets go of me, takes a step backward. Crosses the space between us and Gray like she's slicing through the air decisively.

"What the fuck was that?" Tal demands. She gets into Gray's space in a completely different way than I've ever seen anyone do.

"Everyone thought it would be funny," Gray says instead of apologizing for being part of *everyone*. "Logan was in on it, he didn't care."

"I don't give a shit what Logan cared about!" Tal yells up at him. I watch the steam coming from her mouth float up and slap Gray in the face. "It's not about Logan! It's about the way you just told every queer guy at this school that he's a fucking joke. How could you do something like that? I'd maybe, *maybe* get it if you didn't know who you were hurting, but you do. I thought you cared about Alana."

I should bristle when Tal talks about me like I'm not even here, but it doesn't annoy me. It makes me think that, even if I wasn't here, Tal would still stick up for me like this. Gray looks at me like he expects me to say something, and the worst part is, if this was happening in front of a crowd, if everyone was watching, I probably would. I'd ignore the way that everything Tal is saying could have been ripped directly out of my head last year, and I'd tell her to calm down, say it's not worth it, try and get her to leave before she did something embarrassing like care in public.

But there's no one here. I don't have anyone to answer to but myself.

"You could have told them they were being stupid," I say.

Because they wouldn't have listened to anyone but Gray, and even then they wouldn't care if Gray told them that they were being insensitive, that they were going to hurt people. But if Gray told them they looked *stupid*, that they were being embarrassing and uncool, they would have stopped. We both know it.

"Luke," Gray says, giving me a look like *come on*. "You know how they are. Once they decide they're going to do something it doesn't matter what I say."

That's such bullshit that I almost ask him what he has to gain from lying to me. But then I realize he knows he's not gaining anything from lying to *me*. Behind his head tilts and big eyes there's a look, just for me, that says *what are you doing? Help me out here*. Because that's my job now, right? I clean his messes, right?

But tonight I don't have anything to say. And it turns out that if I don't have anything to say, no one says anything. Tal shakes her head, rubs her eyes so her mascara goes everywhere, but she doesn't do anything to fix it. It makes her eyes look huge and I look away, back to Gray. Back to my boy and his mistakes and all of the impossible things he'd like to be, but isn't. I shrug.

Gray drives us all home in complete silence.

♡

NINE

"So, due in part to capitalism's endless trudge toward our collective doom, you may have noticed we have what I would describe as a crap ton of new students this year."

Last year, some massive company opened a factory ten minutes away. There was a lot of talk about how great it would be for the town, how many tens of thousands of new jobs it would bring, but I didn't give it much thought until school started this year. There's a new development over the way from ours going up. You see the signs where the happy families ride bikes and blow dandelions and whatever the fuck else when you come into town now, big letters proclaiming *Sales office now open!* and *Corner lots available!* People are moving from the city and bringing their kids with them. A hundred new kids starting at our school this year, apparently. A whole new batch of us.

Logan turns to Gray and mouths *What?* But Mrs. DG ignores him.

"The problem with idyllic small-town life is that all of you have known each other since birth," she continues. "So

Mr. Bremner is concerned that these new kids won't stand a chance without a bit of a boost. Enter . . ." She checks a note she's made on a scrap piece of paper. "Tal Stonnard."

"Tal Stoner?" Logan asks. He's genuinely asking, not making fun of her, and that's almost worse. He spent half of homecoming trying to look down Tal's jumpsuit; you would think he'd have a spare moment to learn her last name.

"Stonnard," Tal says, more meekly than I've ever seen her, from beside Mrs. DG.

"Mr. Bremner didn't think it was fair that such a large portion of the student body didn't get to vote for their representation. He's decided having a new representative for each grade is the way forward."

"But none of them voted for her, either," Sydney says.

That's an excellent point, but Gray and I cut our eyes at her at the same time anyway.

"From what I gather, Tal was voluntold for this position by Mr. Bremner personally," Mrs. DG explains. "You'll all help her out however she needs and, ideally, bug me as little as possible in the process."

"We'll try our best, but I can't promise anything," Gray says, and Mrs. DG laughs at him because literally no one is immune to Gray.

"Bremner wants someone on student council to get Tal up to speed," Mrs. DG says. "Show her around the school, let her know what you've been working on, your goals for the year, all that jazz. So fight among yourselves for whoever gets the honor. Tal can make the final call, because while I do care deeply about your collective well-being, I don't actually care too much about this, specifically."

Mrs. DG leaves us alone after that, going back to whatever she's reading on her phone (Logan always jokes that it's porn because to him the idea of an adult woman watching porn—*especially* a gay one—is literally the funniest thing he can imagine), and we all go back to our own things. Sydney leans in close to Logan and lets her shirt expose some extremely-not-dress-code-appropriate cleavage while she tries to explain quadratic functions to him.

I'm expecting Gray to march himself right up to Tal, but instead he goes to talk to Mrs. DG. It's a brave man that interrupts her phone time, so I can't understand why until I realize he's holding that pamphlet for the leadership camp. He's either trying to secure a backup nomination or trying to find out even more about this thing, even though he's been texting me about it nonstop. He freaked out last week because the camp's Instagram followed him back.

We're fine, Gray and I, after homecoming, but I don't know how Tal feels about him anymore. Gray and I made up in our own way, by one of us sending the other a semi-funny meme and the other responding in kind. We don't need to do apologies, because we never do anything bad enough to each other to warrant one, so we don't need to do forgiveness, either. Everything is forgiven before it even happens.

But Gray and Tal don't have that, yet, don't have the history and the rules and background that Gray and I do. She hasn't left the room, even though she could have. She's sitting in the corner watching all of us with her big eyes like she's trying to take notes, and it makes me want to do something interesting so she'll remember me, so she'll think I'm the best of us.

Instead of shrinking back into the corner, like I would, or talking to someone louder and more interesting, like everyone else here would, Tal comes up to talk to me. The back of my neck flushes, because the last time I saw her was homecoming, which means the last time I saw her she was holding on to my arms out in the cold, and before *that* she was in my room, thumb to my lips. I didn't get a good look at her face, so I can't tell what that was, if it was anything. I'm already starting to convince myself that I made it up, that her thumb just slipped and she didn't even notice and she thought it was weird that I flew backward when Gray came in. But there's another, smaller voice, somewhere dark and hidden in me, that keeps reminding me that Tal's thumb moved. It had purpose.

"So," she says, "are you interested?"

It takes me a good long second before I realize what she's talking about, because yeah, I'm interested. I'm way, way too interested.

"It's okay if you aren't," Tal says, assuming my lack of response was negative. "It's not exactly the sexiest job in the world."

She's talking about her new student council position. She wants me to be her partner on it. Not Gray. Me.

Gray and I never made up our own language, but that's only because we're so close we don't usually need to even speak to each other. Sharing a brain like that means that, sometimes, when I speak, it's like it's Gray speaking through me.

It's Gray's anxiety-fueled showmanship that makes me say, "What *would* the sexiest job in the world be?"

Tal gives me a look, so I add, "Besides the obvious."

She considers it for a second, looking like she's really chewing it over. I try to hold in my laugh because she doesn't need to know what a goner I am.

"Something messy," she concludes. "Like, *getting your hands dirty*, y'know?"

That's really not what I thought she was going to say. According to Olivia, there are three different kinds of hot guy jobs: architect, doctor, independent bookstore owner. I always just assumed every straight girl thought that way.

"Sure," I say, and Tal laughs at that because I probably sound as awkward as I feel.

"Anyway," Tal says graciously, "no worries if you don't want to. I'm pretty sure no one's jumping at the chance."

"Don't be so sure," I say. "Helping the poor unfortunate new girl is admission essay bait. And Sydney would kill a man if it meant Yale early admission."

"That's a great resource to have on hand if you ever need to kill a man."

It sucks, honestly, that Tal's this funny. It sucks that she looks the way she does and she smiles the way she does and she's a genuinely good, funny person. If she was a bitch, I'd be okay. If she was boring, I'd be fine. But she's *funny* and I laugh too loudly at her jokes and it makes everyone turn and look at me, just for half a second, just long enough for me to remember where we are and who I am.

"Are you sure you don't want someone else?" I hedge. "I'd be happy to help if you wanted me, but Gray's better at . . . everything."

I swear I don't mean to say that.

But Tal just waves me off. "Oh, I don't think that would be such a great idea. I'd prefer to work with you, if you'd have me."

What the fuck does that mean?

I force myself to snap out of the pit of confusion and anxiety before I even fall into it—Tal doesn't want to work with Gray because it would be weird if they worked together, got together, and then broke up. Not everyone stays tied to their exes forever. I'm being ridiculous.

"You don't have to answer right away," Tal says, again assuming that I'm going to say no while I get lost in my own head. "You can think about it if you want."

"Okay," I say, and I mean *okay, I'll do it* but Tal thinks I'm saying *okay, I'll think about it,* so she smiles and says "I just need to know by next Monday," and I give her a queasy little smile because I've realized that saying yes to this (and of course I'm going to say yes to this) means spending way more time with Tal, means time outside school and time alone and time that I have to be normal during.

"Did you know Mrs. DG *didn't know* about the camp?" Gray asks, marching up to us and looking as offended as he would have if Mrs. DG hadn't known about evolution. "I just tried to talk to her about it and she was all *sorry, what camp? And this is the first I'm hearing of it, Ethan.*"

I look over at Mrs. DG, burying a smirk in a stack of papers.

"Oh, baby," I say. "She was *absolutely* fucking with you."

Gray sputters indignantly for a bit, until Tal starts laughing and he laughs along with her because he doesn't want her to think that he's the kind of person to make a big deal out of something like this even though I know now he's dying to go back up to Mrs. DG and actually talk about the camp.

"Uh, hey," Gray says after he's recovered. It changes the air instantly, awkward now that Gray's saying the unspoken thing. "I wanted to apologize again, Tal. For homecoming, I mean. That was shitty."

"It was," Tal agrees. "But thanks for apologizing."

My eyes dart between them frantically, desperate for at least one of them to become normal again.

"My mom's working late on Friday," he continues. "I was gonna have people over, so you could . . . come, if you wanted?"

The Plan. Smaller group, less high-stakes than homecoming, this time Gray asks her instead of me. Everything coming together just the way Gray decided it would. What is it after this? The three of us hanging out alone. One more step until Gray gets everything he wants. Easy.

"Who's gonna be there?" Tal asks. If I let myself, I can pretend that she's looking through Gray at me.

Gray shrugs. "Whoever you want. Probably most of the people we went to homecoming with."

This time, I don't imagine it. This time I know Tal looks around Gray and at me, searching for something in my face. Approval, I realize. She doesn't know if I'll be okay at Gray's, with all those people she watched hurt me. How is it that she sees it when not even Gray does?

"It'll be fun," I say, because that's my job.

Tal gives me—just me—a little nod.

"I like fun," she says.

TEN

Tal doesn't have fun the way we all have fun.

She gets to Gray's first, before anyone's there except for me, so for a little while it's just the three of us and I know Gray's nervous, can see his knuckles go white on the doorframe when he lets Tal in because this wasn't part of the plan. No extended time with just us and Tal, not yet, not until he knows what she wants him to be.

People start filing into Gray's garage soon enough, though, Logan immediately setting up the old Ping-Pong table held together with super glue and a dream by this point. He grabs cups out of his backpack and gets to work setting up a beer pong game because competition-based flirting is the only way he knows how to interact with girls.

"You any good?" he asks Tal, puffing out his chest. Gray's claim on her isn't strong enough for him yet. Logan's not afraid to be an asshole until it comes time to be an *actual* asshole. He'll flirt with Tal until she's Gray's girlfriend, and then he'll pine from afar but never do anything about it.

"No," Tal says, and it's so direct, so focused and singular, that I bark out a laugh. I've never seen anyone shut Logan down that way. *No* without *you could teach me*. *No* without *but I'll try*. Just no.

Tal doesn't give Logan anything close to resembling the time of day, just turns around and walks over to me.

"So he's just like that, huh?" she asks me, and I know that Logan must hear her but he pretends that he doesn't.

"One hundred percent of the time," I say.

Sav starts playing music through a shitty Bluetooth speaker, and Logan finds people actually willing to put up with him, so the sound of Ping-Pong balls bouncing off the concrete floor tangles with the music and the steadily increasing laughter and makes it sound like a party.

"Have you thought about us at all?" Tal asks me, and I've been nursing the same drink since I got here, so I know I'm not drunk, and Tal hasn't been drinking at all, so I know *she's* not drunk, which means I have no idea what she's talking about, but it makes my eyes go wide all the same.

Tal coughs. "Us, like the student council thing. Do you think you might be into helping me out? Being my guide or whatever?"

I need to stop doing this, this reading into everything and finding meaning where there isn't any. Tal's getting awkward and that's the last thing I want, to ruin things for Gray because I can't take a hint.

"Right," I say. "Uh, yeah. I can help."

Tal's entire face lights up. She has one of those smiles that make you feel like you're the only person in the world when it's directed at you. I swear to god, the music stops and the laughter dies down and the only thing that exists is Tal and the way she's looking at me like I just made all her dreams come true.

"Cool," she says around that smile, and I swallow hard.

She must think I'm a dick with the way I'm barely responding to her, I think, and then I remember that it shouldn't matter what Tal thinks of me. As long as Gray's new girlfriend and his ex-girlfriend more or less get along, everything's fine. Everyone's happy.

"Do you want to do something this weekend?" Tal asks then, and I'm glad I put my drink down because I absolutely would have dropped it if I was still holding it. "We can, like, strategize. Maybe you could give me the grand tour around here."

I snort before I can help myself.

"I don't know," I say. "That would take . . . god, at *least* fifteen minutes."

Tal smiles again, I guess because she hates me and wants me to suffer. "And I know you're a very busy woman."

"I am," I agree. "Between hanging around the hardware store until Gray's manager yells at him and eating three everything bagels for lunch, I don't know how I find the time to get anything done."

"Oh, so Gray's working this weekend?" Tal asks.

Right.

That's not the first time that's happened since last year. Not even close. The girls who talk to me still usually have ulterior motives, and those ulterior motives are 6'1" and objectively beautiful. Everyone knows that if you want information on Gray, I'm the best place to find it.

"Yeah," I say. I get ready to walk away, to find Gray

somewhere and report back like I'm supposed to—*Tal asked about you. Tal wanted to know if you were working this weekend*—but Tal stops me.

"So then you'd definitely be free to hang out."

I blink at her for a second, and then realize how long it's been since someone asked me to hang out. Me, specifically. Me, alone. Me, alone with Tal.

"Saturday?" Tal asks.

My mouth opens to say *yes, of course, literally any day you want, literally anything you want*, but I catch myself in time.

"Can't Saturday," I say. "It's a holy day."

She cocks her head, so I continue, "For me and Gray, I mean."

We both laugh: me awkwardly, Tal gleefully.

"I like that," she says. "I like you guys. All your stuff, I mean. You two seem like a bit of an institution here."

"I don't know if we're an institution." I rub at the back of my neck until I know it's red. "More like an urban legend. The lesbian and her boyfriend."

The only way I can say that word, still, is as a joke. I know what the word for *girl-who-doesn't-like-boys-at-all-and-only-likes-girls* is. But there's something about calling yourself the thing that Olivia used to call girls from burner Instagram accounts in middle school that can be hard to swallow. At least if it's a joke, I'm the one making it.

But when Tal laughs, she isn't laughing at me. You can tell. You get good at telling. And I can tell Tal isn't laughing at me.

"Tale as old as time," she says, and I laugh back, but is it? I have no fucking clue.

"So, Sunday, then," she says after that. I'm grateful for the excuse to stop talking about me and Gray, but then I remember if we aren't talking about me and Gray, we're talking about me and Tal.

"Sunday," I agree, and I let Tal put her number in my phone and I let Tal text herself from it and then I put all of that away because I can't think about it, any of it, too hard or I'll explode.

The problem is I don't really know how to make friends with someone who hasn't just been in my life since I was born. The problem is I still think Tal's going to realize she's too cool for all of us and walk out of Gray's garage and never speak to any of us again. The problem is whenever I catch myself thinking about Tal, I have to crush my own stupid heart all over again and remind myself who she is and who I am and what I'm supposed to be doing.

I refocus. I can't do any of *this*, but at least I can do my job.

"Gray'll be sad he missed you," I say. "He was saying he wanted to hang out the other day."

That's not strictly true, but I have to imagine that Gray telling me he thinks Tal would be on board with us having joint family vacations in the future means he'd probably want to hang out with her at some point.

Tal nods. "Yeah, I'll find him tonight and we can talk."

It's different.

I can't tell if it's because Tal's not from here, so she doesn't fully understand Gray's pull, or because she's too cool to let me see her want someone. But if I'd said that to any other girl here, they would have done a backflip, scurried off to find

Gray right away and bask in his glow. Tal's noncommittal, like she's not against the idea of making a friend, maybe. Like maybe her and Gray could get along, eventually.

God, if Tal's not interested in Gray, I don't know what he'll do. Well, actually, that's not true. He'll be great about it. He'll say that he really hopes she'll still be his friend and mean it. He'll keep inviting her to stuff like this and give her space if she needs it. He'll be Gray: perfect, always.

"You should," I say, because I'm no quitter. "He's great. Like, really."

Tal pauses for a second before she nods this time.

"I will," she says. She starts to look around the room and my heart sinks, because I know what a person looks like when they're trying to find an excuse to leave.

"I'm gonna . . . I have to pee," I say. It's the first thing that pops into my head and then I want to guillotine myself, but Tal, unfazed, gestures for me to go on.

I don't have to pee, but Tal wanders off to talk to someone else and that's all I needed. She won't be paying attention to me, anyway. I figure I'm in the clear, now, to get myself another drink, so I find Gray's stash and rummage through it until I find a passable hard seltzer.

"Are you okay?" Gray's beside me in an instant, so quickly it almost makes me jump.

I take a sip of my drink and grimace. "This tastes like lemon-flavored static electricity," I tell him. "But otherwise, yeah. Why?"

Gray swipes his thumb against the back of my neck.

"Lighting up the room with this thing."

I do it when I'm uncomfortable, rub my neck until it burns red. Only Gray notices, usually.

"I'm fine." I smile up at him to try and prove it, but he narrows his eyes.

"Was Logan being a dick to you again?"

I know Gray must have seen that Logan was talking to me *and* Tal. I *know* he saw that Tal and I were just talking for a long time. But he can't possibly fathom the idea that Tal might have been the one being a dick. He's too far gone.

Not that she *was* being a dick. But it's not like I could tell him *sorry, she's too hot and it made me nervous.*

"When *isn't* Logan being a dick?"

Logan was actually fine, but if I have a chance to blame anything on him, I'm going to take it. He could always use being knocked down a peg by Gray.

Gray assesses me for a second longer, but he doesn't seem to find anything he needs to fix right away.

"Do you think Tal's having fun?" he asks.

We both watch her for a second. She's making drinks for Rachel and her cousin, the girl that Gray must have at least made out with before either of us even knew Tal existed.

"Why did you invite Rachel?" I ask. "And . . . Rachel's cousin?"

Gray rolls his eyes at me good-naturedly. "Her name is Flora, thank you very much."

"Oh, *excuse* me."

"And I didn't, actually. Tal did. I guess Rachel's in one of her classes and I told Tal she could invite whoever she wanted. And I guess Flora wanted to come, too."

"And you're not panicking at the thought of Flora telling Tal you're a horrible, horrible person for hooking up with her and then going after Tal right away?"

"No," Gray says. "Because Flora and I didn't hook up, *actually*. Party flirting, that's it. Harmless. You'd know that if you hadn't ditched us."

That makes sense, actually. Gray isn't the type to hook up with a girl and then lose interest that quickly. I mean, the first girl he ever had a crush on, he dated for three and a half years.

That ended well, right?

"Aren't you clever," I say.

"I am, thank you."

Gray and I sit in the old folding camp chairs he keeps in here even though they smell like mildew. If you've had a couple of drinks you don't notice.

"But seriously," he says. "Do you think Tal's having fun?"

We both watch her for a long minute, pretending to shake cocktails for Rachel and Flora. She fits here in a way I didn't think she would, alongside us, making fun of Logan, carving out a spot for herself. If I let my eyes unfocus, I can see it. Can see her here. Can see me there.

But when things become sharp and clear again, I see Gray seeing her. Picturing the same thing with her. And I know which of us is actually seeing the future.

ELEVEN

"You cannot convince me that this isn't just a very small onion."

"It's a *shallot.*"

"Okay, so it's an onion that thinks it's better than me."

I throw one of the extra shallots at Gray's head, but of course he catches it. He barely looks up to do it. I wonder what that must be like.

"We're doing a shallot pasta for tonight," I say. "Then two fucking massive batches of soup. And then stuff for fajitas you can just throw in the oven. Then three lasagnas. Four if you can pay attention for that long."

"So three lasagnas."

It had been a relief, and then not, to say no when Tal asked to hang out today.

Truthfully, most of my days belong to Gray. He's where I am, and as long as we're together, it doesn't matter what we're doing or who we're with or what else is going on in the world. Today was an excuse, but it was also a saving grace. Somewhere both of us can go and I don't have to think about Tal. I only need to think about Gray, and here, and this, and us.

Gray and I have a lot of days, but none of them are quite as sacred as Meal Prep Day.

"If you're very very nice to me, I could be persuaded to make you a bunch of burger patties to freeze, too," I say to him now.

In his cramped kitchen we're practically ass-to-ass, but that's fine because it makes it easier for one of us to reach behind ourselves, find something to hold on to if we need it. A whisk, a shoulder. If I lean back on a Meal Prep Day, Gray's there to hold me steady.

"Have I mentioned how beautiful and charming you are today?" Gray asks, and I roll my eyes even as I laugh at it, bump him out of the way with my hip because I don't trust him to properly dice a shallot.

When you're us, when you're *an* us, when a person's been so much a part of your life the way Gray and I have been with each other, you have a mythology. You can look at something and say *doesn't that remind you of . . .* and the other person is already laughing because yes, of course it does. Meal Prep Day is like that.

We were young. I used to know exactly how old we were because I cared about that kind of thing, but now I forget. Eight maybe? Ten? Too young to cook full meals, anyway. Too young to be trusted in a kitchen unsupervised. But we were both at Gray's and his mom had to run across the street because she'd been helping the old lady who used to live there back then, before she died, but she was also supposed to be watching us. Gray had asked what we were having for dinner and we both remember, so clearly, the look on his mom's face. The utter exhaustion. The panic when she realized she hadn't thought about dinner yet.

She only left for, like, twenty minutes. But it was long enough for us to fill a pot with too much water, throw in way too much boxed spaghetti, and slosh hard pasta and water all over the kitchen floor as Gray put the pot on the stove.

We thought we turned the stove on, but ended up setting the oven to preheat instead. Not so bad when you think about what we could have done. That's what Gray's mom said to us when she got home, when she saw Gray stirring the cold pasta around too quickly on the stove and me trying desperately to clean up a smashed jar of marinara sauce that I'd dropped. She said of course she wasn't mad at us, which is wild because I think I would have been *so* mad at us. She said she was only glad we didn't mess with the stove, didn't turn the gas on and blow us all to high heaven. She kept saying *if anything had been different, you two could have . . .* but it wasn't, and we didn't.

"I'll make you a grilled cheese." I reach behind me and smack Gray on the ass. He swerves out of the way and pretends to gag.

We waited another couple of years before trying again. Thirteen, I think. Old enough to stay home alone. Old enough to cook things. Not quite old enough to understand how food safety works.

We'd tried with grilled cheese, because both of us knew how to do that. We waited until Gray's mom left for work and then we used a whole loaf of bread and dozens of shiny, rubbery cheese slices, slathered butter on them until our fingers were greasy, and got to it. We figured we could just freeze the ones we didn't eat. I'm pretty sure Gray's mom quietly threw them out after a while, but Gray found one in the back of the freezer three months later and had to miss school the next day. He hasn't had a grilled cheese since.

It's different now. Of course. I wouldn't let Gray and his mom eat rotten grilled cheese. I have standards. But now it's a production. Now it takes all day. Now, when Gray's mom comes home, she's actually happy that it's Meal Prep Day.

Gray did the grocery shopping this morning before I got here, so I got to sleep in. And by sleep in, I mean I got to lie in bed and think about Tal's hands and Tal's voice and what Tal's favorite color might be. I picked up my phone at least fifty times to text her but stopped myself every time. Meal Prep Day should remain sacred. I don't know how well I'll be able to stick to that if there's a conversation with Tal sitting in my phone, waiting for my return.

I haven't told Gray that Tal and I are hanging out tomorrow. He's working a double shift, going all day Sunday to save extra cash to take his mom out for a nice dinner on her birthday next week. I don't know when me not telling him becomes me lying to him.

I drop the shallots into the pan and get Gray to press garlic in as well, and then the room smells like garlic and onion, the best smell known to man, and I take a deep breath in through my nose. My shoulders finally detach from where they've been glued to my ears.

I lose myself to chopping tomatoes for the next batch of soup. Like this, it's easy. Like this, I know where Gray is, what he's doing and why and when.

"So, I might ask Tal to hang out with us sometime this week," Gray says. My shoulders snap back up.

"No Tal talk," I say without looking at him. It's not especially what I wanted to say, but it's what I'm thinking.

Gray laughs, a little incredulous. "No Tal talk? Is that the new MPD rule?"

I have to stick with it now. I focus as hard as I can on the tomato in front of me.

"Yup. No Tal, only soup."

Gray doesn't say anything for a bit, and I don't look up from where I'm chopping and smelling and doing whatever else I can do to distract myself. But after a second, he comes up behind me. Puts a hand on my shoulder like he isn't sure if he can, which is stupid. When I don't flinch away, he pulls me against his chest, brings his other arm across my front, and leans his head on my shoulder.

We stand like that for a while, and I let myself sink into it before I really mean to. We fit so easily like this, on muscle memory alone.

"No Tal," Gray agrees against my temple. "Only soup."

I stiffen a little and wiggle away, back to everything on the stove and everything I need to cut and chop and season, everything that does what I ask it to if I ask in just the right way. At first it's annoying, to have Gray assume that I'm so delicate that I can't even handle the thought of him hanging out with someone else even though I'm the one that had to go and ruin everything with us. But then I feel worse, because I'm the one who ruined everything with us and he's the one still trying so hard, still treating me so delicately.

"Y'know I'm not gonna, like, up and leave you for Tal," he says. "Right?"

I scoff. "Whoever you end up with is gonna hate me so much. Imagine you start dating someone and they're like *by the way, you'll never measure up to my high school ex-girlfriend*."

"Well . . . she *won't* measure up to my high school ex-girlfriend."

If it were any other day, if it were a couple of weeks ago, that would have been hilarious. We would have talked about how this poor hypothetical future girl is gonna get us all on clickbait news sites when she goes to ask the internet how to deal with the fact that her boyfriend comes with a codependent lesbian. But I can't do that with Tal. Either I'm getting in the way of her and Gray by being so miserable about the situation, or I'm making everyone uncomfortable with my big obnoxious gay crush on her. Either way, I don't find much of it funny.

"Are you okay?" Gray asks, and I know what I'm supposed to say. I know that this is my chance to tell him that Tal and I are hanging out tomorrow. To make it stop feeling like a lie.

"I'm good," I tell him, instead of that. "I'm worried about you killing your mother because you don't understand how to use different cutting boards for chicken and shallots, but I'm good."

"I did that *once*."

And that's how it works. We agree to ignore it. Gray knows

I'm not okay but he also knows I'm not talking about it and that's where we land on that. So we cut and we cook and Gray laughs and he either doesn't notice or doesn't ask when I don't laugh as much as he does.

The thing is, I can't be upset with him. I'm the one who told him I'm good. I'm not his girlfriend; I can't tell him I'm fine and expect for him to keep digging.

Gray's mom comes home a few hours later, after we've finished cooking but before we've started cleaning, so Gray starts chattering about how *don't worry, we're gonna clean it, sit down, don't worry about it*, which probably stresses her out even more. Lianne gives me a hug that I don't mean to melt into, but she smells the same way she always has and it's too easy to do this the same, too.

"You're just who I wanted to see today," Lianne says to me, warm eyes crinkled at the edges.

"I bet," I say. "Who would make sure your firstborn doesn't burn the house down otherwise?"

Gray's birthday is in March. Mine's April. He's her first-born, I'm her second.

"Actually," Lianne says, "I was hoping you'd have *information* for me."

At first I don't know what she's talking about, but I grin and lean in because that's what she's doing. I realize just a second too late.

"Tell me all about this Tal girl," Lianne says. "Do we like her?"

I mean, yeah. We like her.

The worst thing, the very worst thing, is that I look up at

Gray for help the same way I would have if she'd asked me about why she heard Gray and I had skipped class. The second worst thing is the fact that Gray jumps in to help me just the same as he always would.

"I got an email today!" he says, and the fact that that was the only thing he could think of to save us from this conversation makes me laugh before I can help myself.

"Me too," Lianne says. She smirks at me. "I've heard that, actually, lots of people get emails every day."

"I thought that was just a theory!" I exclaim.

"I got an email from UMaine today," Gray clarifies. He sticks his tongue out at both of us. "I forgot to tell you earlier, Luke."

He walks over to the little round kitchen table where Lianne and I are sitting across from each other and bows. "Ms. Alana Lucas, will you accompany me to the UMaine open house taking place exactly three months from today?"

I roll my eyes. "Obviously," I say. "You don't need to ask for my dance card."

"I *would* ask for your dance card. I'd do the little bow and everything," he replies, because he accidentally got hooked on *Bridgerton* two years ago. "I'll ask for your dance card at the end-of-leadership-camp dance and then we'll make everyone wildly jealous of our grace and elegance."

"There's a *dance* at this thing?" I groan. "Why are there always *dances* at these things? Who told these people that we're all itching for structured socialization?"

Maybe I should have known that there was a dance at the end of the leadership camp. I mean, first of all, I'm not exaggerating—these things *always* come with some sad little dance on the last day that people inexplicably go all out for. But also, if this camp is the thing that's gonna push my and Gray's UMaine apps over the edge, I should probably be paying more attention to it.

Gray goes back to the kitchen because he still has cleaning to do (we both make the mess, but I'm the only thing standing between us and utter chaos; so Gray cleans), and Lianne assesses me. She's done this since I was a little kid, just looked at me sometimes and smoothed back my hair and stared at me like she already knew everything I was going to do in my life. I remember being twelve and wishing that she would just tell me already.

"So, you're still in on the UMaine plan?"

Her voice is casual, but it's also too quiet for Gray to hear over the sound of his dishwashing playlist (it's a lot of Wham! and I hate it).

"Of course." I shrug. Honestly, it doesn't really matter to me where I go to college. If Gray wants to go to UMaine and he wants to go there with me, I'm sure I'll be just as able to have whatever existential crises I'm bound to have at college at UMaine as I would anywhere else.

For the plan to change, a change big enough to acknowledge would have to happen. And for us, with us, between us, that hasn't happened. So the plan is the plan.

"How do your mom and dad feel about you following in their footsteps?" Lianne asks.

She's asked me that before, but it's a different question now. I know what she's asking. I'm not stupid. I've seen the pictures my parents keep in a scrapbook in a trunk in their room, Lianne and my parents twenty years ago, obviously drunk, occasionally high, sitting on ratty couches and hanging upside down on bus seats. I've seen my parents at their high school graduation, arms around each other, smiles wide and open. I know the story because it's also a country song and a made-for-TV movie and anything else that relies heavily on clichés. My parents met Lianne at UMaine. Her and my mom got pregnant around the same time. My dad stuck around. Gray's didn't. My mom dropped out. Lianne didn't.

"I guess I'm not totally following in their footsteps," I say. "I'm sort of . . . adjacent to their footsteps."

My favorite thing about Lianne is she doesn't push it. I know what she's thinking, but at least I don't have to hear her say it. I don't have to listen to her ask me why I'm still here, what I'm doing, what about her son is so special that I can't leave even though I was actually, technically, the one who left in the first place.

Instead, Gray finishes washing the dishes and he kisses the top of my head on his way back to us. Instead, he rests his foot against mine under the table when we eat and Lianne tells me over and over again how great dinner is.

It's the first hour I've spent not thinking about Tal since I met her.

When I get home, she's texted me three times about tomorrow and my heart bursts, painfully. Like it's going to leave shrapnel behind.

♡

TWELVE

I wake up the next morning with a headache. Something about the bustle of MPD and the stress of keeping something from Gray is all adding up to feel like cotton in my brain.

I also wake up to a text from Tal.

> Hey, sorry, I tried calling!! Is it cool if I come get you like now?

Well, fuck.

I text Tal back, say *yeah of course, see you soon!!!* And then pull the duvet over my head. I used to do this when I was younger, hide out under the blankets if something felt like too much. It's quiet here, and if I don't think too hard about anything else it feels normal.

And then my phone rings.

I answer without looking to see who it is, because only one person would call me before noon on a Sunday.

"Hi, baby," I say to Gray.

"I'm dying," he says. That's not unusual—in fact, it's pretty much the way he says *hello* when he's hungover. But he's not hungover. His voice sounds like he spent the morning gargling nails.

"Jesus, did you blow Pinhead last night?"

"Don't make me laugh," he says miserably. "It hurts to laugh."

Gray is objectively perfect, but he has one standard boy trait: When he's sick, everyone in the world has to baby him.

"You just woke up like that?" I ask. "Have you called in to work?"

"Yes and yes," he whispers.

Gray's dramatic, but he wouldn't miss out on double-shift money if he didn't absolutely have to.

"Baby," I coo. "Do you want me to bring you anything?"

"Mimi's. Banana milkshake and onion rings."

I honk out a laugh. "Not that you knew I'd ask or anything."

"You take care of me," he says, but he stretches out the last word. *You take care of meeeeeeee.*

"Don't forget it," I say. "I'll be there within the hour. Take medicine. Love you."

"Love you."

Once we've hung up, I get pulled out of my Gray Zone and realize what I've just done. I throw the duvet down off my face and stare at my bedroom ceiling.

"Shit," I say to no one in particular.

My phone starts ringing again. I roll my eyes. Gray's *definitely* going to ask for a burger to go with that milkshake and onion rings, even though it's nine in the morning.

"Hi, baby," I say again.

". . . Hey?"

Oh sweet Jesus.

I laugh, because it's all I can do right now. What *is* the appropriate response when you accidentally call your best friend's future girlfriend/your horrible, horrible straight-girl crush *baby*?

We all call each other *baby* in our little group. I think it started as a way to make fun of Gray and me, but it stuck. In the dark corners of my brain where I let myself fantasize about me and Tal as Me and Tal, though, I don't call her *baby* like that. It doesn't mean *you're my friend and I love you* with her.

"Shit," I say, still giggling nervously. "Sorry, I thought you were Gray."

"That's adorable," Tal says. Gray and I get that a lot. "Sorry to disappoint?"

"You didn't!" I say, too quickly, too intensely.

Tal's quiet on the other end of the line for just half a second too long. My eye twitches.

"Uh, anyway," she says. I cringe. "Do you live next door to an old lady who likes to glare at teenagers minding their own business in their cars?"

I smile, totally out of my control. "I do."

"In that case, I'm outside."

"In that case, I'll be down in a second."

We hang up without saying goodbye, same as me and Gray.

"*Shit*," I repeat, a little louder for emphasis.

I don't exactly know what I'm gonna do, but I do know that I can't just leave Tal waiting outside forever. There's no time to shower, so my hair, stuck to my whole body with late summer sweat, gets wrapped and wrapped and wrapped around itself until I can put it in a bun, and then it feels like there's room to breathe. I know there are bound to be mousy little wisps coming out of it, but I'm hoping the effect is more *casual messy bun* than *woman on the verge*. Deodorant next, a shit ton of it and it still can't cancel out that sun-and-smoke, sweat-and-sleep smell on me. Oh god, I probably smell like onions after MPD. I take a deep whiff of my armpit and, when it doesn't seem obviously disgusting, know I have to let it go.

In a way, this could be better, this rush—I can't freak out about what I'm going to wear when I don't have the time to. I grab a sundress that was laying on my desk chair and that'll have to be good enough. I haven't worn it in a while and it rides up high on my thighs, so I hike on a pair of bike shorts. I glance at myself in my dusty mirror and try to see past the panic, to look at my not-brown-not-blond hair and the freckles on the bridge of my nose and my pale brown eyes that are currently wide and frazzled. I used to understand that Gray thought I was pretty, but I only appreciated it in an it's-nice-that-someone-thinks-I'm-pretty kind of way. I have no idea what anyone else might think of me.

Not that I need to know what Tal thinks of me, of course. The idea makes me hack out a depressing, hysterical laugh, and I stuff bits of loose change and my debit card into my backpack and fly out the door, where I nearly collide head-on with my dad.

"There's someone outside," he says.

We blink at each other for a second.

"Probably a vandal," I say. "A vagrant."

He wants to ask *new friend?* and I want to say *yeah, no one* and then I want him to tease me about it, to tell my mom over dinner *Alana has a new* friend.

But that doesn't happen. We don't know how to do that yet, and anyway, even if we did, that's not what this is. That's not who Tal is.

"Probably," he says. "You should go check first, though. Before we call in the SWAT team."

I nod, jerky; smile too tight.

I'm halfway out the door, Tal's car in sight, when I realize I don't have makeup on, and I panic before I remember I shouldn't be panicking about that, which makes me panic more. I feel like I'm forgetting something, and I know that it's Gray.

I don't think I can name a time in my life when Gray didn't know where I was. Not because he asked, not because I have to tell him. Just because why wouldn't he? If he wasn't there with me, he knew why. If there was something separating us, it usually had a name, a place.

I guess it still does.

Tal looks up from her phone and spots me from inside her car, and then it's too late to run back inside. She smiles, and then the absolute last place I want to go is back inside.

"I like that dress," she says when I get into the car, shut the door tight, and then it's whisper-quiet, just my heart pounding.

"I have a very specific and deeply strange favor to ask," I tell her, because otherwise I'd have to think about the fact that Tal likes what I'm wearing and of course she does, people say that to their friends all the time, but also *Tal* likes what I'm wearing.

Tal laughs that big Tal-laugh, head back, fillings catching the light. She has three, I think. Two on the left, one on the right.

I direct her to Mimi's, this diner everyone goes to on Saturday nights because it's the only place in town open past midnight. We don't actually live in Bangor, the way we tell people we do, but outside, the quiet bits no one knows. We have Mimi's, and the hardware store, and the old arena, and a liquor store. Drive another fifteen minutes and you'll hit the Walmart.

"I have to grab breakfast for Gray, and then I'm gonna need to go to his house for ten to fifteen minutes and then we can go."

I haven't thought this through. Obviously Tal's going to want to go in and see Gray. Beyond the fact that they're clearly destined to fall in love, she's a decent human being who would want to check on a sick friend.

"Can't Gray get his own breakfast?" Tal asks once we're in the drive-thru line, not mentioning any of that. "Isn't he working today, anyway?"

"This is a special circumstance," I say. "I swear I'm not usually Gray's errand girl. He's sick. Apparently with something only a banana milkshake and onion rings can cure."

"I come down with that every time *Love Island*'s on."

I snort, and try not to let myself be freaked out by it. Tal can hear me snort because Tal never needs to be attracted to me. In fact, letting her hear me snort right now is a good thing, because it puts more distance between us.

I am very quickly losing focus.

"What's good here?" Tal asks.

"Nothing," I say, and Tal laughs, so I do as well, but I'm not really joking.

"I'm getting a veggie burger," she announces, apparently just as unaffected by the confines of a normal eating schedule as Gray.

"Are you a vegetarian?" I ask, ready to squirrel it away. Ready to know it when no one else does.

But Tal shakes her head. "I just feel like you can really judge a place based on their veggie burger. They can be a bit of an afterthought, y'know? So if it's good, the rest of their stuff is probably good, too."

I order Gray's food after Tal orders hers, slide my debit card over and buy Tal's burger without even thinking about it and then force myself to continue absolutely not thinking about it.

I sip on Gray's milkshake while Tal drives the three minutes to his house, and then she drives by it, parks by the sidewalk at the end of the road.

"I'll wait here," she says, perfectly content. She even leans her head back onto her seat.

I blink. "Are you sure? You don't want to go in?"

Tal shrugs. "This feels like something between you guys. Plus, if he's sick I'd rather not get his cooties."

She grins and I grin back. Half in response, half in relief.

I didn't tell Tal that Gray doesn't know about today, but I guess she's figured it out. I don't know what she might think about that. If she thinks it's weird, she's not letting it show.

I walk down the road and let myself into Gray's house. His mom's not home, no car in the driveway, but Gray left the door open for me. If it's a weekend and Gray's not at work, the door's open for me. (Even if it wasn't, I know the garage door code.)

"Is there a sad boy in this house?" I bellow, and I hear a grumble from the end of the hall, past the kitchen, where Gray's bedroom is.

"As requested." I plop the bag onto his bed and a hand darts out to grab it.

Gray says something like *I love you*, but it's scratchy and through a mouthful of onion rings. He grunts, emerges from under the duvet. Rumpled, perfect. I doubt that's how I looked this morning, and I'm not even sick. I put my hand on his forehead and I'm shocked when it's actually hot. Sometimes I think of Gray as too perfect to deal with the afflictions of us mere mortals.

"You're, like, legit sick."

Gray glares up at me because I guess he already knew that.

"Don't move," I tell him. "Stay here and sleep. If you go to school sick tomorrow, I'll kill you."

Gray's the only person I've ever met who genuinely hates missing school. He can't be alone with his thoughts for that long.

I sit on his bed and he moves his legs over to make room. Lianne must be working, because if she caught me in here, she'd be pissed. Growing up, we always passed colds back and forth. After we traded strep throat on and off for, like, two months a couple of years ago, though, our parents put their collective foot down and made a new rule: No hanging out if one of us is sick.

So I know that, technically, I shouldn't be here. I also know that if I stay for any longer than this, I'll start freaking out for real.

"I'll let you be very sad in peace," I tell him. He looks a little confused about why I'm leaving so soon, but he doesn't call me on it. I give him my hand and he kisses the back of it, and then pulls me in close, so I kiss his sweaty forehead twice. We squeeze hands and then I can turn around, can escape.

I've never felt like I was escaping from Gray before.

When I get out of his house, I realize fall's finally decided to stick around, that the sky is heavy and dark and the wind cuts through me the way it hasn't in months. I step outside just as the rain starts—big fat drops, nothing like summer storms— ice cold and sharp. By the time I make it back to Tal's car, my wet arms are wrapped around myself, goose bumps up and down my skin and the hair that's fallen out of my bun sticking to the back of my neck.

But Tal's car is warm inside, hot, even, heat blasting, and Tal's got her hoodie off, leaning her head back onto her headrest so there's a clear line of exposed skin from throat to collarbone, curves dipping under her tank top.

"Aren't you boiling?" I ask her, shuddering as my body adjusts to the change of temperature, heat blanketing me.

"Figured you'd be cold," she says. "There's a jacket in the back if you want it."

That's something friends do. That's something I've said a million times to Olivia and Syd and Kennedy and Sav. I can reach behind me and grab the jacket Tal was wearing yesterday, curl into it, and let it warm me up. Of course I can.

But I don't. Not yet. I can't tell if that makes it even weirder, but Tal doesn't seem to care either way. We sit there in silence for a second, listening to the rain pounding the car. Tal's the one to break it because I'm a coward.

"So, I don't actually know where I'm going."

"Oh shit, sorry," I say. Then, "Honestly, if you were looking for the tour, you kind of already got it. There's not much else to see."

Tal chews this over for a second. "You can say no to this," she says. "But what if we went to Portland?"

Two hours from here, maybe longer with traffic. Four hours guaranteed with Tal. Somewhere new, with Tal.

A bad idea, technically.

"I'm all yours," I tell her, and her grin warms me from the inside out.

♡

THIRTEEN

The most surprising thing about driving with Tal is the fact that, at some point, I realize that the hard knot of tension at the base of my neck is gone. Tal plays music that I don't know and keeps the heat turned up full-blast while I undo my hair and shake it out. Eventually I'm comfortable enough to reach out and turn the heating down myself, finally wearing Tal's jacket. By the time I went to put it on, I wasn't even cold anymore. But Tal had offered, and I had wanted, so when we were already halfway through the drive I held my breath and grabbed it and Tal smiled at me. When I used to wear Gray's stuff, it was because I thought that's what girlfriends were supposed to do. Now it's because his clothes are soft and comfortable and smell like home. I think maybe it was supposed to feel like this, though. Like a proclamation. Like something special.

But then, *this* isn't supposed to feel like that. So what do I know.

"Can I ask you a question you might not want to answer, and if you don't want to answer it you can tell me to fuck off?" Tal asks after we've been driving for a little while. Three songs, maybe? It's hard to tell when I don't know the music and everything sort of blends together.

It sounds like something Olivia would say. She's big into the *no offense, but* and the *don't take this the wrong way, but.* I don't think Tal's like that, but it makes me tense again. I don't actually know what kind of person she is, I remind myself. I wouldn't want to spend a whole day in Portland with Olivia. This could get dicey.

"I guess?" I say. Better to be noncommittal, in case Tal *is* anything like Olivia.

"Why did you come out when you did? Like, what was the thing that made you think *okay, right now*?"

"Oh," I say. Oh.

No one really mentions this anymore, because if they did, they'd have to talk about me as separate from Gray, as someone with her own feelings. I think that makes them uncomfortable. And that's without even considering how uncomfortable the idea of me hitting on them makes them feel. I'm not used to answering questions like this so directly. But Tal's face is open and curious. Good-natured. Something I'm also not used to, when it comes to this.

So, I tell her.

"People had sort of . . . figured it out. Figured me out, I guess. Someone told someone, who told someone, who told someone, and I knew it was only a matter of time before someone told Gray. So I told him before that could happen. I guess that's really the only time I officially came out, besides to, like, my parents. They had a lot of questions, after everything with Gray, but they're cool about it, so that's nice."

It sounds extra pathetic to end the story that way, like *isn't it wonderful that my parents don't hate me?* But I don't expect Tal to understand the nuances of all of it, so I don't elaborate.

"Wait, what?" Tal asks, whipping her head to look at me like I'd just told her my whole family had been murdered. "So you were outed? Holy shit, that's awful. I'm sorry I asked."

"Oh, it's no big deal!" I say the thing I've always said. From the beginning, this was my line. Anything else would just make it awkward. "It was going to happen eventually. I was probably going to do it at some point soon anyway. This just sped me up."

"Do you know who did it?" Tal asks.

Yes.

She's never admitted it. We've never talked about it. We'll almost definitely never talk about it, ever. But I know exactly who did it.

"No."

Tal slows as we hit traffic. Turns to face me with her whole body, looks me in the eye.

"Alana, that's really, really shitty. I'm so sorry that happened to you."

She reaches over, puts her hand on my wrist like a salve, and even as it lights my body up, it settles me. I put my hand on top of hers without thinking about it, then jolt and rip it away.

"Thanks," I say, and Tal nods.

"So are you just gonna try and bum me out all day, or what?" I ask after a minute, because I can only stand being everyone's object of pity for so long.

"Yeah," she says without missing a beat. "Which of your grandparents are dead?"

I think my laugh matches Tal's then, wide-open mouth and eyes crinkled at the corners.

"I'm so glad you laughed at that. That was so risky, I regretted it as soon as I said it."

It only makes me laugh harder, louder, and as the traffic clears and Tal starts driving more confidently, the sun starts to peek out from behind the clouds, the two of us leaving Bangor's thunderstorms behind.

"We can go wherever you want," Tal says once she's settled herself in the fast lane.

I shrug. "I don't go to Portland very often."

"Oh, I get it. You just wanted a tour of Portland this whole time."

"This whole time!" I agree, hugging my knees to my chest and enjoying the ride. Enjoying the conversation. Enjoying what might actually be a friendship. Telling myself that would be great, too. It *would* be.

"There's a pop-up sex museum that's still on, I think," Tal says. "I went over the summer but it was awesome, I'd go again. Oh, and someone I used to go to school with does a drag brunch on Sundays, but that's ticketed and I think we've missed it anyway . . ."

Tal goes on, describing performance art I don't understand and concerts from bands I don't know and people I'm sure I don't have anything in common with. Gray's right: Tal's automatically cooler than every one of us. I can't believe I took her to *Mimi's* this morning.

We get off the highway and Tal starts maneuvering city streets with a practiced ease, passing cyclists and darting down shortcut side streets. It's too hot in the car again, a loose piece of my hair sticking to my forehead, but I don't want to move. The ease I felt before, the confidence to turn the heating down, is fading. I don't want Tal to think I'm uncomfortable even though I am, a little, I guess.

But Tal drives us past farmers markets and tightly packed theaters, nabs a spot on the street outside a building with dusty pink awnings, gold script in the window advertising fresh brioche, flavored coffees, a new book with a pink cover I vaguely recognize that matches the painted brick outside.

"Sorry," Tal says. "I didn't mean to dive headfirst into Portland's alt abyss. I think you'll like it here."

Here is a bookstore, I think, a bookstore and café, according to a purple neon sign hanging up in the window. The exterior is brick painted pale pink, a little banner that says *All Welcome (Except TERFs)* in one corner of a big picture window beside the door. Inside, it smells like vanilla; the exposed brick is its original red. Deep green plants in zigzagged, hand-painted clay pots hang from the ceiling. One side of the room has bookshelves stacked floor to ceiling, with a rolling ladder that Gray would kill to swing on. The other side, where we came in, has a wide glass counter stuffed with pastries that I can't look away from, my stomach reminding me that I haven't had breakfast. Music that sounds like what Tal was playing in the car is playing here, too, and my recognizing it makes me feel slightly more at home. The back wall, behind the counter, is covered in stickers, old book covers with titles like *Twilight Girls* and *She Prefers Girls* and, less subtly, *Gay Boys*.

I freeze. Tal thinks I'd like it *here*? Tal thinks this is somewhere I belong? Did she even know that this place existed before, or did she google "where to take a lesbian in Portland" before we got here?

Everything in the building feels like a statement I'm too meek to make myself. Even being in here feels like an expectation, like Tal wants me to be this kind of person, wants me to thank her for bringing me somewhere all the People Like Me converge. But I don't think I'm a People Like This. I don't think, really, that anything deep and important in me has changed between now and before I came out. And before I came out, I don't think I would have come in here at all.

The barista, tall with lots of hair stacked on top of their head and a button reading *Callie, they/them* ☺ on their chest, screams when they see Tal. They rush out from behind the counter, even though someone's waiting for a coffee, and whisk her up, squeezing hard.

"I thought we'd lost you forever!" they say.

"If only," Tal says, and Callie laughs, ruffles her hair.

I breathe out a little sigh of relief that I hope Tal doesn't notice. Tal has a friend here. Tal's visiting her friend. Maybe being here actually has nothing to do with me. Maybe she just wanted to see Callie.

I'm reminded, then, that Tal has a life, had a life before Bangor and us and me, and if she has this, this before, then she's probably already compared it to her now, compared people like Callie to me, to Gray. I wonder how we measure up.

"This is Alana," Tal says now, and I jump, actually flinch because I'd put myself off to the side and Tal's bringing me front and center.

Callie says hi and I say hi back, and then I'm not really sure where I belong in this. Does Callie know who I am? Did Tal say *hey, I'm bringing a gay I found today, enjoy* to them this morning?

"I have to work for the next seven hundred hours," Callie says. "Go sit somewhere and I'll bring you a present."

We follow orders, or Tal does and I follow her. There are mauve velvet armchairs by the window, soft with use but not old enough to be gross. Tal slips off her shoes and tucks her feet up under herself as Callie comes back with a plate, croissants and honeysweet brioche and still-steaming danishes. They roll their eyes at Tal when she reaches for her wallet, tell her to fuck off, and Tal laughs like that's exactly what she expected.

"Sorry, but I'm not going to pretend like this isn't going to be the best part of my day," I tell her very seriously before grabbing one of the croissants and pulling it apart. My croissants never turn out, not like this, not this flaky and gentle in the middle. I make a truly embarrassing sound when I finally take a bite.

"I can accept that," Tal says. She's looking at my mouth, I think, at the buttery flakes I'm sure are covering half my face by now, but I can't even care when the croissants are this good. I hold up a piece of the fluffy middle to look at it up close and pull it apart so I can stare at the way it glistens, try and figure out its secret. I sniff a piece of the exterior and smell nothing but butter, watch it crumble between my fingers.

Gray hates it when I do this, deconstruct my food before I eat it. I always tell him he's like my parents, telling me not to play with my food. But if I don't know what's in it, how it works, how it came to be, it's not the same. There's no fun in that. I grab a danish and dip my finger into the gooey center, tear apart the brioche and inhale.

"Whatcha up to?" Tal asks, a laugh threatening to bubble out of her as she watches me with her eyebrows raised.

I freeze. It's one thing to eat like an animal around Gray, who hates it but deals with it because it's me, it's us. It's entirely another to spring it on Tal.

"Shit," I say, half around a mouthful of pastry. "Sorry. This is gross."

Tal laughs. "It's not *not* gross," she says. "But I was genuinely asking. Do you do this with all your food?"

"Only the stuff that looks really good," I admit. "I just think it's interesting. Like, this was flour! Flour tastes gross! And now it's *this*."

Tal pauses. Looks down at the mangled plate between us. Dips her finger where mine was, scoops out thick blueberry curd and sucks it off in one clean pop. Grins at me with purple teeth.

"Tastes better this way, too," she says, and I feel something break, something splinter, feel the world crack into two.

It would be my luck that my first real crush on a girl after coming out would be on someone at once completely perfect and utterly unattainable.

"You're gross," I tell her so she'll laugh, and she does.

"There goes all my mystery."

"You're still pretty mysterious," I argue. "Intimidating, even."

It's true, but I wasn't going to say it.

Tal laughs at that. "Really? I've got you fooled, then."

Definitely, definitely not.

"So I don't want to overwhelm you," Tal says. Everything about her is overwhelming and it's wild to me that she doesn't see that. "But this student council rep thing. Do you have any thoughts about what I should be doing? Like, if you were new at your school, what do you think would help you?"

I shrug. "I guess that's more a question for you, right? You actually *are* new. What's missing for you?"

Tal scoffs. "A primer on each individual relationship, both current and historical. No offense, but you guys are kind of incestuous."

It's nothing like an Olivia *no offense*. It makes me cackle, for one thing.

"I mean, you've pretty much gotten the gist," I say. "Me and Gray. Gray and everyone else, in their dreams. Logan and everyone else, in *his* dreams."

Talking about Gray reminds me of my job, of his plan. The fact that he isn't here makes it feel even worse, like I need to talk him up even more than I would have to make up for it. If this is the thing that fully pushes Tal over to Team Gray, then today won't have been about me being selfish and wanting time alone with Tal.

"Not that Gray ever really goes for any of it," I continue. "Like, don't think he's this asshole guy collecting all the girls at school, or anything like that."

"I didn't assume that." Tal smiles, shrugs. I'm starting to get why Gray had to recruit me to get Tal's vibe; she's impossible to read.

Still, I press on. Never let it be said that I don't look out for Gray.

"Sydney's having people over on Friday," I tell her. "I know Gray would be really happy if you went."

Tal doesn't seem to be getting it, so I think I need to make it extremely clear. *Gray wants to see you. Gray would be happy if you were there.* Surely that should be more than enough.

But Tal cocks her head. "Is that an every weekend thing? Parties like that?"

I blush. "I mean, you saw where we live, right? There's not much else to do."

I'm ready to tell Tal to forget it, to report back to Gray that we're losing her and we need to figure out a new plan, but Tal laughs.

"So there's no, like, underground fight club I should know about?" she asks. "No local cults to join?"

"I never said *that.*"

Tal snorts.

"But yeah, there's usually something at some point every weekend," I say. "We'd all kill each other otherwise."

"But combining a bunch of alcohol and no adult supervision once a week keeps you all safe and sane."

I realize what's making this different all at once. Tal's making fun of us—gently, semi-lovingly, but she is—but she's making fun of us *with* me. I'm in on the joke.

"So can I make all Gray's dreams come true and tell him you're going next week?" I ask. I don't know when this happened, but I'm leaning on my hand, elbow on the table, much too close to Tal. I freeze, knowing that if I move backward too quickly she'll give me the same look she gave me just before homecoming.

"I'll go on one condition," Tal says. "We can't talk about Gray for the rest of the day."

I know that I shouldn't smile as widely as I do at that.

FOURTEEN

This is how you get ready for a party at Sydney's house.

You shower, and it takes longer than usual because you don't actually want to go, and then it takes even longer because you have a crisis about the fact that Tal is going to be there, and then you have a *second* crisis about the fact that you aren't supposed to feel like that, and anyway you think Gray maybe saw her first, and *anyway you aren't supposed to feel like that*. It's not like you'd ever *do* anything. So you forget it.

You crawl under your bed—all the way under, so you end up with cobwebs in your just-washed hair, but you can grab an almost-empty Captain Morgan bottle and sneak a sip before tucking it away in your backpack for the night.

You crawl out from under your bed, and then you stand in the middle of your room.

I have no idea how to get ready for a party at Sydney's. Not now. Not alone.

This doesn't seem like a good idea anymore. Not after another week of watching Gray watch Tal, not after seeing the way he makes her laugh. Not after spending two lunch periods with her while she went over her plans for student council, because she might actually take it seriously, and I never thought I'd think something like that was hot but here we are. I can't go to a party at Sydney's and be normal around Tal now that I know her smile and her laugh and all the ways she makes my guts twist up.

What *does* seem like a good idea is texting Gray to say I'm not going, putting my phone on do not disturb, and hiding away for several hours. Getting lost in my duvet cave again. Maybe making a genoise and eating it all in one go at some point. I get as far as crawling into bed, getting entirely under the covers, and pulling my phone out when there's an ungodly *bang* as my bedroom door swings open and the doorknob hits the wall. That sound only ever means one thing. I brace myself as Gray launches himself onto my duvet and, thus, me, and all the air leaves my body at once.

"You're such an asshole," I yell up at him, but it's muffled. I flail my arms and legs around until Gray gets up and I can squirm out from my duvet.

"An asshole here to save you from turning into a sad little hermit," he chirps, a far cry from the sickly little Victorian ghost-boy of last weekend.

(Also, I didn't end up catching whatever he had, so take that, parents.)

"Let's cool it on the *assholes*," my mom says. I crane my neck to see her leaning against my doorframe.

"That's a very strange thing to say," Gray says, and I know my mom doesn't want to laugh, but you can't not. Not when it's Gray.

"Be good tonight." She points at both of us on her way out. "Keep the door . . . huh. I guess it doesn't matter, does it?"

"If we *do* close the door, I promise to not get your gay daughter pregnant." Gray beams at my mom and I kick him in the thigh, but she just laughs again and actually does close the door, which is helpful when I see that Gray has his party backpack on.

"I thought you were going to do your fashionably late thing tonight," I say.

That was part of the plan. Get there well after Tal so that she has time to miss Gray. Then he can wander around and be his sparkly self and show her how much she's supposed to love him. Then we get to move on to the next phase. Lucky me.

"I was," Gray says, rooting through his backpack, "but then I decided to be amazing instead."

He pulls out a six-pack he definitely stole from someone's garage during a party over the summer (I suddenly realize where my drunken kleptomania from our last party may have come from) and keeps digging until he finds something palm-size that he throws at me, narrowly missing my face.

I look down. It's lipstick, the cheap kind that drugstores sell on the ends of the aisles with a bright yellow sticker that says *now reduced!* slapped onto it. The glossy plastic it's wrapped in says the color is called Purple Puss, and I can't contain my reaction to that.

"I know." Gray grins at me, the Gray Grin, the one where he knows how good he's doing. "I figured if you weren't going to get invited to Olivia and Sydney's pregame makeup shit, then we could do our own thing. Get on board, purple puss."

Gray's always been an overachiever, and I've always done what Gray's done, so it only makes sense that we end up being too good at pregaming.

By the time we work our way through the six-pack (and a little bit of whatever else I find hidden away under my bed) and stumble our way through the five-minute walk to Sydney's house, we're late enough that everyone's there to see the two of us tumble in, to notice purple lipstick smeared on Gray's cheek, to whisper about us glued together, still, always.

Just before we left, when Gray wasn't looking, I found the bottle of Princess Purple I stole from Olivia's house at the end of the summer, hidden in plain sight on my dresser. I was drunk enough, by that point, to feel like it was staring at me, judging me the way everyone else does now. My hand dances self-consciously over where it's burning a hole in my pocket. Gray doesn't notice.

Sydney has one of the nicer houses in the neighborhood, a few roads over and sitting proudly at the crest of a cul-de-sac. It's dingy in partylight, though, when all the girls' eyes are big and red close up and there's a vape cloud overhead almost too thick to penetrate. Everything is either too bright or too dark, and I yell that in Gray's ear even though he can hear me fine, and he laughs so loudly and says *yes, you're exactly right*.

Gray offers me his arm and of course I take it, when haven't I taken it? And we go into the kitchen because when Gray gets drunk he gets even more charming and he knows it, loves playing bartender and seeing if he can get someone to try orange whiskey and grape juice.

"Sav and Parker Knight to second base," Gray says, right in my ear so no one else will hear him. "A 'Don't Stop Believin'' sing-along, annnnd . . . I get Olivia to do the YMCA."

"*Second base?* What's it like living in a teen movie from 2006?"

Gray grins and stares at me, waiting, until I finally sigh and give in.

"Fine. *Kennedy* and Parker to whatever second base is, a 'Mr. Brightside' sing-along, and you know you aren't allowed to guess shit involving Liv because she's been hard for you since the ninth grade, so don't even try it."

We've been doing this for as long as our friends have been drinking at parties. It's not so difficult to get it right—the same group of girls is always going to make out with the same group of guys, and get enough white kids in a room and play any vaguely recognizable song and you're gonna have a sing-along situation on your hands. But it's fun, something to do at things like this that belongs just to us, and Gray loves it. Doing it feels normal, but it feels *so* normal that if I think about it too hard I'll cry, I know I will, because like this, everything is too close to the surface, and if I stop paying attention, I'll reach for Gray's hand.

"Let's get you a drink," I say to him so I don't think about any of that.

"Are you trying to take advantage of me?" he asks, hand to chest.

"Obviously."

We're tangled together all the way to the kitchen, hands in back pockets and my head tucked into Gray's neck, stepping on each other's feet. Sometimes it feels like if I'm not close enough to Gray to touch him, I'll stop existing. Like he makes me real.

We both stop dead when we see Tal, because she's the brightest thing in the room, and she's not talking to anybody but they *must* all want to talk to her, must want to know everything about her because I can't imagine not wanting that. She's on her phone, smirking at it, and there's a flash and a zing in my stomach that I hate myself for because I know Gray's thinking the exact same, can feel his sharp inhale beside me. We both want to know who she's texting. We both wish that smirk was for us.

Gray's arm drops and it's like a slap. He kisses the top of my head, but I know he's looking at Tal, too. He backs up, fades away into whatever exists back there, and I remember I'm not supposed to be thinking about Tal the way I am. Gray left me because I have a job to do, but Tal hasn't noticed me yet, so I'm stuck standing there gaping at her.

Somewhere between last year and now I became the kind of person who crumples when their boyfriend leaves the room—except now he's not even my boyfriend, so it's even more pathetic—and I don't want that person to be the person that Tal sees tonight. Or any night.

I turn on my heel and retreat the way Gray left. I spot him talking to Logan and a few of the other guys around Sydney's dining room table, so he doesn't notice when I turn the other way and go upstairs.

Technically, we aren't allowed upstairs when Sydney has a party, but that was never the case for people like me, for Syd's best friends. I climb the same stairs I always have, and when I reach the top, it looks the same as it always has, but it's different now. I can't stop feeling like I'm not one of the people allowed upstairs, but I don't feel particularly welcome downstairs, either, now that I think about it.

I got my period for the first time in this bathroom, first of any of the other girls. Sat on the floor wearing a pad I stole from the cupboard under the sink and watched a YouTube video on my phone to make sure I was doing it right. Went back downstairs and pretended nothing was different, even though I wanted to cry, wanted to lie down and sob because now I wasn't like them and all I ever wanted was to be like them, the same as anyone else.

There's a crack in the laminate counter in this stranger's bathroom, just near the back where the mirror attaches. That's where I return Sydney's Princess Purple. She has so many half-empty bottles of it that she definitely didn't notice that the one I took was gone, but at least now I can stop feeling like something is wrong with me, somewhere weird and deep down, for taking it in the first place.

"I saw that."

Tal, leaning against the wall, facing the bathroom's open door. Tal, trying to look serious but swallowing a smile. The two of us look at each other for a while; Tal waiting to hear what I'm going to say and me having no idea what to say.

"Hi," I say.

"Hi," she says.

A long pause, both of us looking at each other. Downstairs, there's a collective cheer as someone starts playing "Don't Stop Believin'." Damnit.

"I guess I steal stuff now," I say to Tal eventually, because what the fuck else am I supposed to do at this point? It would probably be weirder to deny it.

Tal grins. "I know," she says. Widens her eyes. "Earlier, a kid told me he heard that the *real* reason you and Gray broke up was because you took money from his mom's purse."

"Jesus," I laugh. You can't not, after a while.

Tal steps forward, just slightly. She's still far enough away that I don't think I'm being weird. I have to police every single act now. I'm always thinking about whether I'm making someone uncomfortable.

"Yeah, you're quite the topic of conversation downstairs," Tal continues. "I've been researching you."

"I'm sure at least ten percent of it isn't true."

Tal gasps. "You mean you aren't pregnant with Ethan Gray's baby because you begged him for one last time this summer?"

"Oh, no, that one's true," I say. I put a hand over my stomach and fake a toast, drink sloshing out of my shitty plastic cup, and Tal hoots delightedly. I take one last sip for the sake of the joke and then leave it on Sydney's counter. Let her wonder who went up here tomorrow morning.

When I can finally manage to swallow, I ask, "So what other horrible things did you hear?"

I don't listen to it, except I always listen to it. Anyone who tells you they don't is lying. You can't not listen to it, when people are talking about you, when they're laughing, when you become more of a ghost story than an actual person.

Tal shrugs with her whole body. "Nothing that scared me off too badly."

I swallow hard.

"Gray'll be glad to hear it," I say.

Tal gives me this look then. This confused-puppy wrinkle-faced look. And then it clears, like it was never there in the first place. And then she laughs, quietly. Softly. For me. She tilts her head, sees some hazy, wayback part of me, and smiles. Arches an eyebrow. Makes all my blood rush to my gut. At some point, we drifted closer together and now she's near enough to touch me. And then, even though it feels like there's no way it could happen, she does.

Tal reaches out and puts her thumb flat between my eyebrows. I feel sick and I never want to stop feeling it. She presses down gently and it almost knocks me to the ground. I catch myself swaying back and there's that grin again, that flash.

"Did you know you get this little wrinkle between your eyebrows when you talk to me about Gray?"

She smooths out the crease, the one that matches Gray's. My mouth is open and I don't know when that happened. I close it, swallow. Tal keeps her thumb there, resting gently against my forehead, and it's like homecoming all over again, but different. More. There's no mistaking that Tal's thumb is on my face on purpose.

I'm frozen. Since last year, it's felt like I have hollow bones, like I'll float away if I'm not careful, and it takes barely anything to knock me over. Tal could do it without even trying.

"Did you know?" she asks again. Her voice has gone softer, has lost a bit of that teasing edge. She takes a cautious half step forward and this time I don't move back, but I duck my head so that her thumb falls away. I can't focus with her touching me.

"Who were you texting earlier?" I ask before I can stop myself. "I saw you in the kitchen when we came in."

Tal hesitates for a second, so I panic and say, "I'm not stalking you."

Which, for the record, is what stalkers say. So that's cool.

But Tal laughs, and in the dark her teeth look sharp and she licks her tongue over her incisor and my eyes follow it hungrily.

"No one important," she says. "No one more important than seeing what you were up to, sneaking off up here, anyway. You know I like an adventure."

That doesn't answer my question, but it also makes me feel like my chest is going to explode, so I don't press it.

"Are people being nice to you?" I ask, then clench my fist at my side. Are people being *nice* to you? Am I her *babysitter*?

But then this smile, this slow creeping thing, is stretching across Tal's face. We lock eyes and I know I'm supposed to look away but I can't, not when she won't, either.

"No," she says around that smile. "No one's even bothered to show me around."

Fuck fuck fuck fuck fuck.

I lean against the doorframe to try and get out of Tal's space, but she tracks me with her eyes and it feels like she's still right up close. I feel like I'm being hunted. I want her to catch me. Gray, Syd's living room, everyone else: It all feels very, very far away.

"Well, you saw downstairs," I hedge. "That's where everyone hangs out at these things. If you wanna smoke, there's always someone ready to shove a vape pen at you, but don't take anything from Payton, it'll wreck your shit."

"Ooh, the behind-the-scenes tour." Tal leans back against the doorframe so we're standing across from each other, tips of our toes just barely touching. I can breathe more easily now that she's not right in my face, but I also want to pull her back in so badly I stuff my hands into Gray's jacket pockets to stop myself. "I love it."

"If the party's at Olivia's house, we need to use coasters," I continue, starting to smile when Tal does. "Syd lets in all the riffraff. Her parents don't care as long as we all stay downstairs."

Tal makes a big show of looking around.

"Uh-oh."

I laugh. "You have new-kid privilege, I'm sure you'll be okay. People don't come up here anyway, except to—"

I cut myself off when I realize what I'm about to say and all the blood starts rushing in my ears.

"Except to what?" Tal asks, but she has a look on her face like she knows exactly what I was going to say.

"Nothing."

"Except to what?" Tal laughs but in a different way from before, drunker, and it suddenly feels like we're on a level playing field, like she feels like she's been tipped upside down, too. It makes me laugh with her, makes me feel lighter to know that she isn't always put together and dangerous. What did Gray say about Flora last week? Party flirting. Harmless. That's all this needs to be, if that's even what Tal's doing. Maybe she's just like Ken, handsy when she drinks. Maybe she heard downstairs that Alana Lucas never minds how you treat her.

"You know exactly what!"

We're both laughing now, and somewhere in it Tal leans forward just enough for me to notice. Our toes are definitely touching now.

"I have no idea what you're talking about," she says.

"Oh, of course."

"So show me."

It drops the bottom out of my stomach. Tal's looking for a reaction, but I can't give her one, wouldn't even know where to start.

She steps even closer. One foot either side of mine. Surrounded.

Tal kisses me, once, quickly, darting her mouth forward and then pulling back to look at me. She stays close, but it's small enough that either of us could walk away, still, could pretend that it never happened and pretend we're fine with it never happening again.

But that's not what we do. I fall against the side of the bathroom door and Tal falls with me, kisses me again, unmistakable this time, strong, perfect, and my knees could buckle, the way I *want*.

Tal's hand drifts up into my hair and my whole body sparks like there's popping candy under my skin and I think, *this is how it feels, this is how it's supposed to feel*. The thought lights me up for a second, and then Tal's other hand is on the small of my back and her fingers twitch, or they grab, her nails scratching at me in a way that makes me gasp, and that sound is what snaps me out of it.

There's nothing I wouldn't do to keep doing this. There's nothing I could say that could take this back.

We break apart, and Tal's lips are wet.

"Fuck," I say without meaning to. "Fuck, sorry, I forgot I have to go."

Her face falls and I can't look at it, can't look at anything, can't tell Gray I'm leaving, can't let anyone see the way I was just feeling, can only run run run under the streetlights on the three roads between Sydney's house and my bed and convince myself I'll fall asleep if I just stop thinking about Tal.

FIFTEEN

There's a moment the next morning, before I wake up for real, where I can be happy about last night.

It's gauze thin and floating, in that space where you don't know if you're awake or asleep and you don't know why it matters, where everything's a dream if you want it to be. There's a moment where I see Tal's lips and I feel her thumb on my forehead and her hand in my hair, and I think, wherever I am, I'm smiling.

And then my door crashes open.

I wake up so quickly it makes me dizzy, dots clouding my vision when my eyes blink open. I barely have time to remember why I shouldn't be smiling before Gray's launching himself onto my bed, his knee narrowly avoiding my stomach.

"One day I'm gonna be on one of those shows about women who kill," I tell him, but only about half the words come out clearly.

"You would never," Gray says. "Syd would be on it like *we always knew she'd snap one day*, and you couldn't let that happen."

He's right, and holding up a brown paper bag that smells incredible, so I let it slide.

"Give," I say. I open my mouth and Gray laughs, digging into the bag and pulling out a breakfast sandwich he shoves in the general direction of my face.

"So I was right?" he asks.

I hum questioningly around my mouthful of beautiful, beautiful sandwich.

"I figured since I lost you early on, you must've puked or something and gone home."

It's a rule. The most sober one buys the hangover breakfast.

"And, by the way, since you *very* rudely didn't text me, I had to text your mom to make sure you weren't dead. She told me to tell you you're very irresponsible."

I love him so much. Shit.

"Joke's on you, I *was* dead."

"Some kind of lightweight now that you pregame with me."

We just grin at each other for a second, and all I can feel is this heavy dread, like tar in my veins, like it's last year and I'm about to break his heart all over again.

Everyone has a limit, and I've always made sure Gray never hits his with me. I'm hungover enough to be honest, feeling sorry for myself enough to know that Gray is my one perfect thing. You only get one soulmate, and I'm not throwing mine away. I can wait another year to feel like this, can wait until Tal is a distant memory to me and Gray both and then find this feeling again, with someone else, with someone Gray's never met, with someone I actually *can* do this with.

If I'm thinking about it (I'm *not* thinking about it), there's a before and after to my life now. Before yesterday I'd never kissed a girl that wasn't Ken after one too many, never kissed a girl that I also want to *touch*. Now it's the *after*, but I'm the only one who knows.

"Sorry I didn't get to talk to Tal last night," I say, too quickly, too out of nowhere.

I don't lie to Gray. Not anymore. When I came out to him, after the dust had settled and we had both stopped crying, he hugged me and he pressed the words *no more lying, okay?* wetly into the skin of my neck, and I said *okay* and I meant it.

I don't lie to Gray. Except, I guess, now I do.

Gray tilts his head at me. "She's the one who told me you went home last night. I figured you guys went upstairs so you could puke and you left from there."

The fact that Gray even knows that Tal and I were upstairs last night makes my heart shudder to a stop. If the subject doesn't change immediately, I think I'll burst into flames.

There's a time-honored tradition, among girls like me talking to boys like Gray, and I participate in it *enthusiastically* now.

"Oh my god," I laugh, and it's too close to a cough. "I guess I was even more fucked up than I thought. I *did* talk to her. My tolerance *has* really gone to shit lately. Gonna have to up my game before college, huh?"

I used to be able to get away with not talking about something by kissing Gray. Now I have college.

"Oh, shit, that reminds me," he says now, his eyes lighting up just like I knew they would. "My mom can't get off work for the open house, so she wants us to take a bunch of pictures and stuff while we're there."

"Oh god, are you going to be okay with that?" I ask. "How will you possibly withstand a full day of *needing* your picture taken?"

If there's one thing Gray loves, it's a photo opportunity. I say this with the broken energy of being his unofficial Instagram husband, which means standing awkwardly while he poses in a million different ways and screeches *Angles! Get my angles!* at me.

"I think I'll survive," he says.

"God, you're so brave."

When we're at UMaine, it'll be different and the same in all the best ways. That's what we keep saying to each other. It's amazing how I used to feel this dread, this unease, about living with Gray. I kept telling him we had to make sure we were *really* ready, that we were stable and in *a good place* in our relationship. All I really needed was an extra bedroom, and now thinking about it can get me through the day. Me and Gray, the way we were meant to be. I'll come home to a shitty apartment I'll share with Gray, and he'll tell me all about saving the world, and that will be enough.

Of course, that was before I did the stupidest thing I've ever done and preemptively ruined everything.

"Come here." Gray stops chattering about college for a second and opens his arms. I wiggle myself half-upright and over to him without thinking too hard about the pit in my stomach, and he wraps me up tight, leans me back against his chest.

"I don't want to be an asshole, but you look fucking *rough*,

Luke. You sure you're okay? Do I have to go get a bucket? Is this going to be like last winter break?"

"We agreed to never again speak of last winter break."

Gray laughs, kisses the top of my head.

"I'm fine," I say. "Really. I just made some bad calls."

I sure fucking did.

"So I assume that means you'll be able to rally for today," Gray says.

I turn around in his arms to stare him down.

"What's today? If I agreed to do anything last night, I don't think you can legally hold me to it."

"*Today* is the next stage of the plan," Gray announces. "And since you agreed to help with the plan weeks ago, stone-cold sober, I *can*, in fact, hold you to it."

"Fucking lawyer."

I was really, really hoping Gray wasn't talking about a new stage in the plan. If I have to spend time with Tal today, I don't really know what I'll do. I think it's a toss-up between bursting into tears at the sight of her and launching myself at her face.

"Both of us got to talking last night after you disappeared," he says. "Even though that was *definitely not the plan*, I asked if she'd want to hang out with both of us today, and she was super game. She seemed really excited, actually."

"She did?"

It's out of my mouth before I can help it. If she was excited at the idea of hanging out in a group that includes me, maybe she doesn't hate me. Maybe it wasn't a mistake.

"Right? The plan is *absolutely* working."

I smile a nauseous little smile and Gray continues. "So I suggested we do something, like, actually fun, which obviously means nothing around here. So we're going to a museum in Portland. Like, now."

"The pop-up sex museum?" I ask.

Gray laughs, shocked. "Uh, no? Is that a thing? You know you have to tell me about your fantasies if you want me to enact them."

I stick my tongue out at him to cover up my own nerves. Everything has a double meaning now, a new layer. Gray probably thinks I just got a weird ad on Instagram, but my brain's trying to convince me that he's going to figure everything out just because I mentioned that I know about something going on in Portland.

Something tickles at the back of my brain, and I figure it out too late.

"Wait. What do you mean we're going, *like, now*?"

"I mean my mom drove me here on her way to work and Tal's on her way to pick us up right now."

"Jesus *Christ*, Gray!"

Gray actually leans back at that, like I'd slapped him. I don't think I've ever really spoken to him like that. That anger, that sudden outburst.

"Sorry," I say immediately. "You just caught me off guard."

"If you don't want to go, then you don't have to," Gray says, but he's giving me his saddest face, the one where he thinks he's being very brave and cool and trying not to make me feel bad.

"No, of course I'll go," I say. "I can't bail on the plan at the last second, can I?"

Gray doesn't look too sure, which makes me feel worse. It's one thing to do something drunk and stupid. It's entirely another for me to hurt Gray on purpose.

"Baby," I say. "Seriously, I'm sorry. I'm just hungover. Leave me at once so I can at least pretend that I'm a put-together, fun-loving gal," I say. "Go flag down Tal when she gets here."

I squirm out from where Gray was holding me and start rooting through my dresser, pretending that I'm just looking for something to throw on and not like my brain is currently on fire trying to decide how I want to look when Tal sees me for the first time after last night. Trying not to think about the fact that Gray doesn't actually *need* to flag down Tal because she's been to my house before. Add it to the quickly growing list of things I've hidden from him.

"That's more like it." Gray gives me a big, long squeeze on his way out, but he still leaves. I'm sure he's skipping downstairs on his way to greet Tal. Gray's the kind of guy who gets excited about a last-minute trip, about going somewhere even slightly different. In middle school our geography teacher asked us to make a presentation about a place we'd like to visit and the room was full of England and Thailand and Australia and Peru. Gray picked Boston.

I can't even scream into my pillow when he's gone because that's not actually as quiet as you'd think it would be. Gray always lingers on his way out of my house. My dad has to catch up with him like they're old drinking buddies (ever since Gray went from Teenage Boy Deflowering His Daughter back to Best Friend and Amateur Daughter Security Guard, their relationship has hit great new heights).

"Oh my god," I whisper. "Oh my god oh my god oh my god oh my *shit fucking god*."

Two thoughts are swirling and tangling together in my head, branching out into these little tributaries that I'm bound to drown in. The first is that Tal clearly doesn't have an issue with seeing me, even after last night. But does that mean she cares so little that she's already written it off as a drunk fuckup? The second is that now I have to make myself look and act normal even after everything that happened last night. And on top of all of that, I keep having to remind myself that *I'm not supposed to care about any of this*.

It'll be October next week, leaves already changing color, cool enough to be called sweater weather. Gray's already unironically made me go get PSLs with him in Bangor more than once. It feels safer, then, to cover myself up more, ripped jeans and the baggiest of Gray's hoodies that I currently have in my room.

If I take an extra ten minutes to make sure my makeup looks okay, that's between me and god.

SIXTEEN

I built it up so much that I'm expecting Tal to be wearing a shirt that says *Me and Alana Kissed Last Night*, but she looks exactly the same. I don't know how that could possibly be true when I feel like a completely different person. Baggy tank top tucked into high-waisted jeans, the long tangle of necklaces she wore to homecoming, boots Sydney described as *super cute* the other day.

The same, except now I know how it feels when the hand that's waving me over is tangled in my hair, scratching at my scalp. The same, except I don't have to imagine what she tastes like now.

It's way colder outside than I thought it would be, so I hold up one finger to her and Gray, waiting in the car. I spin around and grab Gray's jean jacket—the nice one, the one I always say I'll give back but then never do. I realize, once it's too late for me to turn around, that when people look at us today, they might see a girl and her boyfriend, and some other girl along for the ride with them. I wonder if that's what Tal thought just now when she saw it. The jacket is huge on me, so there's no way she won't know that it's not mine.

"Are you ready for the best day of your life?" Gray demands once I've buckled myself into the back seat, quietly tucked behind Gray, and Tal pulls away from my house.

"Also, hi," she says.

Also, hi? What am I supposed to do with *also, hi?*

I half smile at her, but she's driving, so she doesn't see it. I decide the best course of action is to pretend like nothing's happening while really, if nothing's actually happening, I might die.

"The best day of my life was that day three years ago when Starbucks fucked up my drink order so I got my actual order *and* the fuckup order for free and then we went to Six Flags." I pause. "As I was saying that, I realized how sad it was."

"Cruising right past that," Gray says. "Because we're trying to make Tal believe that we're cool and cultured individuals."

"That ship has long since sailed," Tal says immediately. I snort, and she makes eye contact with me for the first time in the rearview. I swear to god, her eyes get darker when we see each other.

"I know I have a lot to compete with," she says, slowly dragging her eyes away from me and back to the road. "It's, like, what? Ten years of friendship versus me being here not even a month?"

"Seventeen," Gray and I say at the same time.

"Longer if you count our in-utero friendship," Gray says. "Which I do. Obviously."

"Our moms are friends," I explain as Tal merges onto the highway with a look on her face like she had no idea what she was getting herself into today.

"She never had a chance," Gray says. "I was always gonna pop out of my mom and into Luke's loving arms. Probably made the episiotomy worth it."

"You *must* know your mother doesn't think that."

Gray and I carry the conversation (him because he's used to it, me because I have so much nervous energy that's demanding to leave my body through loudly telling stories about Gray as a child), but Tal doesn't seem to mind. She laughs like she means it and gives both of us shit when we accidentally say the same thing at the same time.

It isn't until Tal gets off the highway that I realize we spent the entire drive laughing. That I didn't worry the whole time. That, somehow, there's something that works here, when the three of us are all hanging out together. I look at Tal and she smiles this private little quiet smile I haven't seen on her before, and I know she's thinking the same thing, and it would feel perfect if I didn't know that Gray's thinking it, too. That he's thinking about what good luck it is that I get along so well with his future girlfriend.

In middle school, I used to think about what dating someone would be like. It was never a specific person, because I wasn't quite ready to think about who that person would be (or, more specifically, who they *wouldn't* be). But I thought about what we'd do. I thought about it in class and on long car rides and every night before I went to sleep. I tried to think about it so hard that I'd force myself to dream about it, like my subconscious would do me a favor and explain what I was looking for. To me, when you were very grown-up and very mature and very in love, you went to a museum with a person and they held your hand in front of a piece of art that made you feel something.

That probably came from watching *Ferris Bueller* too many times with my mom, but it stuck in my head anyway.

Gray and I have been to a couple of museums together, but not this one, and not with Tal. Not with Tal making my heart thud whenever she turns around to grin at both of us, not with Tal pointing out her favorite paintings and gesturing huge and bold and open at everything she sees.

"Gay, gay, gay, *super* gay," she says when we walk into a room full of ancient Roman sculptures, pointing at each of them.

"The sculptures, or the artists?" I ask.

"Oh, take your pick."

Gray makes us take pictures of him matching poses. I post one on my story with little eggplant emojis over his and the statue's crotches and another of Tal pretending to lick a bust of the emperor Nero. Syd replies to one of them with *hahaha-haha third wheel life* and a bunch of heart emojis, because Syd thinks adding heart emojis to something means she can say whatever mean shit she wants and get away with it. I'd feel a lot worse if Syd wasn't right—someone here's a third wheel, I just don't know which of us it is.

We set up camp in the museum café for lunch, Tal with a limp veggie burger and Gray and me with chicken fingers we ordered from the kids' menu.

"I would like to propose a toast," Gray says, because now

that we're all sitting still, he doesn't know what to do with himself. "It's probably *fucking wild* to come into a friendship like this, but Tal has held her own all day. She may not be human."

"You two aren't as difficult to deal with as you think you are," Tal says, but she raises her cup anyway.

"How dare you," I say. "We're special babies."

"Loved and feared by all who come across us," Gray agrees.

Tal rolls her eyes, but she's smiling. "But seriously, thanks for being so welcoming. Switching schools this late in the game is a bit of a ride. I had kind of made my peace with not having friends senior year."

"I find that extremely hard to believe," I say. Tal when we first met, that huge laugh, the way she made everyone she came across fall in love with her instantly? That was her on *low*?

Tal laughs, turning her whole body toward me and knocking our knees together. She grabs a handful of my fries and I swat her hand away.

"I need extra!" she exclaims. "My burger sucks."

"Wait, are you trying to tell me that ordering food based on a made-up test to gauge how hardworking a restaurant is *isn't* the most effective method?"

"I would *never* say that."

I'm taking a page out of Gray's book today. Pretend that things are fine and normal and maybe they will be. But I hadn't considered that acting normal with Tal, now that things have changed so much, might actually look like flirting to an outsider. I think about that hypothetical person again, who might see Tal as tagging along with me and Gray, and I wonder if that's different now. Maybe Gray's the one tagging along.

"What's the test?" Gray asks.

I blink away from Tal like she's a bright light in my face. She sucks me in like that. The world goes blurry around the edges.

"I think you can tell how good a restaurant is based on their veggie burger," Tal says. "Which you *can*."

"Oh, that makes sense," Gray says. I think he's full of shit until he adds, "Because they're, like, kind of an afterthought sometimes, right?"

I can't help the laugh that pops out of me. Oh my god.

"That's *literally* exactly what Tal said."

Tal's laughing along with me, and she leans back in her chair and tucks one of her feet up under herself. She brings her hand up to rest on my shoulder, and I know if Gray said anything about it (he wouldn't), she would say she's just trying to steady herself. Maybe that's all she *is* doing. But it's the closest she's gotten to me since last night, and everything in my chest goes hot and cold at once.

"Maybe we need to let Tal into the Love Shack," Gray says.

"For the last time, we are *not* calling it the Love Shack."

"Should I be phoning my emergency contact?" Tal asks.

I roll my eyes at Gray, who pretends he doesn't see. "The Love Shack is what Gray is trying to get us to call our apartment when we move in together in college."

"It's a little old place where we can get together," Gray says sagely.

"Oh, super timely reference," I tell him as he flips me off. "A song that came out in 1989."

"So you guys are going to college together?"

Gray and I break away from where we'd been making fake bitch faces at each other. I look away, nod, and wait for Gray to take over, pretend my mouth is full.

"UMaine," Gray says. "Like our hot-mess parents before us."

I'm suddenly a little embarrassed. Tal doesn't strike me as the kind of person to go to college in-state, to go somewhere where she could come home every weekend. UMaine has never felt like a safe decision until now, when we're talking about it around someone who doesn't seem to play it safe.

"We could always add a third bedroom to the Love Shack," Gray says now. "What are you doing after high school?"

Tal shrugs. "Some kind of design, I think. RISD's the dream, obviously."

"Obviously," Gray says, and Tal and I laugh at him before both of us realize he wasn't trying to make a joke, he was trying to make Tal think he knew what she was talking about.

Gray doesn't seem upset with us, but he excuses himself to the bathroom and I know that he's going to splash water on his face and breathe the way he learned how to do in therapy until he feels better about himself. On his way by, I grab him by the hand and kiss it the way he does for me, press his palm to my cheek for a second until he smiles at me with tired eyes.

"He's really lucky to have you," Tal says once he's gone, and I shake my head before she's even finished speaking.

"I'm lucky. He puts up with a lot from me. Like, I'll call him in the middle of the night if I have a nightmare. I'm that high-maintenance."

I'm trying to laugh it off, but Tal looks at me like she has no idea what I'm talking about.

"Yeah," she says. "That's . . . literally just friendship? That's what being friends is."

It's not that Gray's ever, *ever* made me feel like I'm needy. I think somewhere down the line, when he was the Boyfriend and I was the Girlfriend, I started believing that I was. It always felt like we were little kids playing house when we were together, copying what we saw other people doing. All of Gray's friends complain about their girlfriends being needy sometimes, and I was one of those girlfriends, so I was needy, too.

I need to change the subject, but I need to change it to something that *isn't* last night.

Tal beats me to it.

"I'm so sorry about last night," she says, and my heart goes *no, wait, what? no!* "I think I misread the vibe."

"You didn't," I say, and then I feel my eyes widen, holy shit, why would I say that?

Tal laughs down at her burger. Tongue licking over teeth again. "Yeah, I know. I was giving you an out."

I laugh, surprised. I haven't seen Tal like this, really. Averting her eyes, unsure of herself.

"Have you told Gray?" she asks.

I can't stop how quickly I reply. "*No*," I say. "Definitely not."

Tal nods, once, just a bob of the head.

"Is that . . . okay?" I ask. I don't even know what I'm asking. I think I might be asking if she'd still kiss me again, knowing that. Knowing Gray can't find out.

But that would make me a horrible person, so that can't be it.

"Of course," she says, and it fills me with so much relief that I know I *am* a horrible person, because I was definitely asking if she'd still kiss me.

"But," she says, and my heart sinks again, "why not?"

It's a fair question. If I'd just kissed someone and they told me we could never tell anyone, ever, I think I'd feel like shit. But that's not what this is, and Tal needs to know that.

The problem is, I'm only just about able to think about this. Let alone tell someone about it. Let alone tell *Tal* about it.

"I'm just . . ." I swallow a dry bite of chicken finger. "I came out, and no one hates me or whatever, and that's great. But I know that people are looking at me differently. I know that people are talking about me behind my back. And I know this is shitty, but it feels . . . sometimes it feels like I shouldn't give them more ammunition."

"Ammunition," Tal repeats.

"Like, it's one thing to know Alana Lucas is gay or whatever. It's probably another for the proof to be right there in front of you."

Tal looks sad, but I think it's *for* me and not *because* of me.

"We can talk about it later, if you want?" she asks in that same small voice. I want her back, loud, raucous her. And I absolutely don't want to talk about this if it means Tal apologizing again. If it means undoing it.

I don't have time to answer, because Gray comes back, sliding onto the bench seat beside Tal so she's squished between us. I try not to see the irony.

It's not late when we get home, but it's still way colder than usual for almost-October and the sky is dark and gloomy and it feels like it's the middle of the night. There's that crackling feeling in the car when Tal laughs at something Gray or I say, that spark that makes you feel like there's something worthwhile to go looking for in the night. That feeling that tricks you into thinking that as long as the night doesn't end, everything will always be like this.

I know Gray and Tal feel it, too, because when Tal pulls into Gray's driveway, he says, "Do you guys want to come in?" And Tal's already unbuckling her seat belt like that was a given, then leading the way for both of us through his front door even though she's the one who's barely ever been here.

It's not even that anything particularly magical happens once we get inside. We're having fun, but the three of us don't really know how to be the three of us yet, and there's still awkwardness in the way we all piece together. Gray finds a bottle of truly horrific coconut rum and a deck of cards, and the three of us sit on his bedroom floor and drink from the bottle because his mom is working overnight, and for a second it feels like we do this all the time.

Before Tal drinks, she looks at me like she's asking my permission. I don't get it until I realize that she's my ride, that otherwise we'll have to stay here. I wave my hand and she takes a long pull with her head thrown all the way back. I know I don't have to check to see if Gray notices me staring. He'll be staring, too.

Once it's been established that Tal and I are staying over, Gray manages to loosen up more. At the museum he'd clearly been trying to impress Tal, to seem perfect. Now he doesn't care so much, lets himself relax and wear a Taylor Swift concert tee without making it a whole thing.

"Okay, so you can't be tempted by UMaine and the Love Shack." Gray points at Tal with his hand of cards, showing me all of them in the process, but it's okay because I forget what we were actually playing in the first place. "But I bet that fancy Rhode Island school would like you more if you were considered one of Maine's best and brightest high school students."

"Are you trying to get me to join a cult?" Tal asks. "You do have that clean-cut cult leader look about you."

"It's the fingernails," I agree. "Clean as a whistle. Suspiciously so."

"Well, excuse me for exercising proper hygiene, you animals." Gray looks so genuinely disgusted that Tal and I both collapse laughing, dropping our heads on the side of his bed.

"I was just *saying*," Gray continues, "that our camp could be more fun with Tal there."

He's started calling it *our camp* now, so confident that we'll be there. Rightly so—Bremner handed him his nomination last week. Signed, sealed, delivered, straight to where Gray's always wanted to be. I'm still waiting, but Gray keeps telling me not to worry, that I'll get it, that even if I don't, my application is still strong, that of course UMaine will want me either way.

"Oh, that leadership thing?" Tal asks around a mouthful of Doritos. "Mrs. Abbott nominated me the other day."

"Wait, what?" I ask.

"The guidance counselor?" Gray asks, which would have been my next question.

Tal shrugs. "I had to see her a bunch when I first started. New kid problems, y'know? She said she, quote, *sees something in me*. Very exciting, I'm sure you'll agree."

"Fuck yeah!" Gray crows. He actually pumps his fist into the air, which is how I know the rum's starting to hit him.

"The end-of-camp dance won't know what hit it." I scoff.

Tal rolls her eyes. "Why do all these things always insist on hosting *dances*? What do they think that achieves?"

I hide my smile in a long sip of my drink.

I realize now that I hadn't been excited about the camp until Tal said she was going. It feels less like something I have to do to stick with the plan, to be good to Gray. Now it's time away from here with Tal.

Gray seems unbelievably pleased at the news, too, which dampens my enthusiasm a bit. He gets up, doing a little skip-dance that I whistle at, and announces we're all watching a movie. He picks, sticking his tongue out at us when Tal and I groan at his choice.

We don't complain more than that, though, both of us too comfortably tipsy and sleepy to make much of a fuss. We line up side by side by side in Gray's bed, me in the middle, and Gray gets the movie playing on his laptop.

"Watch this," I murmur to Tal. "Five minutes. Time it."

Exactly five minutes later, Gray is snoring softly beside me. The opening credits haven't even ended yet.

I try to laugh without shaking him awake, but Gray's usually a pretty heavy sleeper. He's nothing but energy when he's awake, always looking to solve all the world's problems, so when he sleeps, he sleeps hard.

I turn to laugh with Tal, only to see that she's asleep as well. Of course.

Normally, I would turn the movie off and try to sleep, too, but there's an itch under my skin that keeps me awake. I let myself look at Gray, ghostly in the laptop's blue light with his mouth a little bit open. He's drooling out of one corner of his mouth and he's beautiful.

In my worst moments, I *so* wish it was him. That it was that easy. People talk about how sad it is when people get married super young, when they feel like they have everything they need as a teenager. But for me, that was the one part of being Gray's Girl that I actually loved. The idea of being done, of having a place to land when we both jumped out into the big wide world? I couldn't find much wrong with that.

I watch most of the movie with Gray's and Tal's steady breathing on either side, and it's only when my eyes are starting to droop that I turn to look at Tal.

I almost jump when I realize she's awake, big eyes looking for me in the low light. I'm suddenly so incredibly aware of the fact that we're lying beside each other, that my entire left side is pressed hotly against her entire right side. I could deal with that when she was asleep, but she's not asleep. She's awake, and she's looking at me, and she's *right there*, like she always seems to be.

There isn't a way to tell who does what first. Whose fault it is. Because Tal lifts her chin as I lower my head. Tal's lips part as my eyes close. And both our hands find the other's cheek when we finally, actually, undeniably, inevitably kiss.

It's different from the last time, both of us much more aware of what we're doing. Both of us making a clear choice, both of us breaking apart and coming back together as quietly as we can because holy shit, Gray is literally right there, right behind me, but then Tal licks across my bottom lip and I wouldn't be able to pick Gray out of a lineup. I pull away first again, but don't run away this time. I lie back against Gray's pillow. I let Tal lean on my shoulder, and listen to my heart pound for the rest of the night.

SEVENTEEN

We don't talk about it.

We don't talk about it in the morning, when Gray swoops into his room with half-frozen toaster waffles and Tal and I quickly detangle our legs where our feet were sleepily rubbing together. We don't talk about it when I roll my eyes and flop out of bed to make us cinnamon rolls from scratch with the emergency yeast I keep in Gray's kitchen. We don't talk about it when Tal drives me home, even though I stare at her mouth the entire time and she knows it and she squeezes my hand twice before I get out of the car. We text, but not about it, this, us, whatever it is. Tal asks if I want to hang out after school on Monday, and I say yes because there's no way I would ever say no, but we don't talk about it. We don't talk about it when Tal smirks at me when we pass each other in the hall on Monday morning, and I do absolutely nothing, the entire time, every second, but think about it.

So when Gray meets me at my locker at the end of the day and says, "Ready?" at first I have no clue what he's talking about. And then he holds up a bag of Skittles and my heart sinks.

I usually help Gray go over his Model UN notes before

his meetings. We sit in the library for an hour, and then once the people who are actually *in* Model UN start filtering in and rolling their eyes at me, I walk home. If I'm feeling particularly pathetic or if the weather's especially shitty, I lounge around the library until Gray's done so he'll give me a ride. Sometimes Olivia used to steal me, and we'd go to Mimi's for chili fries and I'd sit with my back ramrod straight the entire time because I knew, I *knew* that if Olivia ever had any reason to see anything imperfect in me, it would take thirty seconds for everyone else to see it, too.

But none of that matters, really, because I'm always, always at Model UN Mondays after school, trying to get Gray to believe that there's a country called Dickhead Island (main exports: sugarcane, spices, strap-ons) and quizzing him about the countries that actually do exist.

"Shit," I say to him now, Skittles bag still dangling in front of my face. "Sorry, I can't today."

The first twinge of annoyance comes when Gray cocks his head at me. He's genuinely confused. Like I told him I was going to Mars instead. The idea of me not being right there by his side for every moment he needs is genuinely unfathomable to him for a second.

"Sorry," I say again, even though I don't know that this is a two-apology situation. "Tal wanted to talk about student council stuff."

That's not exactly true, but even this, today, feels like some kind of proclamation I'm nowhere near ready to make (not that Tal and I even have anything to pronounce, anyway). Having a cover makes it just a little bit easier.

"Oh," Gray says. "Shouldn't it have been me? Like, as the president, I mean."

I can't decide what I want to do, scream or laugh or cry, when I hear Gray ask *shouldn't it have been me?* There's that same dread I've been feeling ever since I first saw Tal, but now there's something else. Something almost like triumph. Because I can't pretend to know what Tal's thinking or what we're doing, but I know, absolutely, that it's not Gray. It's me. For Tal, at least when it's between me and Gray, it's me.

"She asked me last week," I say, which isn't true and doesn't answer his question but I hope will at least keep him from asking anything else. "We planned it around her schedule. Sorry, tonight was the only day that worked for her."

I've said sorry three times now, but I don't know if I mean it. I don't love how sure Gray was, how positive that I'd be hanging around for him. Waiting for him to bring me to life.

"Okay, I guess."

The second twinge happens here, when it feels like Gray's my dad giving me permission to hang out with a friend.

I tell Gray I'll see him later, and the worst part is I think it's only awkward on my part. I'm the one with the problem, even though Gray's the one who caused it. It annoys me even more. Why does he think he can put me on the shelf like that? Why does he assume I'll always be here to follow him around?

I'm lost in my thoughts, semi-stomping down the hall, when Tal catches me as I round a corner. I almost slam right into her and I know Gray's gone in the other direction, so I let my shoulders relax a bit.

"Ready to go?" I ask her.

"Sure." She laughs, once. Takes a tiny step backward. "Where are you gonna bury me?"

I blink at her and she laughs again.

"You've just got an energy about you right now that I can really only describe as *batshit and frightening*. Kinda into it. Mostly want to know what's wrong."

She starts walking, so I follow her until we're in her car. It smells like clean laundry in here, something fresh and like home. I knock my head back onto the headrest and close my eyes.

"Gray can be an asshole."

"Ooh," Tal says, pulling out of the parking lot. She puts her hand on the headrest behind my head when she does it, and I know that's just how people reverse out of parking spots but it still makes the back of my neck tingle. "I didn't think we were allowed to say that."

"He's not an asshole," I say immediately, feeling new guilt on top of the other guilt I've already been carrying. "I just . . . I don't know. I need him to be, sometimes? Or maybe he is, I don't know anymore."

"Tell me what happened and I'll tell you whether he's an asshole," Tal says. "I'm very wise and not at all biased toward you."

We're not talking about it, but I guess we're joking about it. I guess something, somewhere, is obvious enough to Tal that she can joke about it. The thought of that makes me want to do a backflip, but I don't because we're in a car and I think trying it, even outside a car, would kill me.

I tell Tal what happened and she rolls her eyes at all the

right points. I've never talked shit about Gray to anyone, really. Sometimes, last year, I would make up stupid arguments or issues so I'd have something to talk about with Sydney. Girlfriends complained about their boyfriends, right?

But I've never *actually* talked shit about Gray to anyone. So I'm not very good at it.

Because when Tal says, "Jesus, he's out of line," my back goes up.

"I mean, I see why he's confused," I say. "I do always go with him to this thing. Why would he think today would be any different?"

Tal looks at me sideways and doesn't say anything. I don't know how she could say anything to that, really.

"Am I pathetic?" I ask her. "Seriously."

"Obviously not." Tal scoffs. "I have better taste than that. You guys just . . . have your thing. I know that. Even if I don't always get it. But I don't have to get it, y'know?"

Again. Three times now. *Kinda into it. I'm not at all biased toward you. I have better taste than that.* It makes me want to say *forget about Gray.* Makes me want to say *come here. Stay here.* Most of all, it makes me want to grab on to her shoulders and scream WHAT IS HAPPENING?

My phone buzzes. I look down, expecting Gray, but it's Olivia.

Missing you at UN, baby!!! Where are you??

Olivia doesn't miss people. Especially not at UN, where she can remind everyone that she knows everything about everything and then literally win a medal for it. It's like it was designed specifically for her.

She notices things, and she *definitely* notices things about Gray. She might not know him as well as I do, but she knows him well enough to know when he's upset about something. That plus me not being there isn't too difficult to put together.

Last year, Mimi's had basically become our post-UN tradition. Until she stopped asking me. So now it's pretty clear Olivia's trying to figure it out. Figure me and Gray out, like always.

I reply *Just family stuff! Mimi's next week?*

I'm feeling bold enough to actually try and call Olivia out on her bullshit, but she replies almost instantly, *oh my god PLEASE!!!!!!* And ugh, I kind of get excited at the thought of something being normal again. Olivia has a way of sucking you in, of making you feel like the two of you are the only people on the planet, so it wouldn't even *matter* if you told her what you *really* thought of all your friends or your deepest darkest secrets. You come away from hanging out with Liv blinking into the sun and wondering what, exactly, you just said. I stuff my phone into my pocket and try to forget it exists. It's surprisingly easy to do when I remember who I'm with.

"I need to abuse some dough," I announce once Tal and I step into my house, throwing bags and jackets and boots off to the side in a way my parents would normally yell at me for, but we'll get away with because they're visiting my aunt. "Do you know how to make bread?"

Tal laughs, and then looks at me and realizes I'm not

joking, and then she *really* laughs. "Obviously I don't know how to make bread," she says. "Seeing as I am not a *pioneer*."

"Oh, then my plan to have you churn the butter was a *big* mistake."

I grab everything we need—as if I'd let this house exist without a steady stock of yeast, flour, and sugar—and Tal watches from her spot perched on my kitchen counter as I combine everything.

"Want a job?" I ask, and Tal hops down.

"I need warm water in that bowl." I point to where the yeast, miracle ingredient of miracle ingredients, is waiting patiently.

Tal moves slowly, letting the water run and adjusting the temperature, asking me to test it, letting it fill a measuring cup before she pours it in carefully. She pushes the sleeves of her sweater up around her elbows, tucks a dark curl behind her ear, and my mouth runs dry. I lean my elbow on the counter and watch her, soaking up every second I have of her here, in my kitchen, doing this with me.

We're standing beside each other, and if I look down, it's so normal. We're both in big knit sweaters (she looks cool, I look like I'm humoring my grandmother's craft project). We both have our sleeves rolled up, which is how I learn that fore-arms can be hot. We both have flour on our hands. Tal's hair is down, curls flopping in every direction. Mine's up, but it's fallen throughout the day and I haven't bothered to fix it yet. The night I came out to Gray, I stared at myself for an hour in my bathroom mirror. I thought something would be differ-ent, some neon sign buzzing above my head. But I looked like me, and then somewhere along the line I decided that if I still looked the same, I could always feel the same.

But this, Tal beside me in the kitchen, Tal watching me carefully for instructions, Tal caring so obviously about what I think of her. That's brand new, and it makes me brand new, too, somehow.

"Ready to learn how to knead?" I ask once everything's combined and the dough smells like what heaven must smell like.

"Let's do it."

I take the dough out of the bowl. It's still sticky-wet, clinging to the bowl and my hands and everywhere else. I can't resist taking a big inhale, smelling that perfect smell and knowing that I made it.

"Can you throw some flour on the counter?" I ask. Tal takes me literally, scooping up a small handful of flour and flinging it onto the counter. It flies everywhere, gets all over her face somehow, and in a different world I'd smooth it away the way she smoothed out my forehead in Sydney's bathroom. I take a step forward, even, to do it, but stop myself. Kissing me when we've been drinking, when it's late at night and no one else knows what's going on, is one thing. I don't know how Tal feels about kissing me in the real world. I don't know how *I* feel about kissing her in the real world, beyond *incredibly fucking guilty*.

"This is how I avoid murder," I tell Tal now, plopping the dough down onto the counter and finding my rhythm. "Punching bread once a week results in the levelheaded, serene girl you see before you."

"You sure you don't want to up that to twice a week?" Tal asks, and I hip-check her.

I present Tal with her dough and try to show her how to knead, try to demonstrate the rock and sway, push and pull of it, but she's too interested in watching me, which makes me stumble, and basically no bread is being kneaded correctly.

"Like this, right?" she asks, and proceeds with the worst attempt at kneading I've literally ever seen. She's basically prodding it like it's Play-Doh. I've never been less attracted to her.

"Um," I say, which just makes her laugh. She bumps her side against mine again and sends another electric zing up through my whole body.

I don't know when us not talking about it becomes a rule. Right now it's something that hasn't come up. What happens tomorrow, next week, when we still haven't spoken about it? What happens if it becomes something that we aren't *allowed* to talk about?

"Show me, then," Tal says, cutting me off mid-spiral. "If you're the queen of bread."

"I *am* the queen of bread."

I try to take the dough from Tal, but she blocks my hand with her arm.

"How am I supposed to learn like that?" she asks.

It takes me a second to understand what she's talking about. It's the glint in her eye, the smirk creeping up on her face, that makes it click. My face goes so red it's probably nearly purple.

"You're really gonna make me do this, aren't you?" I ask,

mostly to myself, before I go up behind Tal, on tiptoe. I wrap my arms around her, put my hands over hers, and show her what I mean.

"I'm not making you do anything," Tal says, extremely innocently and also right against the side of my face, head tipped back onto my shoulder, which means she must feel the way I gulp. "You're here entirely of your own accord."

I don't respond to that, but then Tal's voice goes quiet. "Right?"

My hands squeeze hers involuntarily. "Right."

And maybe that's talking about it. For us, for right now. Maybe that's enough.

Except when Tal leaves, just before my parents come home, after we've spent the afternoon half-heartedly talking about student council but mostly laughing about the people she's finally starting to put names to at school, she leans in whisper close. Puts her forehead on mine. And says, "I spent every weekend with my grandma ages five to thirteen. I know how to knead dough."

She presses her thumb to the center of my mouth for just a second, then spins around through my front door. I stare at it for a long time after it closes.

"What the *fuck* is going on?" I ask no one in particular.

EIGHTEEN

The thing about Tal is that when it's just the two of us hanging out, I find it very difficult to care about what we're doing
and who it might hurt. I don't let myself think about Gray,
so sure his plan is right on track. I don't let myself fantasize
about coming clean to him, about telling him what Tal might
be to me, because as soon as I do that, everything Tal and I
have done up until this point stops being hazy and dream-
like and becomes real. Really real. Real enough that everyone
would know about it. Real enough for other people to have
opinions about it. I only come down from my Tal-high after
she's left, when I have a second to remember what we're actually doing here.

It happens again the next week, at a student council meeting. Tal sits between Gray and me, and that makes no sense,
why should the grade rep no one really asked for be in the
middle of us? But neither of us want her to leave, so neither
of us say anything, and all three of us pretend we don't see
the way Logan keeps trying to catch Gray's eye, trying to give
him some kind of look that's either going to say *what the hell
is going on?* or *nice one.* Gray turns away from him, so I turn

away from him, so Tal turns away from him, and all of us get through the meeting in more or less one piece.

It's not the meeting. It's right after—after Tal gives my knee a quick, secret squeeze under the table, after I jolt and probably turn red and then hate myself for it because come *on*, it's just my *knee*, but my body doesn't seem to understand that. After Gray leaves and Tal stands, and then it's just the two of us in the room with Sydney still sitting at the big table. Our meetings never take very long, but we have the room for the whole period, and Sydney usually hangs around in here after, working on whatever it is geniuses do. She looks up at me and Tal, and before I even think about it, I take an extra half step away from her. Just in case. Just to be safe. Tal doesn't seem to mind, nodding at Sydney when she looks up at us.

Tal walks over to her, which means I walk over to her.

"Hey, Syd," I say.

Sydney smiles at me, tight, no teeth, but I ignore it because that's just how she looks at me now.

"Do you know Anton Spratt?" Sydney asks instead of saying hi back to me.

Fucking obviously I know Anton Spratt. Lacrosse team, prom committee. Taller than Gray, but Gray would never admit it. A Hot Guy, by all accounts. I've also known him since I was five years old, because I've known half the school since I was five years old. And Syd would know that, because she's *also* known him that long.

When I nod, Syd plows on. "We're official now. We're trying to figure out a good day for him to come to one of these meetings so we can coordinate prom planning, but he's *so* busy. That's what I get for picking a boyfriend who loves helping people, right?"

I don't know if I'd classify determining strategies for sneaking alcohol into prom as *helping people*.

"That's okay," I say, mostly because I don't know why Sydney's telling me any of this. "I'm sure we'll figure it out."

"It's going really well." She seems to just be incapable of shutting up at this point. "I really like him, y'know?"

And now I think I get what she's doing. Now that I think about it, Syd's been quick to talk to me about whatever guy she's currently hooking up with since last year. Always has to remind me how much she likes guys. Always has to make sure I'm not getting the wrong idea, somehow. Tal, who'd been watching the exchange with a pleasantly blank look on her face, starts to shift. Takes half a step backward. Even in the middle of this, it's kind of nice to know that Tal notices it, too. I'd been starting to think that I was making it up.

Everything has been full of this. Everything has left these little hints, sent these little messages that everyone who used to love me isn't as comfortable with me anymore. Not in big ways. Not in ways you could even call mean. But they're there. They're right there and it feels like I'm the only one who notices them half the time.

"Are you guys done yet?"

Olivia, breezing through the door and coming up behind Sydney to try and see if she can steal any of her homework answers. Of course she's here. Even though Olivia likes to think she's some kind of 2000s-movie high school queen bee, she doesn't actually seem to exist if her friends aren't around.

She was probably turning to dust while Syd was at this meeting, dying without applause like Tinker Bell.

"I know I am," Tal says. Just enough bitchiness just close enough to the surface. Perfect.

Olivia purses her lips and it's like I can *see* the bitchy little cogs turning in her head.

Tal's looking at me like she expects me to say something.

"Yeah, we were just about to go," I say, and then I hate myself for it, for speaking for Tal, for turning the two of us into a unit around Olivia. I can barely handle thinking about that on my own, let alone around other people. Especially not people like Olivia, who watches and listens and waits for the perfect moment to blow your life up with everything you thought she didn't know.

Tal laughs a little, fondly, and that's too familiar and too much and feels too good to have around other people. I try to look away from her, try to put more space between us without it seeming obvious that that's what I'm doing, but I know Tal knows. I know Olivia notices.

Syd doesn't look like she's leaving anytime soon—for all people seem to think *she's* just Liv's henchwoman, she's not going to let someone get in between her and extra calc credit—so Olivia sets her sights on me and Tal. I stiffen when she approaches, but Tal goes aggressively casual, leaning up against the wall and putting her thumbs through her belt loops. This time, I get to hate myself for two separate reasons: the way something in the pit of my stomach goes liquid hot at the sight of it, and the way I immediately wish she'd stop, because I know she looks gayer than Olivia thinks she is, standing like that.

"Remember how you said we should hang out aaaages ago?" Olivia asks me then, smile bright and chirpy.

"Sure," I say, even though that text, that Model UN meeting, was only last week.

"Well, remember how that didn't happen?" Olivia laughs. "Do you want to go to Mimi's after school?"

I look over at Tal before I can stop myself, because Tal and I are supposed to hang out tonight. I *want* to hang out with Tal tonight. But now Olivia saw me asking permission to hang out with someone other than Tal. Now she knows that's something I do.

"Go ahead." Tal smiles, waves me off. "I can text you later and we can figure something out."

"Oh, sorry!" Olivia says. "Am I interrupting plans?"

She is so good at this. If anyone else was here, any adult or anyone who doesn't know Olivia the way that I do, they wouldn't have any idea what she was doing, the careful way she's gathering information, the way she thinks she's figured us out.

"Nope!" Tal chirps. I smile a little to myself because she knows exactly what Liv's doing. "Let me know if you need a ride to my place after, Alana."

It's the tiniest little claim, and I know Olivia's going to have a field day with it, but I can't bring myself to care because it means that, on some level at least, Tal *wants* to claim me.

At the end of the day, my phone buzzes in my pocket. Olivia's already walking away quickly from my locker, expecting me to follow her without looking back once, so I can check my phone and see that Tal sent *let me know if you need me* and I'm warmed right down to my toes even as Olivia walks out the school's back door and a cold wall of mid-October wind smacks me in the face.

Liv doesn't hit me with anything right away. We get into her car and she turns bad rap up so loud the bass makes my teeth chatter, and it's so much like so many other afternoons after school. It's already getting dark out, and if I let myself relax, it would feel like last year, the year before, like we were going to Mimi's to pick up food before we meet everyone at someone's house for a party.

"I miss you," she says when we pull into Mimi's. "I feel like we never see you anymore!"

And I hate this, I *hate it*, but I get sucked in. I get sucked in right away because it doesn't matter what I think or know or feel, being like this is easy. Being Olivia's friend is easy. Being who I was is easy.

"Yeah," I say. "Stuff with student council got busy really fast. Plus, I have to keep kissing teacher ass to try and get nominated for that stupid leadership camp."

"Oh, I can't even bring myself to care about that thing," Olivia says, waving a hand. "It sounds exhausting."

Liv doesn't have to worry about stuff like leadership camps and extracurriculars she doesn't care about and kissing teacher ass because at Princeton they have a building called the Reiner Library. But she would never admit that, because that might make people think she's stuck-up, and if people think she's stuck-up, then how would she manipulate them?

We sit in a corner booth at Mimi's and I don't say anything

when the waitress, a girl I sort of know on the basketball team named Aspen, comes to take our order. I'm at Mimi's with Olivia after school: We're having chili fries. I don't need to say anything, because Olivia orders for us. Always.

"It was so funny what Tal said at lunch," she says, only once the fries are here and I'm stuck. I try to sit up straighter, try to make it seem like I already know whatever it is she's trying to do.

"What was funny about it?"

"Because it's, like, I don't know. *Let me know if you need a ride.* Like you're gassing up the minivan. You two are gonna, like, go to your bed-and-breakfast in Vermont where you make goat cheese and shit."

This is when I realize that Olivia might know more about Tal than she's letting on.

It's also when I realize that Liv's knowledge of lesbian culture comes exclusively from shitty jokes in '90s sitcoms.

She's laughing, and if I started laughing along with her, everything would be normal. But it's been months of this shit and I'm tired.

"Or she's literally just giving me a ride."

Olivia rolls her eyes. "It was just a joke, Alana, Jesus."

"You know you aren't funny."

This is how we talk to each other. All *baby* this and *love you* that, these little bitchy asides that set the pace. Before last year, that was why I liked her. We could keep up with each other.

"Everyone else thinks I'm funny."

"What, Syd and Sav and Ken? Yeah, that's why I don't think you're funny. I don't spend my life up your asshole."

Olivia laughs, and Olivia only ever laughs loudly because that's how you get people to look at you.

"You're such a bitch," she says gleefully.

Sometimes I think Olivia misses me, because I was the only one to ever do this with her. Ken is too nice to ever call anyone a bitch. I've never been. Sydney cares too much about what Olivia thinks of her to tell her to shut up. I never did.

"What's her deal, anyway?" Olivia says, leaning forward the way she does when she's *really* about to lay into someone.

"What's whose deal?" I cut my eyes at her when obviously I know exactly who Liv's talking about.

I may not know where Tal and I stand, but I know enough about myself to know that I won't be able to let Liv say a single bad word about Tal. And if the sharp glint in Olivia's eye is any indicator, she knows it. So this should be interesting.

Liv gives me a bitchy look, tilting her head at me like *oh, come on*.

I swallow. "What do you mean her *deal*?"

Liv shrugs, looking up and pretending to be innocent. "I've just heard stuff, y'know?"

My heart stops. I know what it means when Olivia Reiner hears stuff.

"Don't do that."

"Don't do what?"

"Liv," I say. "Seriously. It doesn't matter if you've heard stuff. It's not on you to say anything. About anyone."

Liv rolls her eyes. "Oh my god, Alana, I was literally just asking a question."

I roll my eyes right back, because it's never a real fight with

Olivia. She'll be a bitch but say she's kidding so often that when you finally walk away, you have no idea what just happened and what you laughed at and how you feel.

"Hey," Liv says now. "When does Gray work this week?"

It's the same as me and Gray, really. Olivia and I don't apologize to each other. Except, with Gray, we don't apologize because we know how the other feels. We know that we'd never hurt each other on purpose. Olivia doesn't apologize because Olivia's never needed to apologize about anything in her life, according to her.

I pick at the mushy fries and look out the window so I don't have to look at her when I answer. "I'm not Gray's mom."

"Yeah, but you know, don't you?"

Of course I know.

"If you want to talk to him, just talk to him, Liv," I say.

"Oh, I have your permission?"

Now that we're talking about Gray, she's gone sharper, rougher around the edges. It's harder for her to pretend like she doesn't care when it comes to him.

Unfortunately, the same goes for me.

"I'm sure he'd be just as happy to reject you today as he was freshman year," I say. "And sophomore year. And last summer."

That's the key with Olivia. You keep all of your information tight to your chest until the perfect moment, the one opportunity to drive it home and catch her off guard. If you don't, she will. You just have to beat her to it.

She blinks at me, and I can tell she's weighing her options. She could deny it, but she'd look worse if Gray actually told me (and of course he told me). She could bitch right back to me, but I've already won. So the two of us just stare each other down for a long moment, and then Olivia laughs, awkwardly, trying to claw back just an ounce of the control she usually has in these conversations.

Olivia would never admit defeat. I would never admit that we were fighting in the first place. So that leaves both of us stuck finishing the shitty fries I didn't even want in the first place, surrounded by people who know Liv and who think they know me. Both of us pretend like nothing happened, but Liv starts giving me one-word answers, and by the time we split the bill and I tell her I'll walk home, no worries, I don't need a ride, she doesn't even bother looking at me as she peels out of the parking lot.

I call Tal for a ride and she shows up so quickly that I know she was waiting by the phone. It should embarrass me after all of that with Olivia, but instead it just warms me from the inside. She's here. She wants to be here.

"Was that as horrible as I thought it was going to be?" she asks once I'm shivering inside her car. I try to let my shoulders relax but find that I can't really.

"Yes," I say.

Tal laughs, but then she sees that I'm being serious. "What's wrong with her? Like, beyond her being a massive bitch. Why is she a massive bitch to you, specifically?"

"Oh, she's a massive bitch to everyone," I say.

"Right," Tal says slowly. "But especially to you."

I've never told anyone this. I never think about that day last May, sitting in Olivia's kitchen, painting Sydney's nails while we waited for a party to start. I never think about Olivia's face while she did my makeup and asked me question after question about Gray that made me squirm because Olivia has this way of looking at you where it feels like she's looking right into the secret core of your being.

In a way, it was almost my fault. I left my phone in the kitchen when I went to pee, and you can't do that kind of thing when you're hanging out with Olivia. I hadn't deleted my search history, and you can't do *that* kind of thing when you're hanging out with Olivia, either. Liv knew my password because she knew Gray's birthday because she's always been into him even when she used to pretend she wasn't, and her phone was upstairs charging and she was trying to prove to Syd that the awful lyrics to whatever annoying song they were listening to weren't what Syd was singing.

I wasn't there, but I can see it happening. I know how Liv ticks. She would have gone online and seen the tab open to the queer helpline I'd been talking to before I got to her house. She would have looked around to make sure she was really seeing what she was seeing, and then she would have put the phone down and ignored Syd asking *well? Were you right?*

I came back from the bathroom just in time to hear Olivia say *so you know about Alana, right?*

"It's not a big deal," I say to Tal now. "But I guess Olivia was technically the person who outed me last year."

If Tal was a cartoon, I'd be able to see smoke and then flames shooting out of her ears.

"Holy shit," she says. "Jesus *Christ*. Are you kidding me?

And she's just wandering around like nothing happened? And you have to see her being everyone's best friend? Oh, fuck that. Does Gray know? No one *did* anything when it happened? Are you okay? How do you feel about it? Do you want me to kill her? Oh my *god*, I'm so sorry—"

"It's fine," I cut Tal off before she can spiral even more. "Seriously. Gray doesn't need to know. I've already blown up his life enough, we don't need to get into a whole thing where everyone in the friendship group has to pick sides now. And anyway, everyone was going to find out eventually. There was only so long I would have been able to keep it up. I'd only figured it out myself a few months before, but I'm pretty sure that as soon as I did, it was obvious to everyone. Like, no one was *really* surprised when I actually came out."

". . . Yeah, because you'd been outed."

"No, seriously! It wasn't a big deal. And, like, what *really* happened after? It's not like I was shunned by society. People aren't, like, *actively* homophobic anymore really, right? Not, like, hugely, y'know?"

Tal blinks at me. "What?"

"Like, it's not like anyone's been super mean to me because of it."

She looks at me sideways, stopped at a red light. "When was the last time one of your old friends texted you? Texted you first."

Well, never, really. Not anymore. Not unless they want something. Syd texted me the other night, but it was because she forgot her math textbook at school and she needed me to send her pictures of the homework pages.

"You may have a point," I admit. "Possibly."

Tal reaches for my hand and I give it to her without a second thought. I let her squeeze it, let her hold on to it for the rest of the ride home. She doesn't ask me to hang out even though we were planning on it. She sees whatever tired mess is written across my face and understands.

She puts her thumb to the center of my lips before I get out of the car, and when I do it back, I feel her smile on my fingerprint.

NINETEEN

Over the past seventeen years, there have been a few times when Gray being Gray has annoyed me.

When we were in middle school and snuck sips of his mom's wine when she was out of the house and he panicked and told her the second she came home. When we started high school and he academically abandoned me by being the best and the brightest while I was content to be the best of the middle. And now, when he's trying so hard to keep me included in the relationship he thinks he's building with Tal.

We hang out more this week as a group than we ever have, after school in Gray's room, carving pumpkins and pelting each other with candy that we buy just for ourselves ("Fuck them kids!" Gray screams, dissolving into the same bubbling laugh he's had since he was a little kid. He barely ever lets that out around people who aren't me). Prowling Walmart for shitty home accessories and matching pajamas and talking shit about the people we know that we see there. Driving around town after dark, Gray's cleaning playlist blasting through the open windows while our teeth chatter in the night air. Tal, to my horror, loves it.

Gray's still being careful about his plan—too careful, if you ask me. I keep telling him to just go for it, and it makes me feel like the worst person on the planet. But if he goes for it, maybe Tal will turn him down. Maybe she'll tell him why. Maybe, after a little time, he'd understand if I told him about me and Tal.

Because there isn't a me and Tal yet, really, but she keeps showing me that there could be. If we wanted to, there could be.

When we're making it rain candy on Gray, she stuffs Sour Patch Kids in her pockets and leaves them in my locker to find the next morning, little heart scribbled on a Post-it note. When we're in Walmart, she holds up potted plants and fake neon signs and novelty posters and only cares about my opinion. She rests her foot against mine under the table while we're at Mimi's. When Gray goes to the bathroom, she puts her thumb on my lips again, this thing we've started and won't stop now. This time, for sure, I know that it's a kiss.

So when my doorbell rings on a Friday afternoon, I realize that for the first time since last year I don't actually know who might be on the other side of it. Gray's working tonight, but sometimes when it's slow he can leave super early, grab snacks from the gas station on his way home, and show up on my front porch in search of dinner leftovers.

It's horrible—really, deeply terrible—how much happier I am when I realize it's Tal.

"I'm very mad at you," she says when I open the door.

"I'm pretty sure you're kidding, but please tell me you're kidding."

She laughs and when she throws her head back, her one dangly earring catches the light. She's starting to become different, somehow, when it's just the two of us. I don't know if anyone else would even notice it, but since I've spent the last two months studying every tiny detail I can find about Tal, I see it right away. There's something brighter about her like this, something just a little louder. The single earring. The faint swagger when she marches past me and into my house, big black boots stomping in a way that should be menacing but *really* isn't. I don't tell her how much I like it, but I think she knows. She smirks when she catches me staring at her, when I bite my lip around her to stop from saying something stupid.

"I'm mad at you because I've been keeping score. Gray's gotten to hang out with you three times this week. *Thrice.*"

It's possible Tal and Gray have also spent too much time together lately, with the way she dramatically spins herself around and wiggles three fingers in my face. If she was Gray, I'd lick them to get her to stop, but that *definitely* wouldn't have the same effect on Tal, and . . .

That's actually not a path I need to go down right now.

"So I've come to collect," Tal continues. She digs into her pocket and pulls out tickets for a band I've never heard of playing in Portland tonight. "If it helps, I can promise your parents that I'm a very responsible driver and will have you back before midnight, virtue intact."

That's a shame is what I'd say if I was a different kind of person.

What virtue? is what I'd say if Tal and I had actually had some kind of significant conversation about last year, if she knew about that one frantic, desperate time with Gray a couple of months before everything went to hell. It's what I'd say if I was sure she wouldn't look at me differently if she knew.

(She won't, probably, I know. But there's a lot riding on that *probably*.)

Instead I say, "I'll go get changed."

I leave Tal downstairs only because I know my mom has a dentist appointment and won't be home for another hour at least. Once I'm in my room, though, I realize how weird it is to leave Tal downstairs. I'll have to come down the stairs to her like it's fucking prom night.

God. I scrub my hands over my face and try to calm myself down. I keep thinking *I wish I could talk to Gray* and breaking my own heart. It took Gray a while to get over his initial shock when I came out (that's another change Tal's caused—I think about things as before and after I came out now, instead of before and after Gray and I broke up). After that, though, he was as close to ecstatic as any teenage boy who just found out his girlfriend is a lesbian could be. He kept telling me how excited he was that now we could talk about girls together. He kept telling me that he was going to help me get ready for my first date with a girl.

It's getting harder and harder to believe that all the times Tal and I hang out aren't dates. It's getting harder and harder to believe that Gray will still do that.

I don't know what to wear to a concert in Portland that isn't some big stadium thing I'm going to with my old friends or Gray and his mom (though I've told them there's no way I'm ever going to a Taylor Swift show with them again after the way they both forgot how to act in society last time). I'm imagining some dimly lit bar full of massive guys with tattoos and mean lesbians who'll sneer down at me because I don't know the words to any of the songs.

In the end, I decide I might as well go for looking good over fitting in. At least if Tal thinks I'm hot, I'll care less that everyone else in the room won't think I belong there. I have to dig to the very bottom of my dresser to find a top I like, cropped and low-cut but short-sleeved and soft, and baggy jeans with a million rips in them (including one right under my ass, which is why my mom thinks I threw these out). I stare at myself in my bathroom mirror for ages, trying to see myself the way a stranger might, the way Tal might.

When I finally come downstairs, though, Tal isn't waiting at the bottom like a horrible teen movie ready to give me a corsage. She's sitting in my living room talking to my mom.

"I thought you were at the dentist," I say. Well, bark.

"I keep telling you our family has incredible teeth," my mom says. She turns to Tal. "Incredible teeth, really shitty eyes. My great-grandma was completely blind, but lived to be one hundred and four with all her teeth."

"Why do you bring that up so often? That's not something people brag about."

Tal laughs, but it's sort of with my mom, and the whole scene is so jarring that my brain can't actually process it.

"Tal was saying you guys were going to a concert tonight?" my mom asks. There's that funny little tone in her voice like I should have told her or she should have met Tal and decided whether she was worthy. She's eyeing my outfit with a careful expression, and I know we have about two minutes before she realizes these are my Ass Jeans.

"I sprang it on her," Tal says before I can say anything. "I owed her one—she helped me out a couple of weeks ago and I haven't been able to pay her back, but I know someone who works at the venue and they snagged me last-minute tickets. I thought it might be fun."

"It sounds fun!" my mom exclaims, too excitedly, like she's going to come with us.

"So we should go before we miss all the fun," I say. Tal seems to finally get it, telling my mom it was *really nice to meet you* and making her way back to the front of the house.

For a horrible second, it's just my mom and me in the room. She opens her mouth to say something and time starts moving in slow motion. She's going to say something horrible like *she seems nice* or *why didn't you tell me* or *you know I love you, right?*

But instead she says, "Have fun," and it's almost worse because now there's this thing hanging over us, this unfinished business. My mom always finishes her business.

Still, it's hard to think about that once I'm in Tal's car, once we shiver out of the October chill and into the fake heat, the soft seats, the faint smell of the long-emptied air freshener clipped to a vent. It's hard to think of anything but the fact that Tal came to pick me up, that she planned something just for me. I know that the word for that is *date*, but I can't even let myself think it. Right now Tal and I are friends who've kissed twice. If I let myself call this a date, then we're *dating*, and that means that I cross the line into actively lying to Gray, and that means I'm a horrible person.

"I've never even heard of this band," I admit as Tal merges onto the highway. "Does that make you cooler than me?"

"Of course not," she says. "I *am* cooler than you, but that's not why."

That. That's it. That's what makes this so hard: Me and Tal are so *easy*, completely effortless but in such a different way from Gray and me. When we were fourteen, everyone told me how obvious it was that Gray was in love with me, and I thought *oh, that's nice of him*. Didn't it work out so well that my best friend could be my boyfriend, and didn't I want that, wasn't that perfect? When Gray looked at me and I could tell he thought I was pretty, that I looked good, that was what I felt. *That's nice of him.*

But now Tal's doing it. There's that face. It matters. It counts. I believe it. And the last thing I'm thinking is *that's nice of her*.

"So," Tal says after a few minutes. It's almost unrecognizable, that quiet voice. I'm still not used to seeing Tal act unsure of herself. "There's this thing next weekend. An open house for RISD. I was going to go, but I thought ... do you maybe want to come?"

At first, I don't say anything. Tal thinks I'm hesitating, so she continues, "Y'know, it's not just visual art there. They do liberal arts stuff, too. If that's something you might be into."

Tal's biting her lip. She knows that little suggestion is bigger than anything else we've done up until this point. If we were smart about it, Gray would forgive me for kissing Tal. I know this is dramatic, but Tal might as well have stood up and objected at my and Gray's wedding. UMaine is the plan. UMaine has always, *always* been the plan.

But I say: "That's something I might be into."

And Tal says: "Cool."

And I say: "I'll make the road trip snacks."

And Tal says: "Sounds like a plan."

And neither of us say anything about it for the rest of the drive.

♡

TWENTY

The back of Tal's hand brushes up against the back of mine exactly three times while we wait for the doors to open.

The first time, she's swinging her arms around because she has to pee, even though I *told her* she should stop somewhere before we got in line. I'm not sure if that one is on purpose, but both of us jump a little when it happens.

The second time is on purpose, I think.

"Top five favorite pastries," she says. "Go."

I gape at her. "That's the meanest thing you've ever said to me."

"You *must* have favorites!"

"Would you say that to a mother? Would you ask their favorite *child*?"

"I would if I wanted to watch someone freak out like this again."

I lean up against the venue's wall dramatically and Tal laughs and follows. The venue is pretty much exactly how I pictured it, this big gray warehouse on the outskirts of town with hordes of girls who look like Tal lined up around the block. They're all in these little clusters, looking like they came that way, like they've always known exactly where to look to find someone like them. My arm's at my side, so she drops hers as well, and on the way, our hands brush and that same electric feeling hasn't gotten any dimmer.

I know for a fact that the third time is on purpose, though.

The third time, we're walking inside, trying not to get run over by a particularly rude group of girls behind us who were laughing too loudly the entire time we were waiting in line. I realize I don't have a ticket just a second too late, but Tal holds up both of ours for the bouncer. We get scanned in, and when Tal's arm drops, she brushes our hands.

But I'm the one who links our fingers.

I'm sure Tal's surprised, but she doesn't show it. We walk ahead holding hands like we've done it a million times before, and it feels like that, like we've done this and could keep doing this, but it also feels like this is the first time anyone's ever touched any part of me and I can't stop thinking about the way it feels like my body is sending all its blood and feeling to that one hand.

I almost drop Tal's hand ten times between us walking in and finding a spot (I'm relieved to discover that Tal isn't a *rush to the front* kind of concertgoer), but I force myself to keep hanging on. I don't know what I'm doing but I know how it feels.

"Tal!"

A voice shouts out from across the way and I drop Tal's hand like it's on fire.

At first, I think *oh my god, it's her secret ex-girlfriend from her old school and she's here to take her back and Tal's been in love* with her this whole time, so she's going to abandon me in Portland and I'll have to call Gray for a ride. She's going to be taller than me and she'll have some kind of really hot tattoo on her neck and I'm going to cry in front of all these cool gays.

But when I follow the voice, I realize I recognize the face it's attached to.

"Rachel!" Tal says, because that's Rachel Milner, isn't it? Rachel Milner who I once went trick-or-treating with but haven't spoken to since middle school because she's in all AP science classes and I'm only halfway decent at chemistry. Rachel Milner who has a cousin named Flora who Gray flirted with at a party a hundred years ago. Rachel Milner who, I guess, feels totally comfortable rushing right up to Tal and giving her a massive hug. Suddenly I want to grab Tal's hand again.

"You guys know each other, right?" Tal asks, because she still isn't used to the fact that there's no such thing as *you guys know each other, right?* where we're from. We all just do.

"I love your jacket, Alana," Rachel says. For a second I think it's a dig, because I'm *still* wearing Gray's jacket. I think Rachel's trying to say *remember you aren't this girl*. But then I remember that Rachel isn't Sav or Syd or Olivia. She doesn't need to say things like that.

"It's not mine," I laugh. "But thanks."

"Literally had to *scream* at the guy at the bar," a voice says. "This better be the best water I've ever had in my life. I'm talking polar bears making love on ancient glaciers kind of top-shelf shit."

Someone with long hair in a tight bun on the top of their

head is passing Rachel a plastic cup of water and then throwing their arm around her.

"Oh my god, is this her?" Tal asks Rachel.

Okay, what?

It's one thing for Tal and Rachel to know each other; we go to the same school, and Tal does, I assume, speak to people who aren't me and Gray, no matter how much the thought might upset the two of us. It's *entirely* another thing for Tal to know Rachel *like this*, to hug her and know that this person who I've never seen before is important to her.

How many Queer Girls of Maine meetings have I missed?

"This is Sadie," Rachel confirms, oblivious to my minor crisis. Sadie squeezes Rachel closer and kisses the top of her head like an agreement.

"She literally never stops talking about you," Tal says, and Sadie laughs.

I realize I've been staring at Sadie at the same time I realize Rachel's giving me a funny look.

"It's nice to meet you," I say, like I'm at a fucking networking event. I have to swallow a slightly hysterical laugh at the thought of lesbian networking.

I'm not looking at Sadie because I think she's hot. (I mean, I'm at least out to *myself* now enough to recognize that she absolutely is, but that's not the point.) I'm looking at her because before she even started talking, before I knew who she was to Rachel, I knew that she was gay. And it wasn't some stupid thing where she was wearing a flannel shirt and I know the jokes about what we're supposed to wear. It wasn't anything special or different about her. It was just something

I knew. Something in me recognized something in her. It feels like I've leveled up.

Rachel, though. I had no fucking clue.

It's not like I've been the only queer person at my school. I know, in theory, that there are kids with, like, blue hair and septum piercings who yell at English teachers about assigned reading that's only about straight white people. I know we have a GSA and they pop up on the announcements or in the yearbook every so often. But they keep to themselves, and they weren't my friends, and something about seeking them out *now* didn't feel right to me. If we weren't friends before I was Officially Gay, why would I be friends with them now, just because now they know we have something in common?

But Rachel doesn't hang out with them, either, and she still seemed to get the memo about finding other people and being part of whatever tangled web means Tal knows her girlfriend.

"This is Alana," Rachel tells Sadie. "We grew up like three streets from each other."

Sadie bobs her head, says, "Hey!" And then goes back to her conversation with Tal, where they're talking like they've known each other for years even though they just met.

I don't really talk to Rachel at the best of times, but I have absolutely no fucking clue how to do it in this context. I think she can tell, because she takes little sips of her water and leans farther and farther against Sadie. I'm suddenly so jealous I could die.

(Again, not because of Hot Sadie. Because of the leaning,

of the landing, of the claiming. Of Rachel knowing Sadie's going to be there.)

The longer I stand there uselessly, the worse I feel, until my vision is starting to blur and I feel like I need to go running right out of the room.

"Hey, can we meet you guys somewhere later?" Tal asks Rachel and Sadie. "I need to ask Alana something."

Rachel doesn't look convinced, but she lets Sadie pull her away and into the crowd. I know we aren't going to meet them later because there's no way I'm diving into that.

Tal leads me into the bathroom, and no one bats an eye when we both crowd into one stall. I've done this before, but with Olivia loudly complaining about having a UTI. Never when there's even a remote possibility that I could be doing what people do when they crowd into bathroom stalls with someone they like as much as I like Tal.

But instead of any of that, Tal says, "Do you need a hug?"

I bust out laughing to hide the fact that that kind of made me want to cry. Tal steps into my space and puts both her arms on top of my shoulders, pulls me in close.

I genuinely can't remember the last time someone who wasn't Gray hugged me like this. Before I can even think about it, I all but collapse.

"What's going on?" Tal asks into my shoulder.

What's going on is that Sadie couldn't tell I was gay and I don't know how to make people understand it. What's going on is Gray has no idea where I am and I'm actually getting used to that feeling and I *hate* it. What's going on is my mom's going to tell my dad that she *finally met the famous Tal* and they're going to ask me too many questions about her and I don't know how to answer any of them. What's going on is I didn't know Rachel was queer, and if I didn't know that about Rachel, why does it feel like everyone knows it about me? What's going on is I thought that I could come here and hold Tal's hand and feel like no one cared, but I still don't feel right in my own body and I have *no fucking idea* how to fix that. What's going on is it's starting to feel like I'll never not feel like this.

"It's a lot," I whisper, instead of any of that.

"What's a lot?"

"Being this."

I don't expect Tal to get it, but she squeezes me tighter like she does.

"Come on," she says. She takes my hand again, leads me out of the bathroom and then out of the venue altogether.

"Are we leaving?" I ask. My stomach sinks at the idea of Tal, disappointed, dropping me off at home when we could have had this entire night. It's not even eight o'clock. Pathetic.

"The concert, not the city," Tal says. "I don't even like this band that much. Callie's cousin had the tickets and I was just looking for an excuse to see you. If you're still game to hang out tonight, we don't need to do it there."

Tal leads me back to her car and only lets go of my hand when she has to.

"I'm sorry," I say when we're driving around downtown and it doesn't seem like Tal's going to say anything.

She cocks her head. "What would you be sorry for? You

weren't comfortable. It's not fun for either of us if you aren't happy."

I recognize where we're going before Tal pulls over in front of the café, and that's another thing that's new. Tal doesn't lead me around Portland anymore. I know where we're going, know which roads to turn down and when.

"Let's see if . . . ha!"

Tal jumps out of the car and runs up to Callie, who appears to be locking up for the night. She says something to them and I hear Callie say, "You are such a dickhead," but they're laughing. They toss Tal the keys and wink at me when they pass the car.

Tal knocks on my window, so I roll it down and she leans in, gets right in my face and makes all my blood scream in my ears.

"I can offer you day-old baked goods and total privacy from anyone you grew up with," she says.

I look at her, backlit by the café's purple neon sign. I look at her, biting her lip because she isn't sure whether this is the right call, whether she's read me right. I look at her, knuckles going white on the car's window frame. I look at her and I want, and want, and want.

I don't say anything, but I roll up the window, get out of the car. Tal locks it behind us and puts a hand on the small of my back as she leads me inside, which means she must feel the way it makes me shudder.

"Callie said not to turn on the overhead lights," Tal says, then makes a face at herself. "Sorry, I know that sounds like a line, but they said otherwise people are gonna think the shop's open."

Tal walks to the other side of the shop, where the books are, and fiddles around with a bunch of plugs until all the little twinkle lights strewn over them turn on. It's so romantic I want to gouge my eyes out.

"Wait here," she tells me. I can see the way she's starting to falter because I still haven't said anything. I sit on the floor, on a soft rug that I pray is at least mostly clean, surrounded by oversize pillows and beanbag chairs, until Tal comes back.

She has a tray of pastries, as promised, and she's looking at me like she's waiting for me to explode on her, to tell her this was a stupid idea.

"I'm not a virgin," I say, instead of telling her this definitely wasn't a stupid idea.

Tal blinks owlishly at me for a moment. "Oh," she says.

She sounds surprised, but I don't think it's because of what I just said. It probably has more to do with the fact that I all but screamed that out of nowhere when Tal *absolutely had not asked*. I'm deep, dark red, flushed down to my toes.

Tal doesn't say anything else for an agonizingly long time, and I'm just about to scramble away from this whole conversation (from this whole night), to tell her to forget she ever heard anything, when she speaks again.

"So you and Gray?" she asks. "Or . . ."

It takes me a second to figure out what that *or* means, but when I do, I blush so hard it actually makes me dizzy.

"Me and Gray," I confirm. "Not, like . . . anyone else."

Jesus, this is going well. If I can't even make an obvious, unfunny joke about how no, actually, I *haven't* been secretly sleeping with Kennedy this whole time, how am I supposed to make it through the rest of this conversation?

Tal puts the tray between us, sitting down beside me.

"How was it?" she asks.

It's not like when Olivia used to ask, leering and wrong. It's not like how I thought Tal might have asked, sarcastic and biting, *how was* that? It's a genuine question, and the fact that Tal's being so sincere catches me off guard enough to be sincere right back.

"It didn't fix anything."

That's not something I've ever said out loud. It's not even, really, anything I've actively thought. But even though I still, at that point, didn't *really* get what was going on with me, I know enough now to know that's why it happened. Gray would have never in a million years been the person to suggest it, always too afraid of saying the wrong thing. Most of our friends had covered sex by junior year, and they assumed the same of us. And somewhere, eventually, when I started to feel itchy and desperate whenever I was around Gray, I thought *maybe this is what we need.*

"Nothing needed to be fixed," Tal says quietly. "You know that now, right?"

I shrug. I do, of course I do, but I also don't like thinking about this whole situation very hard.

"It was embarrassing," I admit. "Is that better?"

Tal huffs out a little laugh. "Not really."

My mouth half quirks up. "Yeah. I just remember being so

embarrassed. Just, like, this massive *cloud* of . . . of shame, I guess? But that sounds embarrassing, too."

I always knew that Gray thought I was attractive, and I know, objectively, that he is, too. But it took us having sex for me to realize that the way he thought I was attractive and the way I thought he was were two *very* different things. Gray had told me I was beautiful and it made me want to throw up, made me weirdly angry. I remember thinking *Jesus, Gray, you can't come up with anything more original than that?* And instantly feeling awful, and then feeling even worse because some unknown amount of time had passed since my first thought and I still hadn't said anything back to Gray. And then I realized I was waiting for it to be over.

"I'm surprised that you guys are still so . . . tactile," Tal says.

I snort. "It took us a while," I say. "We only did it the one time, and it, uh . . . clarified some stuff for me. But then I didn't want him to feel bad, like he'd turned me gay or whatever, and I figured, like, hey, I did it without crying or having a nervous breakdown or whatever, maybe I'm bi or something."

"And then you realized *didn't weep during sex with a guy* isn't exactly a great way to measure attraction, I'm hoping?" Tal says.

I laugh, and I have no idea how she's doing this, but it makes the hammering in my chest relax a little. She's making this into such a nonissue that I don't even know why I felt the need to blurt out my entire sexual history, limited as it may be.

"Pretty much. Once I did finally break up with him, Gray was terrified of being anywhere near me for a while. He thought that he'd done something wrong."

What's the word for "having sex with someone who doesn't want to have sex with you," Alana? he had demanded, two weeks after we'd broken up, when he finally, *finally* asked to see me and I came over to find him coming down from a panic attack, curled up on the couch and hating himself so obviously that it pulled heaving sobs out of me almost immediately.

It wasn't like that! I had yelled, over and over and over again until my throat went croaky. *I didn't know that I didn't want it! I thought I did!*

I didn't know how to make him understand it. I still don't know if he fully understands it. I don't know if I do.

"We're better now," I say.

Tal nods. "Clearly. That was cool of him, to ride that wave."

Understatement of the millennium.

"I think we both finally get that it wasn't anyone's fault," I say. "I just didn't know how it was supposed to feel, wanting someone . . . like that."

I only realize what I'm saying when it's too late. Tal swallows hard, eyes flashing to me, to my mouth, to my flushed throat, back up to my eyes.

I think I would burst into flames if she thought that I was beautiful.

"And . . ." Tal trails off. She's looking at my mouth again. "And now you . . ."

She doesn't finish her sentence. She doesn't finish her sentence because I shove the tray aside and lean into her, get so close our noses are almost touching and our eyes cross. Something sparks in her eyes, and I know she knows, now, that she didn't make the wrong call bringing me here.

I almost chicken out at the last millisecond. I sway back, just an inch or two, just enough for Tal's face to come into focus. But then I can see her, see all of her, see the light bouncing off her earring and the patch of freckles on her temple, and I surge forward, faster than I intended to, so that when our lips finally meet it's more of a collision than a kiss, but that's how it feels with Tal all the time anyway. A collision.

My hands immediately go to her hair, scratching up the back of her neck to grab it at the root there, to keep her with me. It makes her gasp and I swallow it, hungrily—the best thing I've ever made without following a recipe.

It's completely silent in the shop, so I hear every hitched breath and soft noise both of us make. I hear the way Tal's shoes scuff the floor when she stretches her legs out, leans back onto the pillow behind her, and takes me with her. I hear the way my breath stutters when we break apart and Tal kisses me, once, behind my ear. And when we stop for a second and look at each other, it feels like the entire shop shakes with the sound of our nervous, thrilled laughter.

TWENTY-ONE

I'm halfway to Tal's car on Tuesday afternoon when my phone rings.

"Where the fuck are you?" Gray asks when I pick up. "We can't start until we're both here and the freshmen are about to riot."

"Shit," I say. I'd completely forgotten about badminton. "I'll be there in like five seconds."

I hang up and start apologizing to Tal, but she's already waving me off. If it was a couple of weeks ago, I would have invited her to join us. It would have fit right into Gray's plan. But I know that we're hiding now. Tal and I have a history and a status and a *something* to hide from Gray, and if I put both of them in the same room, I don't know how well I'll be able to handle it. Since last week, I've barely been able to look at Tal without feeling like some kind of human tornado, emotions whipping around me too quickly to even identify, followed by the heady, dizzying reminder that Tal's feeling them, too.

I think, given the circumstances, I could be forgiven for forgetting a couple of things here and there.

"Wait, fuck," I say, mostly to myself once I've ripped myself away from yet another flashback of Tal's skin under the café's lights. With all my thinking about Tal and hooking up with Tal and spending every waking moment with Tal, I hadn't thought about what I'd said we'd do next weekend.

It's one thing to go with Tal to a college open house that isn't UMaine—Gray would already see that as a betrayal, no matter how hard he'd try to pretend he wasn't hurt by it—but it's really another thing to do that on *Meal Prep Day*.

"I'm in trouble," I say to Tal. I mean to say it like a joke, but as I say it, I realize it's probably a little true.

"Problems with hubby?" Tal asks. I can't tell anymore when she's joking and when there's an edge to her.

"I have plans with Gray on RISD-day," I explain. "He's gonna hate me."

Tal hesitates for a second. I know that look. I've seen it on Olivia and Syd and Kennedy a billion times. It's the I-know-you-might-not-be-into-this-but-I-literally-cannot-stop-myself-from-talking-shit-right-now look.

"I don't want to be a bitch . . . ," Tal says. Ding ding ding. "But it's . . . not great that you're thinking your best friend in the world will hate you if you change your plans with him one time, one day."

I know that she's right, and I know that I should have known that already, but I've never even considered that. Of course Gray would hate me if I missed Meal Prep Day. Of course he *should* hate me.

"It's a whole thing," I say instead of explaining the entire storied history of Meal Prep Day, the way that it's how Gray knows I'll be there, how I'll stay. The way he cried when I showed up for the first one after we broke up and I thought it was because he was sad, but he was actually just so relieved that I was still right here.

Tal doesn't press it, because she never does, and I don't think too hard about it, because I always do. I sprint back to the gym and plop down in my seat beside Gray, wincing and kissing him on the cheek.

"Sorry-sorry-sorry. My head's fucked today, I completely forgot."

He ruffles my hair and I smack his hand away, but it's fine because he laughs and puts an arm around me. I lean into him without even thinking about it, let out a big breath because even though I'm a horrible friend, I still selfishly appreciate the contact.

Gray blows the whistle I keep telling him I'm going to confiscate, and the gym below us descends into its usual chaos.

"I texted Tal to see if she wanted to come hang out, but she had plans," Gray says.

Yeah, with me. I sink farther into Gray.

"How's it going with her?" I ask, because I hate myself. I can't tell if I'm trying to figure out more about Gray and Tal's relationship or trying to feel better, because I know what the answer is going to be, really, and there's a small mean part of me that wants to hear Gray say it.

"Good, I think!" he replies. I hadn't accounted for the fact that Gray always thinks things are going well, until he thinks the entire world is ending.

"Have you guys hung out or anything?" I press. I think I want him to say yes, even, because maybe if he actually hung out with Tal, he'd realize exactly why things aren't going as well as he thinks they are.

Gray puts a hand to his chest, fake affronted. "You *know* that's not part of the plan, Alana Lucas, PhD."

I have the plan memorized the same way Gray does. I know what's supposed to be next.

"But we had that weekend, right?" I press. "In Portland. Isn't the next step you guys hanging out?"

Gray picks at a hangnail. Right. He's afraid to jump from group outings to just him and Tal, alone, out in the world. To the two of them making a statement to people: We're here, we're together.

I know the feeling.

"Not yet," he says. On the gym floor below us, a gangly freshman tries to serve and ends up throwing his racket clear over the net. Gray and I pause for a second to make sure no one's been decapitated and then continue. "She's busy a lot. I think she's the only one of us who actually takes a student council job seriously, which is annoyingly cool of her. Honestly, I bet you see her more often than I do."

I cough. "We don't see each other that often, really."

That's almost true. I want to see Tal way more than I do.

Gray pulls his phone out, open to a food blog I showed him last year. "I found this recipe—she calls it 'Mexican Lasagna,' which honestly just feels offensive, but I feel like that's too weird to pass up. I thought we could make it this weekend."

He couldn't have given me a better segue if I'd asked, but that means I actually have to do this.

"Could we make it next weekend?" I ask. I don't look up at him, still tucked up under his arm.

"You never want to cook after Meal Prep Day. Last time I asked, you said you would never cook again if I asked you to cook right after Meal Prep Day."

Ugh. "No, I mean, like. Could we move MPD this month? To next week?"

"Oh!" Gray shrugs. "Yeah, sure. Why?"

My brain short-circuits. I hadn't expected Gray to be completely fine with rescheduling. In my brief panic, I figure it's easier to tell him something at least truth adjacent.

"Bremner wants Tal to do this whole big presentation thing for all the new kids," I say. "Like, what they need from the school or whatever. She's pretty stressed about it, so I told her we could do, like, a whole big planning weekend."

That implied Tal will be sleeping over at my house, and even though that isn't even true, the suggestion makes me hide my face even farther into Gray's side.

But his back goes stiff. He turns to look at me, quickly enough that I nearly flop over onto my side where I'd been leaning against him.

"You're canceling MPD for Tal?"

"Not canceling, just rescheduling."

Gray gives me a look. "All right."

My eyebrows furrow. "All right as in *all right*, or all right as in *fuck you*?"

Gray isn't annoyed at me often, but when he is, it always starts like this, with this passive-aggressive bullshit. He needs to sit in it for a while, make bitchy comments here and there until I finally just demand he yell at me. If he's going to be pissed, he should be pissed.

"It just kind of sucks that you're canceling something super important to us for Tal," he says.

I blink at him. "Sorry, what? Did you not just two seconds ago say it was totally fine to reschedule?"

"Yeah, when I thought you had, like, a family thing. Not when you just don't want to bother hanging out with me."

"It's not like I sat down and said *fuck Gray, I want to go walk around Walmart with Tal*," I say. "She's stressed and I'm helping her. I'm being a good friend."

"A good friend to Tal."

I know that my excuse was a lie in the first place, but Gray doesn't know that. He doesn't know I'm ditching him to research blowing up our entire life plan—he knows that I'm trying to hang out with Tal when she needs me. And he doesn't think I'm allowed to. Tal's voice is in my head, saying *It's . . . not great* again.

"Yeah, I am being a good friend to Tal," I say. I'm in one of those moods where I don't know what I'll say until it's already out of my mouth, too late to take back. "I'm being a good friend to Tal, and I thought that I would *ask your permission* to be a good friend to *you* one week later than usual. Like, I'm asking if it's *okay with you* for me to spend an *entire* Saturday cooking a *month's* worth of food for you and your mom, but on a different Saturday than we initially planned. You hear how wild that is, right?"

"If Meal Prep Day is so horrible, you don't have to do it anymore," Gray says. He turns his head to look away from me, to look out at all the badminton-playing freshmen who only know him as someone cool and fun and only know me as that gay girl.

"Jesus," I groan. "You *know* that's not what I'm saying. If you have a problem with me having a friend that isn't you, just come out and admit that."

"I don't have a problem with you having another friend."

"So what is it? You're mad that I'm not at your beck and call?"

"I can't argue with you when you're like this." Gray rolls his eyes.

"Cool," I say. "You don't have to, then."

When I get up and walk out of the gym, Gray doesn't even call after me.

The walk home isn't unbearable, but I'm lazy and try to avoid it as often as I can.

It turns out, when fueled by rage, I barely even notice the distance at all.

I all but kick the door down and stomp inside, shivering when the warmth of my house makes me realize it's freezing outside and I've just walked for half an hour. I throw my coat in the hall and make a note to pick it up before my parents get home.

"Y'know, your dad and I went to a lot of protests in our wild and rebellious youth to try and make it so you didn't need to be this angry."

Of course, walking for half an hour means my mom beat me home. Fuck.

"You should have told Gray that."

My mom's incredibly manicured eyebrows launch all the way up her forehead.

"I don't want to talk about it," I say before she can even open her mouth.

"I wouldn't dream of it," she says, like a liar.

"And I also don't want to talk about how I'm going to Rhode Island on Saturday with Tal."

My mom blinks at me. To be fair, that's a lot of information to take in at once.

"Is there anything . . . going on there?"

I freeze. Maybe if I ignore her, she'll go away.

"Between you and Tal, I mean."

"I know what you meant. I just don't want to talk about it."

She holds her hands up in surrender. "Fine, fine! But you *do* need to tell me why you're going to Rhode Island. That doesn't feel like something I can just let you do without more information."

I flop into an armchair and blow a loose strand of hair out of my face. "Tal wants to go to RISD and they're having an open house. I thought I'd go, too. See the world, y'know."

I lied before. My mom's eyebrows weren't all the way up. They've basically disappeared into her hairline now.

"Does Gray know about these grand plans?"

I scowl before I realize that's just going to result in my mom calling me dramatic and smooth my face over.

"No," I say. "And I don't think he *or* Lianne need to know just yet."

"Are you asking me to lie to my best friend and only son?"

"Absolutely I am, since I'm your *actual* child."

My mom looks at me, assessing. There's a line between her eyebrows, same as the one Tal touched on my face the first time we kissed. Her hair is what mine's going to look like a couple of decades from now, streaks of gray running through light brown, cut above her shoulders because she doesn't like bothering with styling it. I used to look at her and see my future and tell myself that it worked, that it's what I wanted. I could just about see it, until I couldn't.

"It's just an open house," I say. "Gray doesn't need to know everything about my life."

"But he'd probably like to know if you were planning on changing your plan in such a big way."

I know she's right, but that's what pisses me off. She doesn't need to tell me that the things I'm doing right now might make Gray upset. She doesn't need to tell me that I'm a shitty person. She doesn't need to say that she'd be disappointed in me if I went back on everything Gray and I had ever tried to build.

"I mean, isn't RISD an art school?" she says now, mostly to herself, staring off into the distance like she's trying and failing to imagine me anywhere but the place she'd always put me. "What would you major in there?"

"Klingon," I say flatly, and take myself upstairs for the night.

TWENTY-TWO

Oh god, Tal in the morning.

When Tal comes to pick me up for our Rhode Trip (she was the one who named it that, I swear to god), the first thing I notice is that she's dressed differently. It's closer to how she dressed at the concert. She's dressed like herself, jacket covered in a million pins that say things I don't understand at all and hair pinned up and wild. She's dressed like *mine*. She's waiting in the car for me in the fog, not even 5:00 a.m., smiling through a yawn when I get into the car she's warmed for me, when I sip the coffee she's brought for me. My parents are dead to the world upstairs and the street is eerily quiet, so I can't resist lurching between the seats to kiss her, and when she kisses me back, my stomach flips and flips and flips. Tal's eyes light up when I open my backpack and show her the croissants and chocolate chip cookies I made for the trip. Four and a half long, complete hours with Tal, just us, not even the radio on to interrupt.

I've never been to Rhode Island. Never really thought about Rhode Island. If I'd gone here without Tal, I'm sure I would have thought it was fine, but traveling like this, there's something magic about it. It's still the morning when we arrive, half an hour until the 10:00 a.m. introduction Tal wants to go to, so we find a place to park and wander by the river. It looks like a college in a movie, a place where you wear skirts with long socks and carry your books close to your chest. If I let myself think too hard about it, it looks like a place where I could meet Tal with coffee and a snack, something I've made for her, and let her kiss me in the real world where someone could see.

"It's fucking cool here," Tal says when we find a bench to sit on. She's steadily working her way through everything I brought. During the drive she couldn't stop to eat, so I fed her bites of croissant when she asked. Her lips touched the tips of my fingers and I burst into flames. I'm staring at her mouth now, and she must know it because she keeps giving me these little sideways looks.

"It actually is," I agree.

"Don't sound too shocked," Tal laughs. "I know it's no UMaine, but . . ."

"I never actually said I wanted to go to UMaine," I say. It comes out too quickly because I was never supposed to say it at all. "Gray said that it would be perfect and I just didn't disagree."

I've never been an incredible student. Gray has, because Gray puts his whole entire life, his energy, his soul into everything he's ever done. It's not that I don't try—that's the thing, I try almost as hard as Gray does for shittier grades. I can do that anywhere.

People are looking at us, or at least they're looking at Tal. I can feel people glancing our way as we pack up and head into the pretty stone building Tal had pointed out earlier as being the main hall for the open house. We file in with a bunch of people who look like Tal but not like me, and Tal writes my name on a sticker for me and pops it onto my forehead with her thumb. She smooths it over the way she did that night at Sydney's. I pretend like it annoyed me, taking it off and putting it on my chest instead. Tal gets this glint in her eye, and I *know* she's about to say *I can help with that one, too*, but she doesn't get the chance, because a voice speaks up from somewhere beside us.

"You guys are so lucky," the voice says. Someone with close-cropped neon-pink hair and a septum ring is standing beside Tal and me. Her sticker says *Dallas, she/they*, and I'm suddenly embarrassed that I didn't write my pronouns on a sticker.

"I've been trying to convince my girlfriend to come here with me for *ages*," Dallas says. They smile at both of us like they haven't just made my heart simultaneously leap into my throat and fall out of my ass. "But she's totally set on being in New York. Where are you guys from?"

"Maine," Tal says, cheerfully ignoring the part where Dallas thinks we're girlfriends and letting me sputter with my mouth opening and closing like a goldfish.

Dallas hangs around for a little bit longer, chatting with Tal about how Rhode Island is *basically* New York, so she shouldn't be worried about her girlfriend being too far away, and by the time they wander off to find their parents, my hands are clammy and it feels like my knees are about ten seconds away from giving out entirely.

It's not that Dallas thought we were girlfriends, I don't think. It's the fact that no one's ever walked right up to me and assumed I was gay before. I've never been so easily, effortlessly, thoughtlessly seen. I feel like if I look down at myself I'll be transparent, nothing but blood and organs and all the mushy jumbled stuff that makes a person on the inside. I realize I'm wearing Gray's good denim jacket again, and that's, like, *absurd*, right? It's fucked up, isn't it? The fact that I'm Gray's Girl, hidden away under his clothes, tucked under his arm, and everyone sees who I am, except they don't. Or I'm Tal's, and people know who I am except I think they only know it because she's beside me. Like she makes me visible, pulls me into the real world whether I like it or not.

Tal leads me by the elbow out of the room, through a long hallway filled with anxious high school kids and their much more anxious parents. I don't ask where we're going because she has that look on her face, like she's going to be nice to me whether I like it or not.

"Do you want to leave?" she asks once we're finally relatively alone, standing outside the main building but off to the side so no one thinks we're lost.

"This is important to you," I say.

"That didn't answer my question."

The thing is, though, I thought it did. I *don't* want to leave, not when Tal told me about RISD and what it means to her. Not when she thinks I'm special enough to bring into this world. I don't want to leave, but I also can't ignore the rough scrape of anxiety in my brain at the thought of going back inside.

"Is it about what Dallas said?"

Tal looks so nervous when she asks that I want to wrap her up, tell her exactly how I feel and make sure she knows how much I mean it.

Which is how I know it's definitely not about what Dallas said. Not in the way Tal's asking, anyway.

"No. It's just a lot to be here, y'know? Everyone knows exactly what they want to do and I . . . really, *really* don't."

"So that, plus the fact that you had to reschedule Meal Prep Day with Gray."

Tal says it so easily, like of *course* she knows what day it is today. Of *course* she understands what it means that I'm not in Gray's kitchen right now. I'm about to either kiss her or start crying, and I don't think I'm quite ready to do either of those things in broad daylight in Rhode Island.

But there are some things I can do. I can reach over and touch the inside of Tal's elbow. I can let my hand drift down until our fingers are woven neatly together. I can walk inside with her and swallow down the mild panic I feel whenever anyone glances at us, even though I know, it's obvious, that they don't care at all.

I don't learn a single thing about RISD, because I spend every presentation, every Q&A, every dorm tour, and every bite of uninspired dining hall lunch thinking about Tal. Thinking about Tal and her cold hands and the fact that everyone who sees us today has looked at us for half a second and moved on, has seen that we were together, that we were something, and not even cared. They won't remember us. We aren't memorable. The thought makes me feel alive.

On the drive home, Tal pulls off the highway.

"Are you murdering me?" I ask.

"Yup."

"Ugh, finally. Put me out of my misery."

"If you must know, we're looking for a dinner spot," Tal says, then quickly tacks on, "My treat."

I've said that to Savannah. I've said that to Syd and Kennedy (I've rarely said it to Olivia, because she's loaded and usually pays and also I wouldn't pay money to spend time with her). But it's different like this. The way Tal looks at me and the careful way she's assessing all the shitty takeout places we drive past gives it meaning.

We end up at a decidedly average fast-food place, greasy fries blotting the bag and filling the car with their smell instantly. Tal messes around on her phone for a couple of minutes and then the little British lady in her phone tells us to pull out of the parking lot and turn right.

"Don't eat yet," Tal says.

"This is cruelty," I say, but I don't eat yet.

Tal drives for a few minutes and pulls onto a dirt road, fat pine trees on either side and ahead and everywhere I look, and for a very brief second, I wonder if she *is* going to kill me, until the trees part suddenly and a wide lake is all I can see.

"Dinner and a view!" Tal says, obviously thrilled with herself.

I like her so much I think I might *die*.

We sit and eat in comfortable silence for a minute, Tal kicking her feet up on the dash and turning the radio down. Eventually, though, she turns to me with a grimace.

"Is Gray actually pissed off?"

I almost choke on my mouthful of fries at the reminder of Gray, at the way it crashes me back down to earth.

"Nah," I say after a second. "Not, like, unforgivably never-speak-to-me-again pissed off. Annoyed, probably. Maybe confused."

"No irreparable damage?"

"I think you'd have to try a lot harder to do that. Plus, real-istically, he sucks at cooking. He needs me."

"So I haven't ruined your life too much."

She's joking, but she isn't. I do the same thing.

"You have absolutely definitely not ruined my life."

Tal's mouth wrinkles when she tries to hold in her smile. I'm feeling bold enough to reach out and squish her lips with my thumb.

I was planning on telling her she shouldn't hide her smile, but once I actually make contact, I can't really say anything. I let my hand fall back down onto my knee, and I'm just about to jump into the lake and never again emerge when Tal's thumb presses against my mouth in return.

♡

TWENTY-THREE

We have an in-service day on Monday, so I decide to apologize to Gray in person on Tuesday morning. My reasons are twofold:

A) When we're shitty to each other, it cuts deeper than if anyone else is shitty to us. Even when I'm the one pissed off at him, I still feel him missing from me like a phantom limb. When we apologize to each other, it feels like it should mean more than when anyone else apologizes to us.

B) I was still a little pissed off at him on Monday, so I decided I'd let him squirm.

Unfortunately, Tuesday is also our school's Halloween costume contest.

Gray and I have always dressed up, even when we became too grown-up and too cool to dress up. I'm pretty sure Gray is the sole reason anyone in this school ever wears a costume—they all want to have as much fun as he always seems to have. Planning usually begins sometime in early

September, and I just go with whatever he decides. Which is why when I get to my locker this morning, Gray's waiting for me dressed as a giant taco.

"Thank you for still dressing up," he says. "Without you, this is just embarrassing."

I had put my foot down this year, because last year Gray wanted us to dress as marshmallow Peeps and neither of us could fit in our desks for the whole day. I told him that he could do whatever he wanted, but my part had to be subtle and cost me less than $10.

"Bonjour," I say flatly. I'm wearing a blue dress with a white apron. The Belle to Gray's Taco. No one's gonna have any idea what I'm supposed to be unless I'm standing beside him.

"Morning," he says, rocking back on his feet like he's expecting me to yell at him some more. "Also, sorry."

The fact that he thinks he messed up enough to actually apologize tells me everything I need to know. I shove my hands under his arms and squirm into place until I'm nestled under Gray's chin.

"Sorry," I mumble into his polyester taco shell.

Gray lets me barnacle on to him for a solid minute before he gives up and opens my locker for me. My combination has always been easy for him to remember. His birthday. His combo is mine. We set them up the night before we started middle school.

"I was going to let you discover this on your own," he says as he opens the door, "but the longer you wait, the more likely this ends up just being gross."

There's a greasy takeout bag from Mimi's sitting proudly inside (well, actually, it's flopped over to one side because a Mimi's bag really only has a shelf life of like five minutes), and I melt against Gray. I lean my head back onto his shoulder and kiss him on the cheek.

"You're amazing," I say. "I should be a dick to you more often."

"You should, if I'm going to keep being a dick to you first," he says. "Seriously, sorry. It's not fair of me to expect for you to stay right where you were. I love that you and Tal are friends."

"I swear I wouldn't move MPD unless I had a good reason," I say. "I'm sorry, too."

Gray shrugs. I grab the Mimi's bag, close my locker, and turn around to face him.

"You're driving me to the grocery store after badminton," I tell him. "I have so much work to do tonight."

"I actually tried to do MPD without you," Gray admits.

"Oh my god, the *first* rule of MPD is don't participate in MPD without my supervision. Now I have so much *more* work to do. Fixing all your MPD rejects."

"You *could* have come over yesterday to fix all of it," Gray says. "But you just *had* to let me sweat it out."

Damnit. I forgot that Gray would have known that's exactly what I was doing.

"I'll have you know that I actually was very busy yesterday," I lie. I spent three quarters of yesterday in bed.

"If I asked you what the Food Network's lineup was yesterday, would you be able to tell me?"

"Yes, but that's true of any day."

Gray rolls his eyes at me and everything clicks back into place with us.

"I even had *gossip* for you." Gray sighs. "Now I guess we'll never know."

My eyes go huge. Gray hardly ever gossips, so if he knows something that I don't, then it must be big. "If you don't tell me immediately, I'm shoving this paper bag in your mouth."

"Well, that would be stupid, because then I wouldn't be able to tell you."

"Ethan Alexander Gray!"

Gray takes a step back, pretending he's shocked and horrified at the fact that I used his full name.

"That got real," he says. "Okay, *so* what you would have learned yesterday if you weren't making a statement is that Olivia slid into my DMs on Sunday night."

"*No.*"

"*Yes*, Alana Lucas, Professional Reptile Handler."

"What did she *say*?"

I grab Gray's phone out of his hand before he can answer. It unlocks automatically when it sees my face and I navigate to Instagram immediately.

There's Liv, right at the top of Gray's DMs.

So seriously, when's your Alana grieving period over?

"She wants to diddle you!" I exclaim, and Gray seems torn between telling me to shut up and laughing at me.

"I just left her on read," he says. "I have no idea what to say to that."

"Please *god* let me respond for you."

"Absolutely not." Gray snatches his phone back. "I don't know what I'm gonna say yet."

"Wait, you don't know what you're gonna say? As in you don't know whether you're into it or not? Don't be weird."

Gray and I stare at each other for a second longer, so I feel the need to add, "This is weird. Stop it. I forbid it."

Gray laughs. "Noted. It's not like I was about to run off with her or anything. Besides, what a waste of time the Tal plan would have been if I just up and dated Liv, right?"

My answering laugh is definitely approaching hysterical.

Gray and I make it through the day. We make it through lunch and badminton and the grocery store and a small, less-productive version of MPD, and everything is normal. But everything is normal between Gray and me only because I avoid Tal like the plague. I avert eye contact, I answer her questions with one word. By the end of the day, Gray's giving me weird looks whenever Tal comes near us.

I feel bad enough about it that I FaceTime Tal when I get home. If I take an extra ten minutes to freshen up my face before I do it, she doesn't need to know it. I flop onto my bed and find Tal's name on my phone.

"Hey," she says when she picks up. She doesn't look like she's mad at me for being weird, but I still feel guilty.

"I'm sorry I was such an asshole today," I say.

Tal's shoulders relax and she laughs. She falls back onto her bed and holds her phone up so it's like she's looking up at me. My throat goes dry.

"Thanks for apologizing," she says. "I kind of thought I'd freaked you out."

"You definitely haven't freaked me out." '

I say it way too quickly, but it just makes Tal smile.

"Gray and I only just made up," I explain. "I wanted to do a Meal Prep Day with him to make up for missing it, and then I just got thinking about how he feels about you, and I just felt . . . guilty."

Tal furrows her eyebrows. "How does he feel about me?"

My jaw actually drops.

"I'm sorry, you didn't *know*? Gray's massive crush on you wasn't obvious from the very beginning?"

Tal laughs like she can't help herself. "Holy shit, really? Man, is he ever barking up the wrong tree."

"How could you *not tell*?"

"I thought he was just being nice!"

"What about the fact that I tried to shove you two together every day for like a month?"

"I thought you wanted me to like him!"

Both of us laugh, and I dive under my duvet without thinking about it. My small face in the corner of my phone's screen is just barely visible, the light gone soft and yellow.

"Hello," Tal says. Like this, with my phone close to my face, it's like she's right here.

I roll onto my side and Tal does the same. Under the duvet I can almost pretend like we're sharing my pillow.

"Are you going to let him down gently?" I ask. I'm going for joking, but I think it comes out a bit too intense.

Tal doesn't like Gray. Tal absolutely, definitely, 100 percent doesn't like Gray. And Tal's done a *whole bunch* the last few weeks to make it seem as though Tal absolutely, definitely, 100 percent *does* like me. I can barely focus on what she says next, my head too busy spinning.

Tal bites her lip. "I mean, he hasn't actually asked me out or anything, right? I feel like I don't actually have to say anything."

"Yeah," I say. But I can't let it go. "I know this isn't really my business, but why don't you just . . . tell Gray you aren't into, y'know . . . anyone like him?"

I don't actually know that for a fact, but Tal's face explodes into a laugh.

"I mean, fair," she says. "But it's also like, why do I have to, y'know?"

I don't know.

"Sure," I say. "I get that." I wait a beat, then, "I just mean, like, I know *he'd* get it. I would know, right? He wouldn't make it weird at all."

Tal chews on her bottom lip for a second.

"Well," she says. She lets it sit in the air between our phones.

"Well, what?"

"Well, why would I need to? What happens when Gray's out of the picture like that? What happens then? When Gray knows exactly who I like?"

I don't say anything. How can you say anything to that?

Tal takes me in. I see her eyes flashing around her phone screen, assessing me. Looking for something.

"Can I say something?" she asks.

"You can say lots of things."

Tal sticks her tongue out at me, but then gets serious again. "I like you. Like, I want to be super clear. I really, really like you. And I think part of why you got weird just then was because you like me. And I don't want you to think that I'm trying to push you into anything, but I needed to tell you that, after . . . everything."

I freeze. I know that I'm staring at Tal, and I know that she must be freaking out about it, but I can't say anything for a long minute.

Tal makes things real. Tal takes the things that lived in the back of my head and the deleted search history of my laptop and makes them come into bright sharp color. And I knew that everything I thought and felt would be real one day, but I didn't think it would be this soon. Not when I'm still telling people, still telling myself, that it doesn't matter if I'm gay, that it isn't a big deal, please *god* treat me the same way you've always treated me. Even if the way you've always treated me is shitty, just prove that you think I'm the same. But I can't deny I'm freaking out, a little, and doesn't that mean that I'm making it a big deal?

"God, have I just completely freaked you out?" Tal asks, and snaps me back to the present. "I'm so sorry, I just wanted to make sure that, like, whatever we were doing, we get to keep doing it. Ha, so of course I went and—"

"You're right," I interrupt Tal before she can spin out much more. "I feel the exact same way."

Of course I feel the exact same way. I've felt the exact same way since the first time Tal smiled at me, and I became the kind of person who thinks shit like *since the first time Tal smiled at me*. At this point, after everything, there's no use denying that everything Tal's feeling I'm probably feeling times a million. The problem is, the more I feel for Tal, the easier it is to let the feeling trample all over Gray.

The relief is clear on Tal's face. She closes her eyes and laughs. "Thank god."

"But I don't . . . I don't know how to be like this," I say. "I don't know how to, like, be a couple. Kind of with anyone? Everything I had with Gray has this weird fake tint to it now, and it's like I've never been in a relationship at all."

That's true, but I know I'm bullshitting Tal. It's not that I don't know how to be a couple, it's that I don't know how to be a practicing, card-carrying, hand-holding lesbian. I don't know how to become real and clear in front of everyone.

"No, that's fine," Tal says. "We can be slow. Maybe we could go to the café soon. Like, with other people there, this time."

If I didn't feel kind of sick at the thought, I would have made a joke. Would have said *I'm not sure I'm quite ready to involve other people in what we did at the café last time*. We both would have laughed.

But instead I say, "Maybe."

Tal must be able to tell that I'm less than enthused about the idea; sure, Portland is better than here, and the chances of us running into someone we know are a lot smaller, but that doesn't mean it's not still a statement. Exactly the kind of statement I'm pretty sure I just said I wasn't ready for.

"And at *some point*, it would be cool if you wanted to come over," Tal continues. "And we could do this in an official way or a completely *not* official way, but that way you could meet my parents."

"What?" I ask, or maybe snap, too quickly. Tal actually startles at it, but I don't know why, since I literally just told her exactly why that would freak me out. I've seen Tal's house, of course, we've all been in each other's spaces over the last couple of months. I've seen the cute bungalow with its bricks painted dark gray and its yellow door. Going inside wouldn't be an issue, unless there was an issue. Unless Tal's parents were there. Unless they were looking at me and assessing and wondering whether I was worthy of Tal and I'd have to sit there and know that I'm probably not.

"It doesn't have to be, like, a whole production or whatever," Tal says hurriedly, realizing her mistake. "I really, really don't want to push you into anything you don't want to do. I just mean, like. At some point. In the distant future. Or, y'know, whenever."

Some point in the distant future and *whenever* are two very different things, but I don't say that. Instead, I say, "Okay," and I let Tal think that it is. Instead, I focus on Tal's voice and Tal's face close to mine and the way Tal looks at me through her eyelashes, even just on the phone, and I wait for my heart rate to settle.

♡

TWENTY-FOUR

On Saturday morning, a day when Gray's working and my parents are still asleep and it's freezing cold outside but just warm enough in my bed, it's hard to feel guilty about how I feel about Tal. Alone, like this, when I've had just enough time and space to actually think about it, when Tal hasn't brought up meeting her parents or going on a real, actual public date, I can sit in my room and focus on the good parts.

Tal likes me. Tal likes me and she told me and I know, finally, that she likes *me*. Not Gray. Not anyone else. Me.

The only problem with my happy day is I can't tell anyone about it. The only person I want to tell is Gray, and if I think about that for longer than a millisecond I'll start to feel bad again, so I'm not going to do that. I stuff the thought down deep, shaking my head to try and get it to leave me alone.

It's a happy day, goddammit, so I decide to make happy snacks.

My parents sleep in on Saturdays, and normally I do, too, but if I'm already awake, then I can take over the kitchen before my dad gets in there and tries to make pancakes for my mom and ruins them until I finally give up and take over (I swear he does it on purpose). It means I can stretch out and take my time and make something really, really good, and after I can wrap it all up and bring it to Tal and make her love me.

I look around the house as if someone's going to jump out and say *make her LOVE you?* at just the thought, but that's ridiculous, so it doesn't happen and I can ignore it and move on.

Anything worth giving to Tal should be a challenge, I think, so I pull up a macaron recipe I've never been able to nail and rummage around to see what we have until I decide on a dozen chocolate and a dozen orange. Sweet and sharp.

When I have time like this, I separate ingredients into little bowls and make everything look pretty. I put earbuds in and forget where I am. I look over my shoulder to make sure my parents aren't coming downstairs yet and do a lot of hip-centric dancing. I feel, finally, for the first time in weeks, entirely like myself.

My phone buzzes and I smile when I see Tal's name. It almost feels like we could be this. Like I could wake up early and make macarons for her, and when she texts me I'd just feel happy.

> *Hey. Sorry for the long message. Basically, last night someone vandalized the café in Portland. Apparently it's a mess. They broke a lot of shit. It's so fucked up, I honestly can't even believe I'm saying this. I'm on the way there right now—I just stopped for gas and thought you might want to come help clean it up? I don't know if you have plans. Don't cancel anything for me or*

anything, but if you don't have plans you could get the
bus, right? I think we're gonna need a lot of hands on
this.

I slump. I know this is going to make me sound like a bitch, but I don't know if I *do* want to pay for a $50 last-minute bus ticket to spend the day cleaning up garbage in a place where everyone loves Tal but no one really knows who I am. Tal would introduce me to everyone, I know, and a couple of weeks ago I would have loved that. Tal welcoming me further into her world. But after our conversation the other day, I'm not so sure. I don't know if I can handle a day of hanging off Tal's arm and waiting for her to speak to me before I become a full-fledged person.

(And yes, okay, there's also the fact that everyone Tal knows is going to assume that we're dating, and that's a mess for a whole bunch of other reasons. I'll go from quietly out to screaming, flashing, sparkling out in thirty seconds, for a start. Plus, Tal's friends know her. They know her history better than I do. That night in the café, after everything, she had said *there was just one other . . . for me, too*, and I don't actually know what that means in this context. One other person? One other time? And while I know that Tal would never actively compare me to that other person, there's nothing to say that her friends won't.)

I was only just reaching a point, today, where it felt like I could reach for myself and just about grasp it. Like I knew what I was doing. I've only just realized I don't need my old friends. Maybe I don't need Tal's new friends, either. Maybe

I'm making my own life, and maybe I get to choose what I put into it.

I wince as I type, as if that absolves me. *Hey, I'm so sorry but I have a family thing today. Let me know when you get home, okay?*

Tal sends back a thumbs-up. She's probably back on the road already now, my agonizing taking much longer than intended.

I put the first batch of macarons in the oven and try very hard not to check on them or breathe near them or think about them because I always fuck up my macaron feet when I'm not careful. I'm just trying to decide whether I should have orange filling with the orange ones and chocolate with the chocolate, or if I should mix and match, when my parents stumble downstairs. They both have the telltale signs of two people pushing forty who snuck booze into the movie they went to see last night (they think I don't know that that's their favorite date night. Like, I'm a teenage girl in America. I know what people look like when they're trying to sneak alcohol into a public place).

"My god, it's one of *those* days," my dad says, blinking wearily at the state of the kitchen.

"Y'know, some teens experiment with drugs and alcohol at this age," I say.

"And our angel has never had a drink in all her life," my mom says, trudging to the breakfast bar and holding her head up in her hand. "Certainly not from the secret bottles she thinks she hides underneath her bed even though her mother is the one who vacuums the carpet in her bedroom."

"I'm just saying, you don't have to sound so devastated. I'm cooking macarons, not meth."

"I suppose we can't complain when we get to enjoy the fruits of your labor." My dad takes a seat at our island and props his head up on his hand.

"You can snack on the rejects," I concede. "These aren't for you."

"I'm sure Gray can spare one or two," my mom says.

I look away. "They aren't for Gray. I'm bringing them over to Tal's later."

My parents exchange a look that I ignore, and, thankfully, I think they're both too hungover to try and force a conversation out of me.

It's another four hours before Tal texts to say she's home and I carefully pack away my (semi-perfect, not as glossy as I would have liked but the best feet I've ever produced) macarons in a little box for her. I consider adding a ribbon and then remember that I have no access to ribbon, and also that is unhinged, so I bundle up against the absolutely-about-to-snow gloomy day.

Tal doesn't live in my subdivision, but she's close enough to school that the walk's only about twenty minutes. Where I don't always find it worth it when I'm going to school, it feels very worth it when I'm walking toward Tal.

She answers the door looking exhausted, but she smiles at me all the same. Her hair is flat and she isn't wearing makeup and her eyes are red and tired, and as soon as she opens the door, she takes a step into me and just stands there until I wrap my arms around her shoulders. I squeeze her tightly, like if I can wrap her up close enough, no one can bother her anymore. I walk us backward and she shuts the door without letting go of me, and we both laugh but neither of us want to let go. Eventually, we break apart. I haven't made anything better, but Tal's still there in front of me, the way she was there for me last week.

"I brought you a present," I say, already grinning. The corner of Tal's mouth twitches up.

I open the box and unveil my basically perfect macarons. "They took me, like, all day to make, but I think it was worth it."

Tal's hand freezes where it was reaching toward the box. "They took you all day?"

"Yeah, I was up at, like, the crack of dawn, so I figured I'd make the most of it."

"I thought you said you had a family thing."

"I mean, I was with my parents for most of the day," I say awkwardly. I laugh at myself. "Sorry, I'm an asshole. I was just so exhausted when I woke up this morning. There's a lot going on in my head right now, y'know? I didn't think I could handle being so, like, *in it* today. I really needed a second to myself."

"You needed a second to yourself."

"Yeah," I say. Halfway through saying it, I realize that Tal has stepped very far away from me.

"So I asked you to be there for me today and you blew me off?"

This isn't going the way I'd planned. "I didn't realize you needed me there. You said it was fine if I already had plans."

"Yeah, if you already had plans. Not if you just didn't feel like going."

"So why was it fine for me to be hanging out with my family? What's the difference if I was at home making macarons? Making macarons for *you*?"

"Oh, thanks so much. That makes today all better!" I've never heard Tal use this voice, this horrible, hard, sarcastic voice. "You clearly knew that there was something wrong with blowing me off to *bake*, because you told me you had a family thing. If you really thought there was no problem, you would have said *nope, sorry, I'm making fucking* macarons."

"Okay, we both need to stop saying macarons."

"This isn't funny, Alana! I'm not laughing!" She's right. In fact, I notice with horror, her red eyes are going wet around the edges. "I texted you because I needed you. Today I needed you instead of you needing me, and you just didn't show up. Because you just weren't really feeling it."

"I mean, is the café okay?" I ask. "You guys cleaned it up, right?"

Tal looks at me like she doesn't even know me and suddenly I can't swallow.

"Do you know why we moved here?" she asks, then laughs hollowly. "No, you don't. You never asked."

"Well, why did you move here?"

I'd always figured one of her parents got a job or something.

Same as everyone else who just moved here. Why would I have questioned Tal being dropped into my lap the way she was?

"I had to leave my old school. My parents pulled me out and researched school boards with better policies for protecting queer students, because my life used to be a fucking nightmare."

I don't say anything. How could I say anything when I never shut up about how no one is homophobic anymore and how I've never had any issues?

"I had this reputation for having a big embarrassing crush on this girl. She was like your friends, y'know? Smart and sharp and interesting and mean. Also *massively fucking queer*, but I was the only one who knew that part. Like, tale as old as lesbian time, right? I was right *in* there the same way you were, tied up in those super intense friendships where it feels like if you say one wrong thing the whole world will end, and if they ever stopped talking to you, you would actually die. And every time everyone else turned around, she was right there to kiss and touch and tell me how much better I was than our other friends, and I thought that's what love was. I thought I was so special."

Her breath starts to shudder and she stops herself sharply, swallows something down.

"But I was too into it. I was okay with being that in real life and she wasn't. So she laughed with everyone else when our friends started joking about how I was obsessed with her. And she ignored it when our guy friends would ask us to make out at parties. And when someone finally caught us kissing in her room, she told them that I had come on to her.

"And things were fine, except suddenly no one would look at me. Things were fine, except none of my friends would change in front of me or invite me over or tell me secrets anymore. And those douchey guy friends thought it would be funny one night, when they were all drunk, to take my face and stick it on a bunch of lesbian porn. And it was just on the internet, right? And it didn't happen during school hours, so no one did anything. I was totally, completely, utterly alone."

She doesn't stop it now, when the tears in her eyes spill over. The second I see her start to cry for real, my eyes start to sting, too.

"The only place in the world where I stopped feeling like I actually, literally wanted to die was Callie's. It was the only place in the world where no one looked at me differently. It was where I learned how to be myself. It was where I learned how to *like* myself. And someone tried to take that away from me. And you didn't care."

"I didn't know," I say, but it sounds pathetic even to me.

"But you knew I loved it there," she says. "You knew it was special and you knew, even though you *love* to pretend like you're above all of this and queer shit has nothing to do with you, you knew that you were safe there, too. I mean, Jesus, you must have felt safe enough the night of the concert. Even if you didn't know how special that place is to me, I don't think it's unreasonable to assume it might *possibly* be special to you too now."

"I'm sorry," I whisper, the feeling of dread that can only

come from knowing I've actually, genuinely fucked up starting to blanket me.

"If you were too busy to deal with all that today, then
you're probably too busy to deal with me right now, too," Tal
says. "You should probably go."

She opens the door and ushers me outside just as it starts
to snow.

♡

TWENTY-FIVE

Something I admired about Tal was the way she was always so good at telling me how she was feeling. There wasn't any beating around the bush like there always seemed to be with my old friends. If she was hungry, she asked for food. If she was tired, she'd go home. If she liked me, she'd tell me (basically) to my face.

But that means that when she decides she's done with me, she makes it extremely obvious.

At first, I think this is something that we can get over. I think that if I'm nice enough to her, if I apologize and then text her like nothing's different, she'll eventually start acting the same way. Eventually, we'll get back to normal. We'll get back to us.

Instead, I text her fifteen times over the rest of the weekend and she ignores me fifteen times. I spend all of Sunday in my room with the window open even though it's well below freezing because then I have an excuse to stay under my covers all day. I eat toast and mashed potatoes and anything else I can make without any flavor because I don't feel like I deserve to taste things, and I know that's fucked up but it's what I do.

I look like such a mess that my dad drives me to school on

Monday. I'm pretty sure my parents think someone's dead. I don't talk on the entire drive, and when my dad says he loves me before I get out of the car, I almost start crying.

We have a student council meeting at lunch. I almost don't go, but then I figure if this is my only chance to see Tal today, then I might as well take it. Not putting myself in situations where I'm around Tal is how I got myself into this in the first place.

We're the first two in the classroom, Tal sitting at a desk and turning away as soon as she hears me come in. I can see her jaw tighten, gearing up for a fight the way she used to do around my old friends when she thought they were being mean to me.

I sidle up to her and ask, "Can we talk after the meeting?"

I didn't think she would look at me, but instead, she snaps her face right over to me. "What do you want to talk about?" she asks, fake-bright and bared-teeth smile. "Do you want to talk about what we did on our weekends?"

"I want to apologize again—"

"Because I was *super* busy this weekend," Tal continues like she didn't hear me. "Cleaning spray paint off walls. Helping Callie order new windows. Y'know, since someone threw a brick through them. I sort of doubt whoever did it saw the irony there."

I also don't see the irony there, but I don't think Tal needs the reminder that I don't know anything about being gay.

"We filed a police report as well," she says, then rolls her eyes. "Not that that's going to do anything. But Callie's landlord was freaked out because they'd been getting all these threatening letters. Someone's been leaving them in books and under tables for months. Figured we'd start a paper trail in case they decide to *really* go hate-criming."

"What?" I demand, my heart picking up speed without my permission. "Do you think that might actually happen? Why do you keep going back there if someone's going to, like . . . hate crime you?"

Tal gapes at me.

"Because it's important to me? Because it's somewhere I feel good about myself and maybe it's more important to fight for that than to run away when something gets difficult?"

We stare at each other for a long moment. Tal glaring, me opening and closing my mouth, trying to think of something to say that's going to make this better.

"Why didn't you tell me?" I finally say.

"Would you have cared?"

Of course I would have cared, but Tal won't believe me now. There's not much point in arguing that I would. I turn around and sit in the first seat I find, away from Tal. Sydney eventually comes in and sits beside me, deep into something on her phone.

Gray comes in, says something I don't hear that makes everyone laugh, goes through whatever opening statement he has to go through. My role's never been a big thing in these meetings. I don't know if I made it that way or everyone else did.

"Gonna turn things over to our fearless and capable new student rep," Gray says. It's Gray-dramatic enough to let me know he's still a little uneasy around Tal, still trying to impress.

"Thanks, guys," Tal says, and the whole room snaps to attention. I know, now, that she doesn't think that she does this. She doesn't know she carries this weight, that everyone in every room wants to hear what she has to say. She doesn't see the way everyone watches her. "I know it might feel kind of weird to have a student rep just for new kids, but it's also weird to come into a school where everyone's already so close. I think it's probably safe to say some of the new kids here still might not feel entirely at home. I know I don't."

She doesn't look at me when she says that, but she might as well have.

"I was speaking to a couple of people the other day who were asking about resources for queer students," she says. "A few of them had interesting thoughts. I know we have a GSA, but people aren't always comfortable joining in with things like that. Do you think there's space to expand those resources?"

Logan rolls his eyes, which means Syd won't say anything, but Gray leaps up and tries to answer Tal like a grown-up, talking out of his ass. Last week it probably would have annoyed me, but it's sweet, actually, how hard he's trying. Tal probably would have said that he should have been trying harder and for longer, but I don't know. If *I* had no idea about half of this stuff, why should Gray?

But the longer the two of them talk, and the more I watch Tal being almost normal, the farther I sink into my seat. Maybe if Tal had all these resources she keeps talking about, she wouldn't have had to leave her old school. Maybe it wouldn't have mattered that some asshole vandalized the café. Maybe we never would have met and we both would have been happy anyway.

The thing that fucking sucks about being part of A Community, apparently, is that when something bad happens to one of you, it feels like something bad happened to all of you. And before today I never felt like I was an *all of you*, but the boulder in my stomach today suggests otherwise.

I don't say a single word for the rest of the meeting. I only even realize that everyone's leaving when Sydney's chair scrapes beside me and makes me jump. She gives me a look like she's thinking about asking me whether I'm okay, but then she seems to remember that we aren't actually friends anymore. She leaves with Logan, talking loudly about whatever definitely-not-as-funny-as-she's-telling-it thing Anton said to her this morning. Which, I realize, means that as far as Sydney's concerned, I now rank alongside *Logan* in terms of conversation partners. Way to kick me when I'm down.

"Alana, could you hang back for a sec?"

It's not Tal, the way I'll imagine it was tonight when I'm trying to fall asleep. It's Mrs. DG, technically our faculty advisor, who was just as silent as me the entire meeting. She has a pamphlet in her hand and I recognize it immediately. Gray squeezes my arm, excitement radiating off him in waves. He kisses my temple on his way out and I barely register it.

Logan was right: Mrs. DG is my ticket to Gray's camp.

"We're supposed to have our nominations in by today," she says to me. "So, as a proud member of the leaving-things-until-the-last-possible-second club, allow me to bestow upon you this nomination."

I take the information package from her and feel absolutely nothing.

"Thank you," I say. I'm depressed, but I'm not *rude*.

"Normally, this would be the part where I'd tell you all about the benefits of the camp and encourage you to go. But I know with one hundred percent certainty that Ethan's done a better job of all that than I ever could."

"That's . . . probably true."

Mrs. DG smiles absently at me and then goes back to whatever it is she's doing. I snap Gray a picture of the package and he immediately quadruple-texts me, messages heavy on the capital letters and exclamation points.

This is fucking IT, luke!!!!!!

And I guess it is. I try to smile at my phone, even though all I'm thinking about is how Gray's gonna want to hang out with Tal at this thing and I'm not going to be able to explain why I can't.

I scrub both hands over my face a few times, which I'm sure definitely helps the barely-put-together look I've got today, and step out into the hallway. Lunch is almost over, so the halls are packed with people grabbing stuff from lockers and chasing after friends and trying to get to class, somewhere, in the middle of it all. Gray's definitely already in class, which is why I jolt so hard when a hand catches my arm, tugs me aside.

In a perfect world, it would be Tal, ready to talk to me.

We all know I don't live in a perfect world.

"Hey," I say to Olivia, because I might as well start the

conversation. I can at least pretend like that gives me the upper hand. "What's going on?"

"Hi, baby," she says, and then, "are you the reason why Gray's stopped responding to my DMs?"

Of course. God, I wish I could tell Olivia just how little I give a shit about whether or not Gray responds to her DMs. But all that would do is confirm to her that she's gotten on my nerves.

"Did he ever respond to your DMs?"

Olivia considers me for a second. "Can I be honest with you? Like, actually no bullshit?"

I shrug. When Liv asks that question, she's going to do whatever she wants. You just have to hang on for the ride.

"When are you going to let Gray go?"

She doesn't sound like she's being a bitch when she asks it, and that's what freaks me out the most. For a second, for this moment, she sounds like my friend. She sounds concerned.

"Last year," I say. I wrap both my arms around my middle like I'm trying to protect my insides from her. "Don't know if you remember."

Liv shakes her head. "No, that was when you broke up with him. When are you going to stop acting like you still have this weird . . . ownership over him?"

I could ask you the same question, I could say, but don't.

"He's my best friend," I say. "Sorry he doesn't want to date you, but that has nothing to do with me."

"You're breaking his heart, you know," Olivia says. It's normally so easy to dismiss what Liv says. This is different.

"Staying right there. He's basically still your boyfriend, except he's single. But he'll never date anyone if he's still with you."

"You have no idea what you're talking about," I say. "He's spent this whole year trying to date Tal. It's not Gray dating I have a problem with; it's Gray dating someone who doesn't give a shit about him. Someone like you."

Olivia thinks about it for a second before she speaks. That's scarier than anything; she always knows exactly what she's about to say. If *Olivia* is thinking twice about saying something to you, you should have run away five minutes ago.

"But we both know why he's not going to date Tal," she eventually says. "Don't we?"

It's the closest thing to a direct threat Olivia will ever make. I pretend that I'm not even giving it a second thought, but when Gray drives me home on his way to work after school, I hug him too tightly before I leave.

TWENTY-SIX

On Friday night, I hear Olivia's voice.

She's in my head from the second Gray comes into my room, offering opinions on my outfit and tossing me lethal-sweet drinks. When he offers to put my hair in braids, something he learned how to do specifically for me when we were in middle school, it's *when are you going to let him go?* When he squeezes me around the waist after we say good night to my parents, it's *you're breaking his heart, you know*.

I can't be breaking Gray's heart. Not like this. Not now that he is really, truly, the only thing I have left. My one perfect thing. I can't have spent the last two months agonizing about breaking Gray's heart if I've *actually been doing it* the whole time.

The party's at Olivia's, tonight, and I knew it was risky as soon as Gray told me yesterday. Being around Olivia at all is dangerous right now, when she's retreated; she's never actually gone, she's just waiting for the pieces of her plan to come together. But a party at her house? Where she controls everything? Where we have to follow her rules?

Basically, I'm nearly Kennedy-homecoming-drunk by the time we get to Olivia's house.

"Fucking lightweight," Gray says fondly, helping me through Liv's front door and out of my heavy winter coat, brought out of the depths of my closet last weekend by my mom.

"It's not my fault your tolerance is essentially, like, elephant-tranquilizer level," I say. I don't know if that makes sense, but I say it loudly and Gray laughs like he knows exactly what I mean, so it works for us, like always.

We do a couple of laps, soaking up the easy party energy. No one's quite on our level yet, but these are our friends, so they just think we're being funny. Even if they didn't, *we* think we're being funny, and that's enough for us.

It can be good, all of this. Me and Gray and everyone else. The way it always was. The way it can be again, now, without Tal.

Thinking the words *without Tal* brings me dangerously close to that razor-thin border between fun-party-drunk and deeply-sad-drunk. I shove them down, squeezing my eyes shut until they disappear from my head.

"Oh, look who's partying with the townies!" Gray suddenly booms. He's grinning so brightly and openly that my heart immediately sinks. There's only one person who isn't me that he looks at like that.

Of course Tal's here. She's gone to our school, gone to our parties, been a fixture in our lives for months. She gets invited to these things without me or Gray needing to take her now. But the reminder that Tal is permanent while *me and Tal* weren't hits me like a sledgehammer to the face.

"Baby," I mutter to Gray. He glances down at me, still

grinning over at Tal. She's smiling politely, and I know it's for his benefit, not mine, but I still stare at her while I speak to Gray because she looks too good to look away from. "I think I might puke."

"Oh shit, really?" he says. He studies me carefully—Gray knows all my tells, so I try to look a little woozy, more unsteady on my feet than I actually feel. "Do you need me?"

"M'fine," I say, trying to slur it a little bit extra so he believes I have to throw up but not so much that he tries to come with me. If he can talk to Tal now, maybe he'll get it out of his system for the rest of the night once I come back downstairs.

I pound the drink Gray poured me when we first walked in, not wanting to carry it upstairs, and trudge up to Olivia's parents' bathroom, tucked away at the back of the house where no one except Liv's best friends ever goes during parties.

It's here, looking at myself in the mirror, that I realize I should not, in fact, have pounded the drink Gray poured me when we first walked in.

"Shit," I say to myself in the mirror, laughing helplessly for a second before remembering that that's what pathetic people do. My makeup is somehow already smudged and ruined. My bra strap has slid all the way down my arm. I look like a walking mug shot.

The only thing that has, of course, remained perfect are my two French braids, courtesy of Gray.

"You don't deserve these," I hiss, pointing a finger at the sewer rat version of myself in the mirror. I hurriedly tug my hair out of both of them, finger combing the kinks and trying to make it look intentional.

I peek one eye open at my reflection and groan.

"Oh, that did not help."

I look like Cousin Itt. Also, I need to stop talking to myself.

I decide to cut my losses, figuring I've been having a nervous breakdown up here for long enough. I try flipping my hair in a couple of different directions and give up—people should be drinking enough by now to not care so much about whatever I've got going on.

From the top of the stairs, I pause to look out over Olivia's living room. I expect to feel all the same awful feelings that have come with these parties ever since last year; feeling like I don't belong, feeling like no one wants me here, feeling like I should just cut my losses and bail. But I'm fine. I know who I belong to down there now. If breaking my own heart with Tal is what it took to figure that out, then fine.

Of course, that's when my eyes pan to Olivia, huddled up with Gray in a dark corner, with both her arms draped over his shoulders.

"Jesus Christ," I mutter, going down the stairs as fast as I can without becoming a cautionary tale.

Liv doesn't move when I go up to them, but Gray looks at me half-helplessly. Sometimes I'm reminded that, perfect as he may be, Gray is still, in fact, a guy. Objectively hot girl is all over him? Pretty easy to forget that he doesn't actually like her.

"Baby," I say once I'm closer. I figure I'll just give him an out, let him excuse himself gracefully.

But Olivia turns around. She looks me up and down. And she says, "He's not your fucking baby."

There's enough bite to it that I take a brief step back. I lock eyes with Gray and he makes a face that immediately settles my nerves; he's just as weirded out by Liv right now as I am.

I scoff. "Liv, I'm not doing this with you. It's bad enough to fight over a boy, never mind fighting over a boy I'm not actually dating. I can call Gray whatever I want, because he's my best friend."

There have been a lot of times, over the years, where Gray and I have joked about the moment when Olivia Reiner Finally Snaps. Someone so tightly wound, who attaches so much to what everyone else thinks about her? Oh, you know she's always one poorly worded sentence away from an absolutely *nuclear* meltdown.

I just didn't realize me saying *Gray is my best friend* would be the straw that finally broke her back.

Liv's eyes flash. She takes a step toward me and I actually take one backward like she's going to hit me or something.

I don't know why I thought that. Olivia's too smart to hit you.

"If he's your best friend, does he know that you and Tal made out at Syd's party back in September?"

There it is. The shattered glass. The record scratch. The thing that pulls me out and away from Gray forever.

My knees actually feel like they're going to give out. I've thought about this moment in my nightmares, wondered how Gray would look at me and what he would say to me if he found out what I'd been doing, what I've done to him. But it never felt like this. It never felt real until it was right in front of me.

I don't even know what to say. What the fuck do I say? So I don't say anything.

"What?" Gray asks. He's smiling confusedly, so sure that Liv's full of shit.

But Gray knows all my tells. He looks at me and the smile falls off his face the second we make eye contact.

"You aren't gonna deny it?" he asks, in a little voice I barely hear over the party.

People must be looking at us, I think wildly. Liv isn't being quiet, and I look like I'm wearing a wig from Spirit Halloween; add that to the fact that it's me and Gray, the thing people have been trying to poke and prod for years, and I'm surprised we haven't attracted a full-on crowd yet.

"She's lying."

All three of us turn around to see Tal standing with a hand on her hip.

It's so unfair, how good she looks in Liv's house. It's unfair, how good she looks when she hates me.

"Come on," Tal says. She rolls her eyes and everything. "Everyone knows she likes you; I knew it after I'd been here for, like, a week. And you know she's not exactly original—like, mean girl queen bee? In 2024? Of *course* she's gonna say the gay girl's in love with her competition."

It's perfect. Logical explanation with the added bonus of making Olivia look even worse than usual. Gray's already looking at Liv, bewildered. I can practically hear him saying *why the hell would you do that?*

It would be so, so easy to let him say it. To take Gray back, my parting gift from Tal.

But then I realize that I know why she's doing this. Tal doesn't want me in her life; I don't think Tal even likes me as a person very much anymore. But before she's anything else, Tal is part of something bigger than herself, and even if she doesn't like it, that *something* includes me. She knows how terrified I was of this leap between coming out and being out, and she's not going to let someone take the choice away from me again.

"Stop," I say. I squeeze my eyes shut. "Thank you, but no. Liv's right."

It takes a second, I can tell, for Gray to figure out what to believe. But that's the thing with me and Gray; we believe each other above everyone else.

"Can we talk about it somewhere else?" I ask him. My lip wobbles like a toddler. "Outside?"

Gray doesn't say anything. I know he half wants to tell me to go fuck myself and hash things out right here in front of everyone.

"Please," I say. "I'll tell you everything, but Tal doesn't need all of her shit aired out in front of everyone. She doesn't deserve that."

I watch everything play out on Gray's face. He knew I was telling the truth, but now, seeing me leap to protect her, he knows how deep it goes. He turns around and walks out Olivia's front door, me running at his heels to chase after him.

I have to stop my drunk brain from scoffing at that. Like fucking always, right? Gray, then me.

People didn't realize something was going on, I don't think. No one's followed us outside, and it's not late enough in the night for people to be throwing up on Olivia's front lawn. It's just me and Gray in the pitch-dark, breath steaming out of both of us.

As soon as we get outside, the pressure of the party leaves me and I can't pretend like this isn't the worst thing I've ever done. I start crying immediately, and when I see Gray's hands twitch like he's thinking about coming over to hug me, I start *sobbing*.

"Just . . ." He looks so defeated. My breath is coming out of me in quick little hitches. "Just tell me it was that. Just that."

And I could lie. I know, at least, that Olivia didn't see Tal and me kiss in Gray's room. She *definitely* didn't see us in the café. And maybe Gray would be more okay with that eventually and maybe he could forgive me sooner.

But there's no fucking point to that.

"It . . . wasn't just that," I say. And then, because Gray's looking at me, because Gray tilts his head, because I know what Gray's asking without him having to ask, I continue. "It's not just that. We kissed on the day we went to Portland."

"When we went to *Portland*? When I was fucking *there*? So, what, you guys just wait until I'm not looking and have this whole *thing* going on?"

"It wasn't like that, Gray, I swear to god."

"Okay, what is it like, then?"

This isn't the way I was supposed to talk to Gray about a girl for the first time.

"We . . . there was more. More than kissing, I mean."

It's something close to agony, to use the past tense like that. To acknowledge that anything I had with Tal is over now. To have this conversation with Gray when this thing that should have been exciting is already gone.

"Jesus *Christ*, Alana," Gray says. "I mean, you know how fucked up that is, right? Beyond the fact that you've been lying to me for *months*, it's also just . . . not very fucking cool to *sleep with* the person your best friend likes?"

"But I . . ." Fuck. It was one thing realizing all of this on my own, but having to tell Gray, now, like this? I can barely get the words out. My throat feels like it's closing up. "I really, really liked her, too. So much. From the first day. Right from the beginning. Like, I was obsessed with her. I wanted to be with her. She's the first girl I've ever met in real life that makes me feel like this. It's the first time I felt like I wouldn't care what people thought, if I could just be with her."

Gray looks bewildered. "So why wouldn't you *tell me* that?"

"I thought it would be easier to—"

"Easier to *what*? To watch me look completely fucking clueless for two months? To leave me behind for someone you've known for twenty minutes?"

"That's not fair," I mumble, half trying to avoid this topic altogether, but then I think about it for a second. I remember the conversation I had with Tal about my old friends. It's *not* fair, actually. None of this is fair, to either of us, but I'm tired of accepting things that aren't fair to me.

"No, that's *not* fair, Gray. What was your plan? When you thought she might like you? You wanted to date her, right? By your logic, how was that not leaving *me* behind? If I'm a shitty friend for wanting to date someone, then you've been a shitty friend all year. I didn't tell you that I liked Tal, but you never asked, either. You haven't asked me about *anything* like that. Maybe you just assumed, somewhere deep down, that what I wanted was always going to matter a little bit less than what you did."

Gray doesn't have an easy response to that, and I know it's shitty but I pounce.

"You were trying to build something new for yourself. Apart from us. But you expect me to be exactly the way I always have been. I don't know if you noticed, but a *lot* of stuff has happened between when we were together and now. And you think I shouldn't have changed at all? I should just sit on the shelf and stay exactly the same and wait for you to need me?"

For a second, it looks like Gray takes that in. But then his face clouds over again.

"Don't try to turn this around on me. There's no version of this where you're the good guy."

It's even worse than I thought it would be, this inevitable crash and burn. I realize I'm crying and that makes me cry harder, because Gray must see it and he doesn't care at all.

"I'm sorry," I say.

Gray shakes his head. He looks out into the road, eerie quiet. He looks back into the house, low lights and Olivia waiting for him, ready to tell him how *crazy* I am for lying to him this whole time. *She* would *never* lie to him.

"I know I fucked up," I say. "I *know*. But it's over. I messed it up. It doesn't matter. She doesn't want anything to do with me anymore."

He ignores me.

"Baby—"

Gray whips toward me. "*Don't* fucking call me that."

"It can be like it was," I continue, even as I shrink back. "It can be like before. Before we even knew her. You and me, before—"

"Before what?" he snaps. "Before you didn't even trust me enough to tell me you liked someone? Before you decided it was better to lie to me and hide an entire relationship from me than to actually fucking *talk to me*? If you thought that was okay, then we clearly had enough problems *before*."

"Then I want to fix them!" I yelp, real panic in my voice now, because if Gray doesn't listen to me, if he doesn't want this, then I don't know what I'll do.

"I can't do life alone."

It's not fair of me to bring out the tiny, sad voice. But I feel tiny and sad, so he'll just have to deal with it.

"You won't be alone." Gray smiles bitterly. "That's the whole point."

Even like this, when everything's dying, I still just want to talk to him like he's my own. I want to say *oh, shut up, I already told you that's not what it's like.* I want to shove at his arm until he laughs and tucks me safely underneath it.

"I thought Tal was something," I say. "And I let myself think that she was important. But she doesn't even want to be around me anymore, and if she doesn't want that, then I don't want it, either."

It'll be true, eventually. At some point, I'll say that and Gray will believe it and I'll believe it, too. High school, Tal— all of this can be a blip.

"I don't want her," I say. I try to look him in the eye, but he looks away. "I want us."

Gray's face goes pinched. I struggle to place it for a second, but then I remember. That party a million years ago, end of summer. *You're the best boyfriend ever.*

"What does that mean?"

He looks exhausted. With me, with this.

I shrug.

"Just that I love you," I say. "If you want to forget any of this ever happened, that's what we'll do."

"Any of this," Gray repeats.

I don't say anything because Gray's thinking about what he's going to say next; really thinking about it, and when he's like this, I can't ever read him.

"How?" he asks. He must see the question on my face, because he elaborates. "You just want me. How?"

My heart breaks all over again.

This isn't the first time someone's asked me a question like that. My parents, Kennedy, Syd, they've all done it. They saw the breakup and they saw that Gray and I were almost exactly the same almost immediately after, and they couldn't comprehend the idea that maybe Gray's the love of my life and maybe I don't want him to be my boyfriend and maybe both of those things can be true at the same time.

But I've never heard it from *Gray*.

"Are you serious?" I ask. "All that time it took me to figure my shit out, all the feeling like a complete *monster*, and now you're like *are you sure?*"

Gray shrugs. "You broke up with me and then pretty much nothing changed about us."

This is how we fight, when it happens. Something reminds us of something reminds us of something. By the end, we don't know who the bad guy's supposed to be.

"I thought that's what you *wanted*." I finally notice how cold it is outside, adrenaline from this conversation wearing off into something worse. "I thought you wanted us to be the way we were before. Friends. That's what *I* wanted, anyway."

"I mean . . . maybe I'm an exception."

My jaw actually drops for a second. My mind goes completely blank for a beat before igniting with rage.

"Oh, awesome thought! Yeah, I never once considered that. I never *once* stayed up all night and cried and hoped more than anything that you were an exception. It never occurred to me that my whole life would have just fucking slotted into place if I could just get whatever broken ugly part of me that couldn't love you like that out of my head."

"There's nothing ugly or broken about it," Gray says, because he has to be the good guy, every time.

"Fuck off, Gray. You don't get to be this perfect ally and say that at the same time."

"What did you think happened to me?" He explodes. He can't even look at me. "What did you *think* happened when we were together and I was so in love with you it felt like you lived in my fucking *bone marrow* and then I had to just *stop*? And you expected me to be there for you, and I *wanted* to be there for you, but I didn't even have a second to get *over* you.

You'd been figuring yourself out for over a year. I didn't have any of that time."

"So, what, the whole time I thought we were okay, you still had feelings for me? You were just going to let me follow you off to UMaine and live with you and the whole time you still liked me that way?"

"No, that's not—"

"I don't even want to *go* to UMaine, Gray!"

I don't mean to say it, but now it's out there. I feel gross. Dirty. Like every bad thing I've ever thought about myself come true at once.

Gray laughs, once. A horrible, brittle, hollow thing. Everything that just happened, everything that we just said to each other, and I know that the worst part of it all is what I just sprang on him. I'm not going to UMaine. I don't want to be in his shadow forever. I don't want all of the things that I've told him I want for the last seventeen years.

"You don't have to," he says. "No one's making you do that. *Especially* not now."

My stomach burns. I don't know how to explain to him that no one was *making me* do that, but I still didn't feel like I had a choice. But now, I guess, it doesn't matter. *Especially* not now. Gray shutting the door. Gray finding somewhere and someone else to call home next year.

That's that, then.

I walk home alone. I don't turn around when I hear Gray calling my name. I don't cry until I'm sure he's not going to run after me.

♡

TWENTY-SEVEN

When I wake up the next morning, my mom is standing over my bed holding a plate of scones.

"How many of these did you make?" she asks.

"I think I lost count after the second dozen."

She puts the plate down on my nightstand and sits gingerly on the edge of my bed.

"And . . . I'm afraid to ask this, but *when* did you bake several dozen scones?"

I shrug. "When I got home last night. It was pretty late. You guys were asleep."

My mom blinks at me. "So, you got home from a party in the middle of the night . . . and baked a variety of scones."

"I was upset."

"So . . . scones."

"Yes."

My mom looks from the plate of scones, to me, to the plate, back to me. I pull my duvet up to my chin.

"Those are brown sugar and cinnamon, if that helps my case any."

I watch her internal struggle between parenting her delinquent child and enjoying said delinquent child's perfect scones. The scones, as always, win out.

"I can be convinced to not lecture you about your out-of-control lifestyle choices," she says eventually.

"Wow. I didn't think I was *that* good a baker."

My mom rolls her eyes. "Contrary to popular belief, I'm not that much of a pushover. You just seem . . . well, honestly, you seem like you're barely hanging on these days."

She says it gently, but then it's a pretty harsh thing to say no matter how gentle your tone might be.

"I'll take the excuse," I say. "Slightly less into accepting that assessment."

"I feel like I haven't seen Gray in weeks," my mom says. "And you've been seeing a lot of Tal, and I'm wondering if those things might be connected?"

I pull my duvet all the way over my head in response.

"Got it," she says. "I just want to make sure you aren't getting too overwhelmed."

"Too late," I say from within my duvet kingdom.

"I thought that maybe you might want to cut down on your extracurriculars," she says. "I know I'm supposed to be telling you to do everything you possibly can so you can go and enjoy your student loan debt, but if you're feeling like this, you need to take a break."

I know objectively that she's trying to be nice, that she doesn't mean anything by it, but it makes me flinch. Now I'm officially so pathetic that my mom doesn't think I can even handle school.

"Do you really think I'm that much of a disaster?" I peek one eye out at my mom, who looks horrified.

"I obviously don't think you're a *disaster*!" she exclaims. "You've just seemed to be a little . . . floaty, lately. Like, the thing with RISD?"

I prickle. "I never signed a contract with Gray saying we'd go to UMaine. I know you and Dad want me to, like, follow in your footsteps—"

"What?" my mom interrupts me. "I've never said that. Have I said that?"

"Well, you were pretty excited when we said that's what we wanted to do."

"Yeah, because I thought you'd found a path for yourself. I thought you were excited about UMaine. You could tell me you found a college on the moon that was perfect for you and I'd be just as excited."

"You'd never visit me if I went to college on the moon. You're afraid of space."

"I just don't think we should be messing around with it," she says for the millionth time, waving a hand dismissively. "*But* I would visit you. You're worth going to space for. Which is why I wanted to make sure you were sure about RISD. I wouldn't want to see you pass up an opportunity just because you're following someone somewhere. Whoever that might be."

She kisses me on the forehead.

"You're grounded if you make any more scones," she says. "There's no way we'll be able to eat all of these."

"Let the record show I've made no promises about cookies."

I don't know how to navigate the new Gray-less world the next week at school.

There's something missing from me, just off to the side. I keep turning around and expecting to see Gray right there, but he never is. I keep picking up my phone to text him when I think of something I know he'd like, but I resist the urge after the first time when he leaves me on read again.

I don't actually know where this ends. I have to believe he isn't finished with me forever (because if I think that, I'll never recover; I'll sit down in the hall and let everyone step around me and I'll stay there for the rest of my life) but I also have no idea how I'm supposed to make him forgive me. It would probably be easier if he would actually speak to me, but even then, I don't think I'd get anywhere. There's not much else I can do but apologize, and he doesn't seem to want to hear that.

Maybe he'd forgive me if I swore off all things Tal, if I promised I would go back to how I always was and I would stand beside him at UMaine and I would find myself a girl he liked but not *too* much to be with and I would do it all on his terms. And maybe, if Tal wasn't looming so large in my brain and body and self, I could do that. But even now, even knowing that I'm not anything to Tal anymore, knowing that she doesn't want me the way I (still, maybe always) want her, I could never do that. Even if she isn't going to be a part of my future, she's so much my present that I wouldn't have a hope of dismissing what we were.

I make it until third period without seeing Gray at all, but I know I'll have to see him at lunch because today is Friday and he always, always leaves school to bring his mom lunch at work on Fridays. All I have to do is wait by the student lot and he'll have to come out eventually.

I try to casually wander to the lot without making it seem like I'm actively stalking Gray, but it probably doesn't look very convincing because I'm walking at a glacial pace and every time I think I see Gray, I duck, as if that would hide me from him. When I finally get too cold to deal with being outside, I go back into the building. I stand aimlessly in the hall while all the people who *haven't* systematically destroyed their lives over the last couple of months flit around me.

A laugh that sounds much more like a cackle rings out, and I flinch before I mean to. That's Olivia, Olivia when she's trying to draw attention to herself, Olivia when she thinks she's life's main character and she wants you to know it. I turn around even though I don't want to, because the last thing Liv needs is a bigger audience, and immediately regret it.

She's walking down the hall with Gray, and when I see him, I duck into an empty classroom and peek through the window at them. Olivia's still laughing even though she doesn't think Gray's that funny (she doesn't get him and we both know it), and she slips a sneaky little arm around his middle as they walk.

Gray doesn't shrug her off. He swings his arm over her shoulder and they keep walking and I see red.

It's one thing for me to want to be with someone else. It's one thing for Gray to want to be with someone else. It is *entirely another* for Gray to be with Olivia.

"Bitch," I mutter out the window.

"Alana?"

"*Holy fucking shit*," I yelp. I really thought this was an empty classroom, but I whip around and see Mrs. DG sitting at the teacher's desk at the front of the room.

"Sorry," I say once it registers what I said before and the fact that Mrs. DG isn't an axe murderer. "I didn't think there was anyone in here. You scared me."

"I gathered that."

The two of us stare at each other for a second. I don't really know how to end this interaction.

"Do you want to talk about why you're muttering obscenities through my classroom window?" she asks. "You aren't supposed to call your peers bitches anymore, you know. Girl power and all that."

"If it helps, I was actually saying it to Gray."

"Ah." Mrs. DG nods. "Breakups can be tough, huh?"

Wait, what?

I laugh, too loudly, and then laugh again awkwardly at how weird the first laugh was.

"Do you not know what . . . happened there?"

Mrs. DG has been in every student council meeting this whole school year, and she oversaw the elections last year.

She saw me with Gray and she saw me without Gray and she *must* have heard what people were saying, Logan's jokes and Sydney's distance.

"I don't want you to take this the wrong way, but despite what movies may have taught you, most teachers don't actually have any idea what their students get up to on their own time. Sorry for the ego bruise, but I didn't actually care about the details when you broke up with your boyfriend."

She's kind of blowing my mind. I wasn't walking around thinking that everyone knew what I was up to at all times, but then maybe I was. I realize now that I was picturing teachers sitting around in the teachers' lounge saying things like *well, good for her* and *poor Ethan*. But maybe not every look is a Look. Maybe not every whisper is about me.

"That's . . . fair," I say, instead of telling her any of that.

"I hope this information brings you peace." Mrs. DG smirks.

"We broke up because I came out," I blurt. "Or, was outed, technically, I guess. Whatever. But we're still best friends."

She raises an eyebrow. "I, too, enjoy calling my best friend a bitch while actively hiding from them."

I've never really heard a teacher swear casually, like Mrs. DG has been doing this whole conversation. Normally when they do, they're trying too hard to be cool and relatable.

"Yeah," I admit. "Things . . . got complicated."

Mrs. DG bobs her head in a little nod. "Not that this is any of my business, but we *do* technically have a zero-tolerance policy for homophobic bullying. Outing counts. I made sure when the board was creating the rule. Just in case you wanted someone out of here."

My gut twists uncomfortably. This is exactly what I *didn't* want. To make it a big deal. To admit that Olivia hurt me. It's the same as with Logan, that night, that faraway, years-ago night at Olivia's party, just before this school year started. You can't let them know when their shots hit.

"I don't know that I'm really the *revenge-booting-someone-out-of-school* kind of gay," I say to Mrs. DG instead of enlightening her on the finer points of my friendship ecosystem.

That nod again. "That's fine. For the record, though, I am. So if you change your mind, you know where to find me."

I smile tightly and will a sinkhole to remove me from this situation.

"Oh, and remember that I need all your camp forms filled out by next week," she says. It's not a sinkhole, but at least it's a subject change. Mrs. DG is back at whatever it is on her desk, piles of papers and a red pen.

I haven't given the camp any thought. The forms are on my kitchen table. I'm 100 percent positive one of my parents has signed everything they need to sign. I just need to remember to pick them up and take them to school.

But I haven't done that. I've walked by them and glanced at them and thought *later*. Always *later*.

"Actually, I don't think I'm going," I say. "Sorry."

Mrs. DG looks up from the papers on her desk. She assesses me for a second.

"I don't think that you're the kind of person to not do something because of a boy," she says. "Or a girl."

I shrug. Maybe I am. But I don't think that's exactly it.

"I just . . . I don't think it's my kind of thing."

As I say it, I realize how true it is. I don't want the ice-breaker games. I don't want the networking. I don't want to spend a week surrounded by various versions of Logan Bailey. I don't want the *fucking* end-of-camp dance.

"Fair enough," Mrs. DG says. She shrugs, and gets back to what she was doing.

I'm still completely alone, but now I feel lighter. I think, maybe, I can start doing things just because I feel like it.

And right now, I feel like I want a danish.

♡

TWENTY-EIGHT

I've only taken the bus to Portland one other time in my life.

Gray and I, fifteen years old, wanting to be grown-ups. We spent weeks convincing our parents that it was fine, that we wouldn't do anything stupid. My mom sat me down and tried to talk to me about safe sex and I screamed that she was being disgusting.

Savannah gives me a ride to the bus station. She doesn't ask, but I'm sure people at school tomorrow are going to be shocked to see me, thinking I've finally run away to join the gay circus.

"Thank you," I say when she drops me off. I toss her whatever's in my wallet for gas money, but she waves me off.

"Yeah," she says. The whole drive to the station, she was looking at me out of the corner of her eye. Stealing little glances. A few months ago, that would have terrified me. Now I just want her to ask. Better I tell her exactly what's in my head than have her make it up.

"Can I tell my parents I'm at your house?" I ask. I know it's not really fair to involve Sav in all of this, but also it wasn't very fair of Sav to dump me along with everyone else, so I don't feel too bad.

"Yeah," she says. "Of course. You can always do that."

I blink at her. Savannah's always been nice, but we've never been the type of friends to be like *got your back always, love you forever!!!!*

"I'm sorry," she blurts out, and then looks out into the parking lot in front of her. So she's sorry, but she's not going to look me in the eye while she says it.

It takes me one second longer, but then it clicks. Sav was *so* ready to drive me all the way out here, even though we haven't actually spoken in months. The weird, sad little looks she was giving me. This is her apology for last year.

I used to think about this, what it would be like if someone ever apologized to me. The fantasies ranged from satisfying (them doing it at a high school reunion where I'm clearly the hottest person in the room) to mediocre (I'd mutter *yeah, thanks, whatever*).

I *used* to think about this, but I don't know when I stopped. Because now, seeing Sav like this, I realize I don't care. I don't need an apology from her. Is she still my friend? Not really, but she probably wasn't really my friend before, either.

"It's fine," I say. "Really."

Savannah beams at me, absolved. She can look at me again. I barely resist an eye roll, but I climb out of her Jeep and manage to just make it onto the Greyhound that's about to pull away, nearly empty because who's doing this trip at 3:00 p.m. on a Monday?

Tal's this entire city, for me. She's in every road and light and street sign, every puddle and cloud and person. Knowing how little she wants to do with me doesn't take back all the time we spent here. I still know my way to the café, and it's stupid and overly dramatic to think this but I'm pretty sure you could drop me here in ten, twenty, thirty years and I'd still know it.

My heart's pounding by the time I round the corner toward the café. I have no idea what I'll say to Callie. I have no idea if they'll even recognize me. I have no idea why I came here, actually, but the next bus isn't for an hour, so I'll have to do *something*.

I stop dead in my tracks when I see the café, its boarded-up windows and scrubbed brick. Tal must have been doing that, when she was here. She got almost all of it, but there's still a stain. You can see exactly what whoever did it thinks of us. The lights are off, but I can't remember if Tal told me there was damage to them or not. There's a handwritten sign on the door—painted a different color now, and I can guess why—that says *Closed until we fix this*.

It seems like a lot to fix.

"She's not here."

Callie, from inside. Peeking at me through a cracked sheet of plywood. They don't look thrilled to see me, but they also didn't immediately tell me to fuck off, so I shuffle from foot to foot while we stare at each other.

"I know," I say. Or I guessed, anyway. "I wanted to talk to you."

Callie rolls their neck, stretching out what I assume is days of being hunched over scrubbing things. They wave their hand out to me. *Go on.*

"I'm sorry," I say. "I should have come to help when I heard about everything that happened."

Callie looks at me for a long time. They look so, so tired.

"Okay," they say. "And why are you telling me that? You've always been nice enough to me, but I wasn't exactly sitting here wringing my hands wondering where you were. Kinda had other stuff going on."

"I just . . ."

Thought I needed to. That's how that sentence was going to end. Fuck. Now I'm Savannah.

"I just wanted to know if you needed any help now," I say. "Or, y'know. Ever."

They turn around and disappear into the dark café. My shoulders slump for a second, but then they kick the door open. They have an industrial-size tub of paint in one hand, and two rollers in the other.

"I was taking a break," they say. "But if you're offering."

I don't always think I'm the smartest person in the room, but I can take a hint when I see one. I take one of the rollers from Callie and get to work, pink over pink on the bricks on the outside of the café.

Callie gets started up beside me, both of us working in silence. Every so often, someone walks by, and they either avert their gaze or speed up.

"If they don't have to look at it, they don't have to do anything about it," Callie says.

I know what they mean, but I also know that anything I say to that is going to sound like bullshit, so I don't respond.

But Callie doesn't let me get away so easily.

"Is that what you thought?" they ask me. "When this happened?"

I'm almost positive everything I say is going to go right back to Tal, but it's not like she's my biggest fan right now. Might as well be honest.

"Yes and no," I say. Callie waits as I dip my roller again and start a new section. "I didn't want to see it. I didn't want to care about it. But I think that's because I didn't want to *have* to care about it? Like, if I have to care about it, then I have to be part of this whole community. And if I'm part of that, then when something like this happens, it's happening to me. And I don't know if I was ready to deal with that."

Callie makes a face like they maybe might be impressed, so at least there's that. If all of this *does* get back to Tal, maybe she won't think I'm as much of a complete and utter fuckup.

That would be nice.

I laugh, embarrassed at myself but figuring the point of this little school night journey was to lay my cards out on the table.

"I don't even know what this place is called. Tal would bring me here and I would kind of duck my head on the way in, like someone was going to see me and . . . I don't even know."

"Tell someone you're a card-carrying homosexual," Callie finishes for me. I can't tell if they're making fun of me, but they nailed it, so I guess it doesn't really matter. "It's called Lavender Menace."

I look at the wall I'm painting. "But it's pink."

Callie takes that in for a second and then laughs. Not at me, I don't think.

"I'd actually never really considered that," they say.

"I guess it's a reference that I'm not a cool enough gay to understand, though, right?" I ask. I'm only a little bitter. I know that it's mostly my fault that I don't know about any of this stuff; I've avoided it like the plague for most of my life.

"Did you know I went to your high school?" Callie asks instead of answering my question.

My eyebrows almost fly off my forehead.

They chuckle. "Yeah, I know. So I get it. You fucked up, but so did she."

A terrible part of me so badly wants to reach out and take that, to think *well, Callie thinks we both fucked up* and use it as an excuse to stop giving a shit, to turn it around on Tal. But beyond the fact that that's shitty, Tal would actually have to agree to speak with me for me to do that.

"I graduated ten years ago this June," Callie says, and then laughs like they can't believe that. "Not to be all *you kids don't know how good you have it* or whatever, but if I wanted to see a queer person on TV, I had to watch *Glee.*"

I shudder. "My condolences."

Callie snorts. "It wasn't great. You had to either band together with other freaks, or suffer on your own."

"What did you pick?"

"Neither. I went with secret option three: Stuff yourself into the closet so hard you can't breathe and don't think about any possible long-term repercussions on your mental health."

"Oh, hey, I know that one!"

Callie laughs, and I start to relax a bit. Look at me, holding my own in a solo conversation with a real actual queer person!

"I got through it by imagining this great big future," they say. "I thought everything would have been worth it if, at the end, I was this massive, untouchable thing. Richer than god and twice as powerful."

"Well." I gesture around at the two of us painting a wall in the dark, surrounded by garbage. "Manifestation clearly works."

When Callie smiles at me then, I can tell they're trying very hard to be patient with me.

"I didn't need that life," they say. "I needed *my* life. I just didn't know what I was looking for, at that point."

"And this was it?"

"Pretty much. I went to culinary school in New York—you don't have to do that, the culinary school thing, but I wanted to be the best and the fanciest, so I did—and I thought I'd be some kind of incredible chef in the city. But then my grandma died, and she left me a bit of money just as this place became available, and I figured *hey, fuck it, we all start somewhere*. But this is it. This is what I was looking for. Community and home."

At some point while Callie was talking, I dropped my roller. Like, not as in I put it down on the ground. As in it fell out of my hand and hit the sidewalk with a quiet little splat.

Ask me to repeat that story, and I'd only be able to say *Callie went to culinary school in New York*. They went to culinary school. They graduated from my high school and then went to a place where they cooked all day, and now they have a job where they cook all day.

"So you went to culinary school?" I ask, trying to sound casual. "Like, you went to school to learn how to cook?"

"I mean, I've been cooking and baking for as long as I can remember," Callie says. "Culinary school just took all of that and turned it up to eleven. Especially my pastry classes."

Huh.

Okay. I knew, objectively, that there were people in this world who go to culinary school. I knew that some people decided that they could cook or bake forever and they could do it as a job and they could go to school for it.

It's just that I may have forgotten that I was also people.

I'm pretty sure this is what it's like to be called to the priesthood.

"Hey," Callie says, nudging me gently out of my trance. "It's getting late. You should probably head home. Plus, you look like you need to think about some stuff."

I can only imagine the crazed look on my face right now, but I don't care. It feels like I float back to the bus station, my mind racing. I can't even focus on one thing, images and ideas flashing around in my head. Me working with food all day. Me talking to people who love baking as much as me all day. Me *finally figuring out macarons once and for all.*

And then, just as I'm boarding the bus, I get a text from my mom.

Are you kidding me Alana where the hell are you

♡

TWENTY-NINE

I figure it's easier to get this shit show out of the way as quickly as possible, so once I'm safely tucked in the back of the bus I call my mom.

"I'm safe I'm fine no one is murdering me," I say as soon as she picks up.

"Not yet," she says, which is a bit predictable but also not unwarranted.

"I'm on a bus coming home from Portland right now," I say. "I'll be home in two hours and also please remember that, prior to this, the worst thing I've ever done is throw up in a pair of your shoes that you literally never wear."

"How often I wear the shoes has nothing to . . . never mind. Why the hell are you on a *bus* from *Portland* in the middle of the night?"

I pull my phone away from my ear to check the time.

"It's eight thirty."

"Alana."

Shit.

I manage to convince her that I'll explain what happened

once I get back, which means I have two hours of headphone-less bus travel, during which, oh yeah, I have absolutely no one to text. The only recent messages are the ones from my mom, and two from Sav saying *shit, your mom just saw me in Walmart and I couldn't think of an excuse fast enough.* And *sorry sorry sorry sorry.*

I roll my eyes without any real heat behind it. I hadn't actually thought this plan through; I was going to have to call my mom once I got to the bus station anyway.

Annoyingly, the trip flies by when I'm not looking forward to what's waiting for me at the end of it. Before I see anything else, I see my mom, standing against her car. Arms folded, trying very hard to look menacing, but we both know she's too short for that.

Once she sees me walking up to her, though, she doesn't say anything. Just gets in the car and waits for me.

"All right," she says once my door's shut. "Spare no detail."

"I went to a café in Portland," I say. "Tal knows the person who owns it, and I went to talk to them."

I clamp my mouth shut as soon as I've finished, and my mom stares at me incredulously.

"That feels like sparing a couple of details."

"It's like . . . ugh, it's like a gay café."

"Why *ugh*?"

Ugh. I can talk to her about why I went AWOL tonight, but I'm not going to discuss the intricacies of coming out in high school.

"It was vandalized," I say. "A couple of weeks ago. I went to go see if I could help. I painted for a while and then I got back on the bus. It was hardly a scandalous night."

"I don't care that it wasn't a scandalous night," my mom says. She finally, blessedly, pulls out of the parking lot, but I know I've got a solid fifteen minutes of solo car time with her before I can escape to my room. "I care that you thought it was fine to go to a city two hours away on a Monday night. Even if you were doing it for a good reason, the fact that you didn't tell us about it doesn't exactly lend you credibility."

"What, so you think I'm lying?"

I don't even ask her that to pick a fight. At this point, I've already been to the café. I've already spoken to Callie. I've already had my lightning-bolt-this-is-my-calling moment. All in all, not a bad night.

"I don't think you're telling me the whole truth."

I slam my head back against my seat, rubbing my hands over my face.

"I went because Tal loves it there, and when it got vandalized I didn't go with her, so she dumped me for being shitty and I was trying to be less shitty."

My mom doesn't say anything to that. I'm sure if I looked at her browser history right now I'd find a lot of "how to talk to my gay teen"–related searches, but I don't think she actually ever expected me to say anything. I think we were all operating on some flimsy assumption that I would just bring some girl home for Thanksgiving next year and we'd never need to actually talk about it.

"I thought you said you'd tell me if something was going

on when you had something to report," she says. She sounds hurt, and it twists something like annoyance up in my stomach. All of that, and she took *why didn't I, specifically, know* out of it?

"There never *was* anything to tell," I say. "Not officially. I ruined it before it could get to that point, so there still isn't."

"Is that my fault?" she asks.

"What, that I ruined it? I'd love to be able to blame you, but that one was all me."

"No," she says. "The way you shut down. The way you're pretending like you don't care even though I'm pretty sure this was your first actual almost-relationship and I know a feeling like that doesn't go away so quickly."

That's a big question for a Monday night.

"No," I say. I'm pretty sure it's the truth.

Neither of us say anything for a minute, but the silence gets to be unbearable and I can't help it any longer.

"Gray liked her, too," I say. "He didn't know we were a thing. He found out last week and then he dumped me, too."

My mom makes some kind of half-choked sound, covering her mouth with one hand and turning away. I peer at her carefully under the streetlights.

"Are you *laughing* at your daughter's pain?"

"I'm sorry!" she says. She's still giggling. "You have to admit, that's a little ridiculous. Like, what are the odds?"

I snort humorlessly. "It's me and Gray. The odds are pretty good."

I didn't want to have this conversation with my mom for a *lot* of reasons, but tonight there's also that pesky oh-my-god-I-found-my-life's-purpose situation that I still need to talk to her about.

"Am I in trouble?" I ask.

My mom shrugs helplessly. "I don't know. Probably not. We've never really had to punish you before, so I don't know how we'd start, at this point. No seeing Gray or Tal?"

She's smiling a little, and I laugh in spite of myself. "Too soon."

My knee is twitching, bobbing up and down because it feels like if I don't bring this up I'll actually explode.

"So y'know, like, college?"

My mom glances at me from the corner of her eye. "I've heard of it."

"Callie—that's the person who owns the café, who I was with—they were telling me that they went to culinary school. That's kind of cool, right?"

My mom brakes so hard I nearly fly through the windshield. I slam back into my seat after my seat belt locks. Jesus, thank god the road is empty.

"That's an *incredible* idea," she says. "I can't believe I never thought of that before! I didn't realize you would want to do your baking thing as an actual career."

"Well, I don't know if I would for sure," I say before she can get out of the car and apply for me. "Maybe I should just stick with the UMaine thing. It's a big school. Even if Gray still didn't want to hang out with me while I was there, I could probably avoid him."

My mom starts driving again, but I hold on to the overhead handle just in case she decides to try and kill me again.

"I just want you to do the thing that makes you happy for as long as you can do it," she says. "Also, realistically, I'd like for you to make money doing it. Such is the curse of late-stage capitalism. But you can do whatever it is you decide to do at UMaine, or you can do it at culinary school, or you can do it anywhere else. I just care that you do it."

"Couldn't you just tell me that I absolutely have to go to UMaine with Gray or you'll disown me forever so that I don't have to make a decision like that?"

We hit a red light and my mom ruffles my hair.

"I'd love to," she says. "But that would make me an asshole."

When we get home, she mercifully lets me trudge upstairs to my room and flop into bed. There's a pile of homework that'll be going untouched tonight sitting in my backpack, and it's not even that late, but I fall asleep so instantly that I barely remember my head hitting the pillow. It's the kind of sleep usually only experienced by the hungover or deeply sedated, so when I wake up in the morning, I have no idea how long it's been or what year it is, but I *do* have a pretty impressive puddle of drool soaked all the way around my head. So that's cute.

I try a stretch, and I'm relieved to find it doesn't make my entire body snap in half. My legs kick out from under my covers, but they hit something, and I hear paper rustling and falling to the floor.

I peek out over the edge of my bed as if something's going to jump out at me, but I have to laugh when I realize what it is.

My mom has gone full mom. Scattered all over the floor are printouts—has this woman ever heard of paperless communication?—for culinary schools. The community college in Bangor with its culinary arts program, but everywhere else, too. Baton Rouge. Philadelphia. Fort Lauderdale. Louisville. New York. She's put sticky notes all over them with things like tuition and scholarships and open houses. On the New York one, she's written *Get to work*.

I didn't feel like I was anybody until I was Gray's Girl, as trapped and frantic as it made me feel sometimes. And then Tal showed me that I didn't have to be that, that I could be hers instead. But maybe it's time to belong to myself.

I get to work.

♡

THIRTY

"I packed you a lunch."

"You packed me a lunch?"

"And I called ahead to the hotel so they'll be expecting you. You should be able to check in by yourself, but if they give you trouble, call me and I'll talk to them. And if they won't listen to me, I can just drive down there and we can sort it out."

"Just drive down the six and a half hours? At that point it would be easier for me to just come home."

If I'm being honest with myself, I think I'd rather just stay home. Stay home and sleep for the rest of Thanksgiving break. Stay home and not hear from Gray. I don't know if I'm not talking to him or if he's not talking to me, but either way we aren't talking. I missed making Thanksgiving leftover sandwiches with him for the first time since I had tonsillitis when I was eleven. Stay home and not hear from Tal, who's still ignoring me. Even if everything was still the same and we were talking and it was good, I wouldn't be able to talk to them. Syd texted me from the bus to the leadership camp at five in the morning two days ago saying *Someone just said they'll make us put our phones in a big fucking bucket when we get there. Send help.*

I'm glad Gray's there. He deserves to go. He deserves this golden ticket to the life he's been trying to build for as long as I've known him, to UMaine and law school and a girl who'll love him the way he needs it. Some fratty roommate freshman year he'll move in with who'll let him call their apartment the Love Shack even though he won't get what he's talking about until Gray hauls his ancient SingStar game to him and they perfect their performance the way we did.

My mom shoves an actual brown paper bag at me. She must have had to go to the dollar store to buy an entire pack of them. I make a mental note to talk to her about paper waste when I get home tomorrow.

"You're *sure* you don't want me to drive you?" she asks for the billionth time.

It's not that I can't drive. I got my license with Gray when we turned sixteen last year because that was part of the plan. I'm technically insured on my mom's Camry and there's nothing actually stopping me from doing this trip by myself. But I usually prefer not to drive, because it feels like this constant test that I'm always just on the edge of failing, and if you fail the test, you *literally* die.

But last week I came downstairs holding the New York printout. The Culinary Institute of America, holding an open house in Hyde Park this weekend, and my mom had the hotel booked before I could even finish speaking, and it felt like something I had to do on my own. Like something I needed to keep close, just for myself, before anyone else could tell me what they thought about it.

New York isn't that far. I'm doing the drive in a day. So in the alternate universe where everything gets better and Tal goes to RISD and Gray's at UMaine, I could still have them. At least, I could have a version of them. I could pocket little moments with each of them, avoid becoming a face in a yearbook and someone you hope you don't see when you're home for the summer.

I've downloaded a playlist so immense it's choked nearly all my phone's memory, but I need it. I need seven hours of the loudest music I know to drown out the texts I'm not going to be getting this weekend and the thoughts in my head and the little voice that's saying *what the* hell *are you doing?* And the way my mom looked so proud of me when she waved goodbye as I pulled out from the driveway. She can't be proud of me, because if she's proud of me, then that means I have the potential to fuck it all up and disappoint her.

The drive is uneventful, probably because I blast music loudly enough to make me forget my own name, much to the chagrin of every soccer mom I stop beside at red lights. I'd left around six and I get to Hyde Park at around one, and I realize that I have never, ever, been alone like this before. Hypothetically, if I wanted to, I could never go home. I could get a tattoo. I could sneak into a bar. I could kiss a girl who isn't Tal. And no one would ever have any idea.

But then I pass the exit for the Eleanor Roosevelt National Historic Site and Tal appears beside me, casual in the passenger seat holding my hand on the center console, knees bunched up to her chest while she draws boobs in her fogged-up window and she says *Eleanor Roosevelt was a dyke, you know* and I want her here so badly I could throw up.

The CIA (my dad hasn't stopped laughing at that since my mom and I told him about it) open house isn't like the Bangor Community College open house my mom made me go to freshman year. It's not one room in the town's only hotel, pamphlets that look like they haven't changed in ten years. This is hordes of people who all seem to know where they're going, moving in a million different directions. Even the people who don't know where they're going—the reedy future freshmen guys and anxious, darty girls—have someone with them, at least. Parents, friends, partners. There are demonstrations being held in immaculate kitchens and instructors with severe faces and burnt fingertips, tattoos of knives and whisks and measuring spoons on their forearms. There are signs advertising campuses in Texas, Singapore, California. Student volunteers with booming, peppy voices trying in vain to direct traffic. I know it's not true, but it feels like I'm the only person here alone. The fact that I could do anything I wanted and no one would notice starts to seem more like a threat than a dream.

I get sucked into a current of kids filing into a massive room, and I figure I must be in the right place because the girl beside me is holding a glossy admissions booklet that says *CIA New York*. I sit down and shrug off Gray's jacket, make myself comfortable just in time for the lights to dim and for me to realize that I'm sitting in front of a giant projected presentation that reads *CIA CALIFORNIA: THE FLAVOR OF NAPA VALLEY* and it's too late for me to get up.

I sink down in my seat as the presenters get their mics set up, as if they'll pick me out of the audience and force me to enroll in a school thousands of miles away if I make myself too visible.

"Thanks so much for coming out today, everyone," says a man in a button-up shirt with the sleeves rolled up and a meticulous beard, once the mics are ready to go. He's got tattoos of grapes and chalices up and down one of his forearms, and I can immediately tell he's everyone's favorite professor. "I'm Gus, and I'm the program coordinator for CIA's California campus. I understand I don't exactly have a home-court advantage, here, but I'm gonna try my best to convince at least some of you to abandon ship and join us on the West Coast."

He clicks onto the next slide and a virtual tour of the California campus starts playing. It's gorgeous, of course, this big stone building tucked away among palm trees, because things that are far away and not meant for me are always beautiful. Everyone watches as the camera bobs through the campus's main building, its herb garden, its entire building dedicated to wine. Gray replaces the girl beside me, then, arm stretched out over the back of my seat easily, and says *oh I get it, that time you drank a bottle of white wine and then sobbed in my bathroom for three hours was just homework*. I blink him away to see the tour is over, but the next slide makes me gulp. Like, audibly gulp. Like, the girl sitting beside me gives me a careful sideways look.

"Something that sets us apart from some of our other campuses at CIA California is that our students have more opportunities to specialize their studies," Gus says. "Of course, we couldn't have a campus in Napa and not allow for wine studies, right? But we also offer specialties in baking and pastry arts."

Baking and pastry arts. *Baking and pastry arts.* I could get a degree in fucking *croissants*.

I don't hear the rest of the presentation, my brain running too wildly, but I manage to watch as Gus flicks through slides, shows off pictures of the campus, and it's there, okay? I see it. I see myself going to classes with names like *Specialty Cakes* and *Café Operations* and *Advanced Baking Principles*. I see myself in California, somehow, like magic, like it was meant for me. I see it the way I can see whatever I'm baking already done in front of me when I begin, like I just need to follow a few steps and make it happen.

I only realize the presentation is over because the girl beside me stands up. She nudges her leg against my knee for a second because I'm blocking the aisle, and I panic when I realize, standing up and basically squishing the two of us together.

"Hello," she says with a little smile. She has to turn her whole head down to look at me.

"Hi," I reply on instinct, like we're just having a conversation. "I mean, shit. Sorry."

I scramble out of her way, but she follows me to the side of the room.

"Are you here alone?" she asks, then makes a face at herself. "Sorry, I didn't mean for that to come out as creepy as it did. I'm not here with anyone, but it seems like everyone else is, right? So I thought you might . . . Yeah. Anyway. Sorry!"

"I'm here alone," I blurt. "I'm Alana, hi."

"Hi," she says. "I'm Jaya. So that's four hellos, any more we should do?"

"No, four seems appropriate. I think it's only five when the other person is a visiting dignitary. But I'm rusty."

Jaya laughs, and that's how I learn I can make other people laugh when I'm on my own. Maybe I don't get all of my power from Gray's electricity, Tal's magnetic pull.

"So why California?" Jaya asks.

I blush. "I, uh. I may have thought this was the New York presentation, and then by the time I figured it out, it was too late to leave."

She laughs again, grabbing on to my arm like she can't believe I just said that. But not in a mean way. In a then-she-takes-a-step-forward way. Her nails are painted a gleaming white that stands out sharply against her brown skin, and I take in the mess of silver rings she has on each of her fingers and clock her, then and there.

"Why California for you?" I ask. I want to step backward, but there's also something about having a girl—any girl, a girl who doesn't know me, a girl who I'm 99.9 percent sure is queer—see me and want to talk to me, want to share space with me, that feels good.

Jaya grimaces. "Honestly?" she asks, and I nod. "I just got dumped. Like, *dumped*. I kind of feel like I need to get as far away from the East Coast as possible."

"I know the feeling," I say before I can stop myself. Tal didn't dump me, because Tal and I weren't together, because I was too chickenshit to be with her.

"I hope you don't take this the wrong way, but I kind of thought so," Jaya says. "You had that listless air of the recently dumped. I say this, of course, as someone also with the listless air of the recently dumped."

We laugh at each other for a second, and there's a question just on the tip of my tongue. I want to know about whoever dumped Jaya, who they were and what that might make her. There's something about the way she carries herself, something in the knot tied in the orange scarf in her dark ponytail and the worn brown leather boots she's wearing and those rings that I know. But I don't know how to ask the question without sounding too interested, or like a straight girl just trying to dig for something to gawk at.

"So who was she?" Jaya asks me, and my eyes bulge out.

Who was she. Who was she. The thing I see in Jaya is the thing Jaya sees in me.

"Oh shit, sorry!" Jaya's misinterpreting the way I'm gawking at her. "Did I just totally misread you? Mine was a she, too, I'm not just, like, pointing the gay finger at you. Oh my god, please pretend like I didn't just say *pointing the gay finger*, I—"

"No!" I say, loudly, quickly. "I mean, no, you didn't misread me. Definitely not. It was a she."

Jaya grins. She links our arms and starts walking us out of the room and toward the kitchens I was too afraid to venture into alone earlier.

"I've been *dying* for more queer friends," she says. "Give me your number later so I can convince you to come to California with me, okay? We can wing-woman each other and both of us can forget all about girls who hurt our feelings on the East Coast and focus on girls who'll hurt our feelings on the *West* Coast."

I spend the rest of the day trailing behind Jaya, following along as she runs her hands over kitchen surfaces and talks about the restaurant she wants to open one day. She talks to instructors and follows me on Instagram and asks me what Maine is like. It feels like being a little kid, meeting someone and becoming friends right away. I can see it, if I let myself. I can see Jaya and me going to parties and laughing about inside jokes and swapping recipes and being friends.

It's just that, if I'm not careful, I can see all of that in California.

♡

THIRTY-ONE

Jaya hugs me at the end of the day, when I'm carrying a tote bag filled to the brim with CIA paraphernalia (about half of it is for the California campus, but I'm telling myself that's just because I was with Jaya all day), and it feels like my feet are going to fall off. The last person I hugged was Tal, standing in her doorway before everything went to shit. Wait, no. It was Gray. Drunk at Syd's house. Before everything went to shit.

At least I'm consistent.

I stop at a drive-thru on the way back to the hotel (you'd think for a culinary school they'd provide more snacks) with every intention of watching something on my laptop until I pass out promptly at eleven thirty. The guy at the front desk doesn't give a single shit that I'm a minor checking in alone. My mom had me thinking I was going to have to participate in *Home Alone 2*–style plotting to get through the door, but the guy swipes my mom's credit card and passes me a key, muttering *pool closes at midnight*. I didn't even know there *was* a pool.

I used to think about traveling alone a lot as a kid. I'd imagine myself boarding flights and wandering cities, waking up late in massive king-size beds with blindingly white sheets and drinking coffee. I don't know what I thought I'd be doing on these trips, but I assumed something important. In reality, it's 11:00 p.m., my right eye is twitching, and there's an extremely unsettling water stain on the ceiling right by the bathroom wall.

Just as I'm thinking of packing it in for the night, Jaya texts. *U up?*

I make a face at my phone and try to decide whether I should ghost her forever or just for tonight when she texts again. *Just kidding. I'm not the worst. Are you still in New York? I'm in a hotel for the night and booorrreeeed.*

I laugh out loud without meaning to. *I'm at a Holiday Inn up the road from CIA*

> *WAIT. Give me your room number immediately I'm either about to visit you or really embarrass myself.*

My grin widens. *244*

It takes about ten minutes for the knock to come at my door, and I'm already laughing by the time I get up to answer it. Jaya's laughing, too, standing in the doorway wearing a literal matching pajama set, which I didn't think anyone outside of senior centers and mommy blogs actually did. But she's the kind of person who wears what she wears so confidently that it convinces you that you should wear it, too, and now I want a matching pajama set.

"Why didn't we figure this out today?" Jaya comes inside

without asking, but I was already stepping aside to let her in. "You mean to tell me I've been watching the Food Network for four straight hours when we could have been doing something actually fun?"

She looks around my room as if it would be any different from hers, and normally I'd balk at the intrusion, but Jaya already seems to fit into my life.

"We could go swimming," Jaya says after some careful consideration.

Swimming with my old friends didn't actually mean swimming. It meant floating, or preening, or tanning. They'll only get in the water if it means someone's watching them get in the water. But I have a feeling swimming with Jaya isn't going to be like that.

I tell her I don't have a bathing suit and she rolls her eyes and escorts me to the hotel gift shop, which is how I end up cannonballing into the pool in a truly horrific neon-green baggy one-piece ten minutes later. The pool's empty except for a group of Business Bros hogging the tiny hot tub.

"How is that enjoyable?" Jaya mutters, looking over at them. They essentially have to form a huddle for all eight of them to fit, arms overlapping arms. They're all laughing way too loudly, but they seem harmless enough. "Like, we get it, you want to touch each other without it being gay."

I snort, and before I can help myself, I think, *Tal would love her*.

"Scale of one to ten," Jaya says, all business, and before I can ask her what she means, she's diving down into the water and throwing her legs up in a clumsy handstand. I can't stop the grin that spreads over my face. I haven't rated someone's underwater handstand since middle school.

"Seven," I say when she comes up. She looks absolutely outraged. "Seven was generous! Your knee was bent, your toes weren't pointed, you were moving around. It was all over the place. You've gotta get it together."

"Oh, you mean business," she says, and then tries again.

We go back and forth like that for ages, long enough that the Business Bros get out of the hot tub. A couple of them stop to watch us until Jaya yells, "I'm twelve years old," and they scurry off. Long enough that the charming man from the front desk comes in and reminds us that the pool closed five minutes ago.

"Do you think there's ice cream to be had in this town?" Jaya asks, and I'm so glad that she doesn't want the night to end, either. As soon as we stop hanging out, I stop being some fun girl with a new friend and I go back to having *the listless air of the recently dumped*.

I drive us around until we find a Dairy Queen open late, and we drive back to the hotel and sit in the parking lot.

"Tell me about your girl," Jaya says around a mouthful of Oreo Blizzard.

"Tell me about yours," I counter.

Jaya makes a face. "She's not mine. When I asked you about yours, you got this look on your face like a tortured rom-com character. That tells me you're still into her. So she could still be yours."

"Optimistic," I say. Jaya rolls her eyes and gestures for me to keep going, so I roll my eyes back. "Her name's Tal. She's perfect and I fucked it up. The end."

"Did you cheat on her?"

"God, no. We weren't even actually together, first of all. But no, there's definitely no one else."

"Oh god, one of *those* things."

"My breakup was extra fun," I say, "because it was actually two-in-one. Her and my best friend."

"You were dating her *and* your best friend?"

I snort. "No. Well, kind of. Separately. I had a boyfriend, last year. We broke up for, uh, obvious reasons? But he's my best friend in the entire universe. He always has been. Like, literally since before we were born. But he was mad at me, and now I'm mad at him. It's a whole thing."

"What does that have to do with your girl?" Jaya asks.

I grimace. "I guess it shouldn't have anything to do with her. But it does. He liked her, too. I never told him that I was into her, so the whole time Tal and I were together, he was trying to be with her. And *then*, after I fucked it up with Tal, Gray kind of implied that he still wanted to be with me. Which is *wild*, considering how much I fucking *hated* myself for breaking up with him in the first place."

Jaya takes all of this in. That's how I know she's actually going to be my friend—the fact that she hasn't already run away screaming.

"I mean, you're still into this Tal girl, right?"

I snort. "Understatement."

"And how long did you and the guy date?"

"Like . . . almost three years, I guess?"

Jaya raises her eyebrows. "So doesn't that make sense? That it took him a while to get over it? Three years is a *long* time."

I know she might be right, but that doesn't mean that I want to hear it.

"When I get you to California, I'm putting you on the apps, like, immediately. Day one. Get ready."

I realize two things at once, then.

The first is that I don't care about girls. I don't care about all the plans Jaya is already making for us, about meeting someone on campus or at a bar or on an app. I don't want to think about those girls and who they might become to me and what we might do together. Maybe one day I will, but right now I don't care about girls. I care about Tal.

I care about the way Tal puts her hand on the back of my headrest when she's reversing out of a parking spot. I care about how Tal can always find me in a crowd, about the secret way she looks at me and the electric brush of our hands. I don't want other girls, I want the fillings in Tal's mouth and the jut of her collarbones and the flash in her eyes and the chip on her shoulder. Maybe there'll be other girls one day, but right now it's only Tal. It's only been Tal, and I feel that in the ache of my chest and stomach and shoulders, and that ache only gets stronger because as soon as I realize this, as soon as I know in every inch of me that Tal is what I want, I realize the other thing.

I realize that I want this, too. I want to eat ice cream in some parking lot at one in the morning with Jaya. I want to learn to cook the way the students doing demos did today, like everything they were touching was just an extension of themselves. I want to pull apart my food and know, exactly, precisely, 100 percent what it is that makes it taste good. I want to learn about wine that wasn't stolen from Gray's mom, and I want to do more and more and more and more until I can carry myself the way the professors did today, burn scars up and down my arms and a posture I've never even seen before.

I realize I want to *do this* in a way I haven't wanted to do anything ever before. I want to go to class and be the best and learn everything I possibly can. I want people to think of me the way they think of Gray now, always trying to be the absolute best. I want classes about pastries. I want to make beautiful things that taste good. I want, I want, I want.

I realize that Jaya's right. I need to go to California.

THIRTY-TWO

I feel hungover the entire drive back home, like I've been turned inside out and now every touch hits the raw, inside, nervy parts of me. I was supposed to check out of the hotel at ten, but I do it at seven after a night of not sleeping in a king-size bed with a scratchy comforter that smells faintly like bleach, going over conversations with Tal and Gray and Tal-and-Gray in my head and wondering how I got here.

My mom said she'd be waiting for me when I got home, but that was when she thought I'd be home at five. I walk through the unlocked door and shuffle out of my boots and coat, and when I look down there's a pair of yellow Vans sitting at the front door. I drop my overnight bag with a thud and bolt up the stairs to my room.

I stop short in my doorway when I see him. Gray, asleep in my bed. Gray, with his face squished up against a greasy take-out bag. Gray, in my space where he's always fit so perfectly. Gray, Gray, Gray, Gray, back here for me.

I take a running leap and flop on top of him, laugh when he grunts and swears and tries to throw me off before he remembers where he is.

"Do you have a key to my house?" I ask him.

"Your mom gave it to me for emergencies."

"This was an emergency?"

Gray presents me with the bag, cold and damp and wilted, and when I take a bite of the breakfast sandwich inside, it's the most disgusting best thing I've ever tasted.

"This was an emergency," he says firmly. "Shit, Alana, I'm so sorry."

I raise both my eyebrows. "Whoa. Alana. You haven't called me that since . . ."

Gray hasn't called me Alana since we broke up. Before, he'd call me Luke to get a rise out of me, to make me laugh and swat his arm. The next time we spoke, after everything had settled, after I'd broken his heart, I was Luke, or I was Alana Lucas, full name. Period. But we didn't talk about that.

"I kind of couldn't, before," Gray says. "Alana was my girl-friend, y'know? Luke's my best friend."

I squirm. "I'm sorry," I say. "I should have realized."

"I should have told you."

"I wouldn't have wanted to hear it."

We look at each other for a second.

"I want to hear it now," I add.

Gray takes a breath. He hasn't slept, either. I can see it in the bags under his eyes and the slouch in his shoulders and in the way he keeps rubbing his hands over his face.

"You knew who you were when we broke up," he says. "I mean, like, that's *why* we broke up. You'd figured out some-thing about who you were and that person couldn't be with me. But I hadn't figured that out. I didn't know who I was without you. So I needed you to still be there, like that. I needed to put you there or else I wouldn't have had any clue who I was. And that sucks, but it's what happened."

I want to hug him. I want to tell him how much I love him. I want to tell him that it's okay, that we're okay, that I'll do whatever he needs if it means I'm allowed to keep him.

Instead, I say, "I can't go to UMaine with you."

He doesn't want me to see it, but the air goes out of him. He takes another breath.

"I kind of guessed, when you drunkenly yelled it at me," he says eventually. I laugh, covering my face with one hand. "So you're going with Tal? That place in Rhode Island?"

I shake my head. "I don't think I should follow anyone. I found a place just for me."

Gray's already wincing. "Why am I getting the feeling that that place is very, very far away from here?"

"Y'know how you're always saying how much you'd love to go to California?"

Gray laughs like he's admitting defeat. "I've never once said that."

"Well, you might have to start because I want to go to culinary school in Napa Valley."

The last part comes out in a rush, all one word, but Gray's always spoken my language. He takes a pause that's almost too long.

"Well, fuck," he finally says. "That's perfect for you."

All the stress and agony of the weekend melts off me, and I let all my weight drop onto Gray's chest.

"You're perfect for me," I say.

Gray laughs. "I think we've established that I am not."

He shoves me off him and we adjust so we're sitting beside each other the same way Tal and I were a million years ago, backs to the wall, feet out in front of us.

"I hope you know how much I wished you were," I say. "How much I used to wish I could love you the way I l—"

I cut myself off before I can finish the rest of that sentence, before I can say something I can't take back. But Gray leans back to look at me, eyes wide, smile tugging at his mouth. Gray's always spoken my language.

"Holy shit, you were going to say *the way I love Tal.*"

I realize it as I say it. "Holy shit, I was going to say *the way I love Tal.*"

Gray bro-shoves my arm so hard I nearly fall over. "Holy *shit*, you're in love with Tal."

"Shut up."

"You're in *love* with *Tal*!"

"Shut *up*!"

I let Gray shove me again, let him flop on top of me. When his weight settles, I let it press the breath out of me, relief coming off me in waves.

"So I have a confession," Gray says. "You were going to find out eventually, so. Might as well tell you now."

"Please *god* tell me you're gay. That would be so incredible."

"Sorry to disappoint." He kisses my forehead. "But you should know that Liv got sent home from camp early. She's in deep shit."

"What did she do?" I ask. Olivia is an expert at getting away with things. It must have been something really bad.

Gray winces. "Please don't be mad."

I realize exactly what happened, instantly. "Oh shit."

"Tal and I had been talking," he says. "Trying to pretend like we weren't both just thinking of you, I guess. And Olivia came over to us and, uh . . . kissed me. And after she left, Tal just, like, couldn't hold it in. She told me what Olivia did to you. And I couldn't just let her float around that camp and get everything she ever wanted just handed to her. Someone needed to know what kind of person she actually is."

I could be mad, I think. I could be really pissed off that Tal told Gray and that Gray did something about it and that now my sexuality is A Thing that people are going to talk about and think about.

But I'm not.

"How much trouble is she in?"

"Mrs. DG said you told her you didn't want her expelled. So she's just not allowed to join any team or club for the rest of high school. And, because I'm Mrs. DG's favorite no matter how much she tries to deny it, she told *me* that she'll be making calls to every school that accepts her for next year."

"*Jesus*," I say. Before I even know it, I'm laughing. "Holy shit. Oh my *god*."

"She deserves it."

"She does!" I'm still laughing. "She deserves it! She fucking sucks!"

To be honest, saying Olivia sucks is a thousand times more freeing than coming out ever was.

"Thank you for saying something," I say. "I wouldn't have. But I'm glad you did."

"Oh thank god," Gray says. "I was so worried you were going to hate me."

I shake my head, squeezing him more tightly. I tried hating him. I didn't like it.

"Thank you for not hating *me*," I say. "You could have hated me."

"No, I couldn't have," he says. "I thought about it. I tried to for, like, a day. Couldn't do it. So I had to figure out how to love you the way I was always meant to."

"I love you," I say. "I love you I love you I love you."

"I love you," he says, then grins. "But not as much as you love Tal."

I groan, burrowing into his armpit. I don't need to worry about being in a boy's armpit with Gray because he's used the same deodorant since we were twelve, the one I picked out for him in CVS the summer before seventh grade.

"It doesn't really matter," I say. "She hates me now anyway."

I explain what happened, Lavender Menace and its small magic, the text from Tal, the way I ignored her. I don't say anything that she told me about her old school—I at least know not to do that now—but I tell Gray, in excruciating detail, just how much I ruined it.

"So anyway, she hates me and she's glad to be rid of me and now I'll have to make it through the whole rest of the year with her just being around and it's going to be horrible. So that's fun."

Gray laughs like he can't help it. I glare at him and he holds his hands out in front of him.

"I just spent the weekend with Tal," he says. "And she did *not* have the energy of a person super happy to be rid of you."

"You're lying," I say. Then, "But please also tell me everything."

At least I have him again. At least he'll be there now when I try to find someone who makes me feel the way Tal does, when I need to cry for hours or hate her. I can picture introducing him to Jaya, the two of them teasing me about a girl I'm talking to when Gray visits in California.

"Syd asked me why you weren't coming and Tal *whipped* around in her seat and was all like *Alana's not coming? Why isn't she coming? Is she okay?* And then she moped around the whole time we were there."

Gray leans over. Puts a hand on the side of my face that I lean into, feeling the little ridges he's carved into his palm with his fingernails over years of trying to calm himself down by balling his hands into fists. He kisses me on the forehead and finds a spot for himself in the new life I've found for me.

"So what are you gonna do?" he asks after a long stretch of silence.

"About what?" I ask.

Gray looks at me like I'm missing something big. "About Tal? About the girl you told me you're in love with twenty seconds ago?"

"She doesn't want me anymore. Do you not recall that depressing yarn I just wove for you?"

"Do *you* not recall the fact that I just told you she was miserable without you all weekend?"

"So, what, I totally disappoint her and *then* I steamroll over all of her boundaries because I like her?"

"First of all, stop pretending like you didn't just say you *love* her." Gray grabs my head and touches our foreheads together like he's giving me a pep talk in an intense movie about football. "Second of all, you aren't worried about her boundaries. You're telling yourself that she doesn't want you so that you don't have to go through the scary shit where you have to tell her how you feel and give her the chance to break your heart."

I break eye contact. "Well, you weren't the biggest fan of having your heart broken."

"I also wouldn't have been *the biggest fan of* being married to a miserable lesbian. Shit happens, and it usually happens in the direction it's supposed to."

"Did you just *everything happens for a reason* me?"

"Alana." Gray gets serious. "What do you want to be to Tal?"

The person beside her in the car. The person holding her hand. The person sharing pastries with her at Lavender Menace. Someone to kiss on rainy days. Someone to kiss on sunny days.

"Everything," I admit. "God, that *sucks*."

Gray leaps up from my bed and stands in front of me.

"Then let's get fucking brainstorming."

Gray loves a plan.

THIRTY-THREE

There's a benefit to teachers being obsessed with Gray.

I mean, there are a lot of benefits. The time I forgot to do a science project and Gray talked to my teacher and got me an extension. Last year when a teacher caught the two of us with a water bottle full of rum at homecoming and let us off with a warning. And now, today: the fact that Bremner trusts him with a key to the school.

We get there early, a week and a day after that morning in my room. Early, early. Middle-of-the-night-using-our-phone-lights-to-guide-us-before-we-can-find-the-cafeteria-lights early.

No one uses the caf in the morning, really. Everyone hangs around by their lockers or runs around in classrooms having before-school team meetings or does drills in the gym or has practice in the weight room. The caf is usually empty. At least, it's empty enough for our plan.

Gray finds the lights and throws them on, and both of us scream when we see a body lying on one of the tables. Gray all but leaps into my arms.

"Zoinks, Scoob," Rachel says, leaning up on her elbows.

"Why were you just *lying here* in the dark?" Gray demands.

"I'm an immortal creature of the night," she deadpans. "Also, it's five a.m. and I got sleepy."

She's covered in glitter, because she was sleeping on all of the posters that she brought. Thankfully, none of them look damaged upon my inspection, so Rachel can live another day.

Who am I kidding, I owe Rachel my life for helping with this.

Gray throws me a pack of balloons that we got at the dollar store last night, and both of us get to work blowing them up. Rachel claims that she has a lung condition that prevents her from inflating balloons, but when I ask her what it is, she says *it's called I-don't-want-to disease*, and she knows that I owe her my life, so I have to let her get away with it.

Rachel is sarcastic, I've learned over the last few days. She's biting and funny, and she loves Sadie so much that I have to look away when she talks about her and their life and their plans, and we've only been something that skirts the edges of friends for, like, a week, but she already feels like she could be permanent. If Tal ever talks to me again, I hope we can go to Callie's with Rachel and Sadie, spend an entire day eating and window-shopping and laughing with Callie and being with people who get it.

I've never done any kind of gesture, grand or otherwise. When I was with Gray, neither of us ever needed to. We were both too afraid to lose each other to ever do anything that would require something like this.

I look at Gray across the table, where he's on easily his twentieth balloon, and my heart swells. No matter what happens today, he'll be there. He stayed up all night with me to figure out the details of this. He's asked me about Tal. He's told me he wants to go to Portland with me and Tal again, joking about *knowing* he'll be the third wheel this time. He's started a new savings account for his first flight to California, even though I haven't even applied yet. He used his key to break us into school.

"I love you," I tell him, and he lets all the air out of one of his balloons into my face, but I know that means *I love you, too*.

My phone pings. Jaya, home in Connecticut, sending me a picture of herself even though it's way too early for anyone else to be awake. Hair in a silk bonnet, tongue out. Caption: *get your girl!!!!!!!!! Tell Gray hi!!!!!*

Jaya and Gray love each other. That's something else I've learned. Jaya and I talk every day about what we'll do to our dorm when we live together in Napa and the places we'll go and the day trips we'll use to explore. She's FaceTimed me and Gray three times this week, and they make each other laugh so hard that last year it might have even made me jealous. She's sworn off dating for the rest of the year, but she's already sent me a list of places the internet told her are queer-friendly in California. I've had to tell her which ones are actually near Napa and which ones are hours and hours away. I think that might be our thing? She plans the wild adventures and I tell her what we can actually do. I think we work like that. I think we work, period.

"Okay," I say once everything's set up, once the posters are on the walls and the balloons are everywhere. "Okay, you guys need to leave."

"We don't get to watch?" Gray demands.

"It's bad enough that I'm doing a public gesture!" I exclaim. "The last thing I need is for her to feel pressured to react in any specific way because people are watching. That's why I need you to guard the doors."

"That was not included in our initial agreement," Rachel says, but I know she'll do it because she agrees it wouldn't be fair for Tal and me to have an audience for this.

Seven rolls around too quickly. I thought I'd have more time to sit down, to take a second and try and convince myself that this is a good idea, that it'll go well and everything will be fine. But I look at my phone and it's 7:00 a.m. and now I have to actually do this.

"All right, action," I say. Rachel's made up a crisis with Sadie, asked Tal to meet her at school early today.

Rachel grabs her phone, holds it up to her ear.

"Hey," she says when Tal picks up. She does an incredible fake in-crisis voice. "Can you come to the caf? I couldn't find an empty classroom and I don't want to tell you everything out in the hall."

Tal must agree, because Rachel thanks her and hangs up.

"Look alive," she says, and then she and Gray scurry away.

For a minute, I'm alone, sitting on top of the table where Rachel had been napping earlier. When the caf's this quiet, you can even hear the clock ticking, announcing each second between now and the time when Tal might completely destroy me.

The doors open and I scramble to my feet so quickly that

I get my leg caught in the table's attached bench and fall on my face.

"Fuck, fuck," I say, both because I've completely ruined my big moment before it even started and because *fuck* it hurts to land on hard linoleum on both wrists.

"What are you doing?" Tal asks.

I can't read her. She stopped letting me when I ruined everything, and now I don't know if she's happy to see me or if she'll let me say what I wanted to say or if she's about to tell me to go to hell and never talk to her again.

"Showing you the kind of intense glamour and sophistication that could be yours," I say, mostly to myself, but Tal raises both of her eyebrows when I say *yours*.

"I see you've recruited Rachel," she says, crossing her arms. "I should have known better than to believe something was wrong with her and Sadie."

"Yeah, that one's really on you," I say, but Tal gives me a look that reminds me I'm not really in a position to joke with her. I shake my head at myself and get serious again.

"I know you're mad at me," I say. "You should be mad at me. I was so shitty to you. But I've done something to try and make it up to you. To try and do something good. Can I explain it to you? Or do you want me to go? I can go if you—"

"You can explain it," Tal says, voice smaller than I've ever heard it. "Wouldn't want all this plastic pollution to go to waste."

She gestures at the balloons, and I want to destroy all of them, but I realize there's the tiniest suggestion of a smile on her face and it spurs me on.

"So, before I met you I thought that I was exactly the same as I've always been. I thought that just because I'd come out, it didn't mean that anything in my life had to change. I mean, I essentially kept dating my boyfriend. And I've realized that I did that because if I had to think about the things that *had* changed, I'd be just, like, so sad. All the time."

Tal takes a cautious step closer. Her hands aren't balled up at her sides anymore, I notice. That's something, maybe.

"And then when I met you, you, like, punched me in the gut. I've never understood what people meant when they talked about meeting someone and wanting them right away like that until I saw you. I didn't even know I could feel like that. So it started feeling like, actually, maybe things had changed for the better? Like everything was going to be better now.

"And it kind of was! I got to feel that thing people talk about when they talk about being in high school and having a crush on someone, and it was fucking awesome. But it scared the shit out of me. Because if things were getting better, that still meant that things were changing. And then when everything happened with the café, I realized that if I was going to enjoy being a part of something, I have to be there when it's not fun, too."

"I just wanted you to want to be there for me," Tal says.

"And I wanted to be, too! I do, I swear to god," I say. I take Tal speaking to me and not screaming at me as a good sign and take another step forward. "I didn't realize then that of *course* something happening to the café meant something happening to you. To all of us. I get it now."

I reach behind me for one of the posters Rachel made last night, the one with more glitter than I've ever seen before. Half of it falls off onto my clothes, and I can hear Logan making some shitty joke about how now I'm so gay I'm actually sparkling, and I don't care.

"I went to the café," I say. "I talked to Callie and we figured something out. It'll be our student council project for the rest of the year. But I thought, I mean . . . Look."

I hand the poster to Tal and watch her read it. An alt-prom fundraiser to help fix the café. An officially school-sanctioned event, thanks to Gray convincing Bremner we could use it as our school's annual fundraiser.

"I want you to feel safe," I say. "I want you to have somewhere that feels safe. And I want . . . Fuck, can I keep going? Is it worth it for me to keep going? Do you want me to stop?"

Tal hasn't looked away from the poster.

"Keep going," she says.

"I want . . ." I take a deep breath. "I want to be your fucking girlfriend, okay? I know that might be selfish, to do this now when I'm trying to apologize, and I swear this isn't connected to the apology, like, forgive me or don't, we'll do the fundraiser either way—"

"Get back to the girlfriend part," she says to the poster.

"I'm applying to culinary school in California," I say, instead of getting back to the girlfriend part. "I feel like I can have this big huge life there. Or, like, I don't know, maybe not even a big huge life, but it feels like I can start figuring out what kind of life I *want* in the first place. It feels like something I can be good at and it feels like I *finally* have something that makes sense for me, and I want you to be the girlfriend that everyone hates me for out there because all I do is talk about you and FaceTime you, and I hope you think I'd be worth doing long distance for because you are, you *so* are, and I love you—"

Tal drops the poster.

Tal drops the poster and steps on it because Tal's closing the space between us and Tal's grabbing me by the back of my neck and Tal's kissing me, actually, for real. Tal's kissing me in real life, I think, and that doesn't make sense but it's how it feels. Like now this is real and we're real, and more than that, I want us to be real. I want people to see us and know us and even have opinions on us, because at least that means they have something to have an opinion *on*. I yank Tal closer, an arm swung around her shoulders and the other in her hair, and step as close to her as I possibly can.

"I love you," I say against her mouth, barely decipherable but I know she'll get it.

"Holy shit." She laughs, pressing her forehead to mine. "I love you, too."

"Oh my god." I laugh, too, then, lit up by Tal and Tal's hands and Tal's mouth and Tal's everything else.

"Can we please come in yet? We are *dying*," Gray shouts, peeking his head through the caf doors. Rachel's head is underneath him, and underneath her is Gray's phone, Jaya's pixelated face trying valiantly to come through on the school Wi-Fi.

Tal waves them over and they crash through the doors,

sprinting over and scooping both of us up. Gray's cheering and Rachel's laughing and Jaya's screaming, "Point me at them! Gray, you're pointing me at the floor, I want to see! Ethan Gray, I swear to god!" Everything goes blurry around the edges in the best way, sparkling like a beginning, and when I look around, I see all the perfect things I'm allowed to have.

SEPTEMBER

TWO WEEKS BEFORE NAPA

"If you cry again, I'm just going to hit you. I seriously cannot do it again."

Gray sucks in his bottom lip, trying his absolute best to not start up all over again. It kind of just makes him look like a pouty toddler, but it's still such a *Gray* face that it makes me cry anyway.

"We *just* got here," Lianne says, coming into the room with a massive tub on wheels where Gray's tossed all of his earthly possessions. He's already told me he's going to visit his mom every weekend, so I don't know why he felt the need to bring the lamp from his bedroom at home, but hey. He's a delicate ecosystem.

"Shouldn't you be weeping about your son growing up and moving out?" Gray asks. "Spreading his wings? Leaving the nest?"

Lianne sighs, smiling ruefully. She walks up to Gray and puts both hands on either side of his face.

"When I got pregnant with you, I was really scared," she

says, and oh shit, Lianne never talks about this, should I leave? "But do you know what helped me?"

"What?" Gray asks, his voice thick.

Lianne gently taps Gray's cheeks twice. "The thought that having a baby at twenty meant I'd be an empty nester before forty."

I spit out my Gatorade.

"Hey!" Gray sputters, half at his mom and half at me. "You're cleaning that up."

"It's hardly the first *or* last bodily fluid this carpet's gonna see, Gray, you're fine."

"I'm not trying to hear that," Lianne says, and, huh, I guess that's where Gray gets his Dionne impression from.

We're here first—Gray matched up through the school with some guy who seems half-decent, and they've been messaging on and off. I mean, he's no *me*, but I'm sure he and Gray can get along.

Gray takes ages to pick out which bed he wants, though, which means that by the time he's actually made a decision (it is, of course, the first bed he chose when we walked in, but I don't say anything), the guy's already here. His name is Mo, which I already knew from weeks of online sleuthing with Gray, but he still introduces himself to me and smiles at me and Lianne.

"Do you think he thinks you're his sister or his girlfriend?" she asks me under her breath while Gray and Mo clap each other on the back and talk about Room Things.

"Do you think I could convince him I'm his court-appointed chaperone?"

"Ooh, if you want to do that, let me know and I'll back you up."

It's good, the fact that Gray's move-in weekend is two weeks before I need to fly out for CIA orientation. My good-byes get to be spread out. I get to be here to snicker along with Lianne so she doesn't break down in the middle of this dorm. I'm visiting her next weekend to do one last giant meal prep push before Gray has to take over for real.

(It's possible that that made me more emotional than the thought of leaving Gray on the opposite coast.)

It's the move-in day Gray always used to talk about. He puts little reminders of us on every shelf. He makes his bed perfectly. He takes pictures *everywhere*.

"Only thing missing is your room, huh?" he asks, sidling up to me at the end of the day. The sun's already setting, and we're going out for dinner with Mo and his family before Lianne and I have to drive home. I spent three hours yesterday making a let's-not-cry-so-hard-we-crash-the-car playlist for us to listen to.

I look up at Gray, completely beautiful in this lighting (in all lighting, but the sun does love him). I squeeze his hand.

"Just kidding," he says unconvincingly. "Didn't want you here anyway."

"I love you," I say, because I don't need to do any of that with him today.

And it's peace, and history, and warmth, and family, and something deep down and permanent that I feel when he says, "I love you, too."

Tal and I have been awake for about half an hour, lazily rubbing our feet together in her extra-long twin bed, when I finally break our comfortable silence.

"Did you know," I say, "that I spoke to three people here yesterday while you were in class?"

"Yeah?" Tal asks into my neck. I bring my hand up to scratch into her curls and she shudders and tries to wrap herself even more tightly around me.

"And all three people said *oh shit, Alana* Alana? *Tal's Alana?*"

I can feel Tal's smile against my collarbone. "Am I supposed to be embarrassed by that? I stand by it."

"Definitely not," I say. "Huge fan of being called *Tal's Alana*, by the way. Considering a legal name change."

"Let's not get ahead of ourselves," Tal says. "Plenty of time for legal name changes after we graduate."

I flush down to my toes and don't say anything, just hook Tal closer and squeeze. The other day, Gray explained the concept of *ring before spring* to me, and now Tal and I can't stop saying it to each other. I'm, like, 60 percent sure we're kidding. Most of the time.

"What do you want to do today?" I ask into her hair. Tal kisses me right in the middle of my chest, and yeah, fair, she makes a strong argument.

"Jump onto your back so you can't leave," she says.

This is a side of Tal I didn't know existed until we started dating for real. A Tal that isn't afraid to be a little needy. It might be my favorite version yet.

"I'm coming back for Thanksgiving," I remind her. "And Christmas. And you're coming for spring break. You're gonna be sick of me."

"Not possible," Tal says.

She's still speaking into my neck, but she detangles herself just enough to stretch up and look me in the eye.

"Hey, you know I'm joking, right?" she says. "I don't want you to leave, but I'm *so* fucking proud of you. Like, I'm glad you're doing this. I believe in us."

The wild thing is that I do, too. I try not to compare Tal and Gray anymore, but I remember thinking that there was no way Gray and I would make it if we ever had to be long distance. With Tal, the doubt just isn't there.

I take advantage of the fact that Tal's still looking at me to kiss her, twice, slowly.

"I love you," I say.

And it's strong, and sharp-toothed, and electric, and mine, and something massive and wonderful that I feel when she says, "I love you, too."

NAPA

I get in the car.

I go.

ACKNOWLEDGMENTS

They say to write what you know, so I wrote about a teenage lesbian stuck somewhere between knowing herself and being herself. First and foremost, if that's also you, I hope that someday soon you'll be seen in exactly the way you want to be.

Thank you to my agent, Claire Friedman, for seeing this book when it was a crumpled-up proposal I could barely look at and knowing that something was there. Thank you to Rachel Diebel and Jordan Tyson, two of the most thoughtful and precise (and funny, and nice, and, and, and . . .) editors in the universe. Thank you to my publishing teams at Feiwel & Friends and Puffin for their countless hours spent making this book something I'm even more proud of than I already was.

To my somehow-increasingly-incredible wife, Gabi: Thank you for the countless hours of work you put in so that I get to do this. Thank you for our life and, crucially, for letting me rip off our first kiss for this book. (To anyone who was also witness to Halloween 2015: Thank you for never speaking of it again.) Thank you to my sons, Arthur and Oscar, for being perfect in every way (it's in print now, no take-backs).

I don't think I could have written a character like Gray if I hadn't had the friends that I had in high school; thank you to the Commune—Katherine Bieniek, Danielle Monaghan,

Sally Medland, and special thanks to Doug McPherson and Carl Pike, my emotional support straight boys.

Finally, thank you to Rebecca Barrow and Rory Power, for sticking with me and this book for the last six years and listening to every single absolutely bananas thing that's ever popped into my head for even longer.

ABOUT THE AUTHOR

Maggie Horne is a writer who grew up near Toronto, Canada. After graduating from university in the UK, she imported her best-ever souvenir; her wife. They now live outside of Ottawa, Canada with a collection of dogs and children. She is the author of books for middle grade readers, including *Hazel Hill is Gonna Win This One*, as well as young adult books, including *Don't Let it Break Your Heart*. Maggie loves writing the queer stories she wishes she could have read growing up.